I Did It For You

Also by Amy Engel

. . . .

The Familiar Dark

The Roanoke Girls

The Revolution of Ivy

The Book of Ivy

I Did It For You

A Novel

. . . .

Amy Engel

DUTTON

DUTTON

An imprint of Penguin Random House LLC
penguinrandomhouse.com

LIBRARY OF CONGRESS CATALOGING-IN-PUBLICATION DATA
Names: Engel, Amy, author.
Title: I did it for you: a novel / Amy Engel.
Description: New York : Dutton, an imprint of
Penguin Random House LLC, [2023]
Identifiers: LCCN 2022042465 (print) | LCCN 2022042466 (ebook) |
ISBN 9780593187395 (hardcover) | ISBN 9780593187401 (ebook)
Subjects: LCGFT: Novels.
Classification: LCC PS3605.N4354 I3 2023 (print) |
LCC PS3605.N4354 (ebook) | DDC 813/.6—dc23/eng/20220909
LC record available at https://lccn.loc.gov/2022042465
LC ebook record available at https://lccn.loc.gov/2022042466

Printed in the United States of America

1st Printing

BOOK DESIGN BY SHANNON NICOLE PLUNKETT

For my mother, who read me my very first book

As long as you live, there's always something waiting; and even if it's bad, and you know it's bad, what can you do? You can't stop living.

—Truman Capote, *In Cold Blood*

I Did It For You

Ludlow, Kansas

She returned at dusk, just as the sun was sinking into red fire. Drove straight into town and took a right on Elm, rolling through the stop sign the way she always had. She was older now, her face thinner, eyes guarded, but instantly recognizable, even after all these years. Ludlow never forgot its own.

The first call came from Mrs. Allard, who looked up from raking her last pile of leaves in time to see the car sail past. "She's back," she told Chet after she'd rushed inside, cell phone clutched hard in her hand. "About time, too."

"I'm sure she's had her reasons for staying away," Chet said, and Mrs. Allard huffed. Typical. Chet'd always had a soft spot for Greer Dunning. They all had, truth be told, especially after the murders. How could they not when there was no way to avoid seeing how hard her sister's death had hit. At first, all Greer's grief spewed outward in frantic claims that the police had missed something, that there had to be more to the story. She stopped anyone who would stand still long enough to listen, hands plucking at sleeves, wide eyes imploring, begging to be believed, even as all the evidence said otherwise. And then, as the weeks passed and it became clear the police had the right man and he'd acted alone, they watched as she drew into herself. Turned quiet and wary as something closed off in her, tightened up like a hard shell. She became unknowable, and over time people stopped trying because Ludlow only liked secrets it could eventually pry loose.

After Mrs. Allard hung up, Chet spread the word. One call turning into ten, those ten multiplying into thirty. The news winding its way through town, easing under doors and over backyard fences. By morning everyone would know. Everyone would have an opinion. Resentment that the big-city girl thought she could show up after more than a decade and fit right back in like she'd never left. Compassion at the thought of her returning home, maneuvering around parents who'd given up a long time ago. Jealousy that no matter the reason behind it, at least she'd managed to get away. Hope that, this time, things would be different.

And above and around and through it all, Ludlow listened. Breathed and remembered. Back to a time when the Dunning sisters rode their bikes down the middle of the street, pigtails flying. Ate corn dogs on the Fourth of July wearing matching dresses spangled with stars. Grew apart as the years passed, robbed of the chance to ever stitch back together.

It watched her make the final turn onto her street, slide her car up to the curb, and turn off the engine. Hands clenched on the steering wheel, eyes closed on a shuddering breath. *I've been waiting for you*, Ludlow whispered as she stepped out of the car, a soft breeze against her pale cheek. *Welcome home.*

Chapter One

didn't attend the execution, although I was invited. "Invited"—such a civilized word for a string of events that began with my sister's brains being blown out and ended with his veins pumped full of state-sanctioned poison. I heard later, through the grapevine, that his final words were "I shouldn't have done it." A pretty half-assed apology, if you asked me. That same grapevine reported a last meal of chicken-fried steak and twice-baked potatoes, capped off with fresh strawberry shortcake. I wondered, for a long time, if it had been the kind made with biscuits or the kind made with angel food cake. Those were the type of pointless details my mind snagged on to keep it from having to think about uglier ones. Like how long it took him to die. Twelve minutes, for the record. I wish that brought me some pleasure. Or at least more pleasure than it does.

After he was gone, I put him away. Did my best to shove him into the cobwebby corners of my mind where I stored most of my memories about Eliza and that long, sultry summer before she died. And then my father called, left a rusty-voiced message that I had to strain to hear, bourbon breath boiling through the phone. "It's happened again, Greer," he said. A noise that might have been a sob, might have been a cough. "He did it again." I got the details off of the internet, not from my father, an unreliable source on even his best days, of which there were few. An eighteen-year-old couple shot to death where they were tangled together in the front seat of the boy's car. Ludlow, Kansas. My hometown. Change the date, change the names, and it could have been a story about my sister and her boyfriend, Travis. More than a decade of time wiped away in an instant. Back to the moment when my world spun off its axis. Although that's not quite accurate. Less spinning off and more splitting open—all the hairline cracks turned to sudden yawning fissures.

But despite my father's drunken ramblings, Roy Mathews hadn't done it again. His trigger finger was as dead and buried as the rest of him. These were two other kids. These were two different murders. Copycat, the reporters said. Sick. Disturbing. But not directly connected. And yet it felt like someone reaching out to me, opening a door, waiting to see if I would walk through. A whisper slithering out of the dark. *Come back.*

Leave it alone, I told myself every night as I took long, tepid baths, trying to escape the lingering late-summer heat. "Leave it alone," I whispered under my breath as I poured a glass of wine with dinner. Glass. Singular. Eliza's death might have torn my family apart, but I'd be damned if I let it turn me into my father. *You've been doing well*, I lectured myself as I lay in bed chasing sleep that wouldn't hold still long enough for me to catch it. Okay, "well" might be overstating it. But I had a job, an apartment, a small circle of acquaintances. I went to museums, and movies, and the occasional ball game. I voted and saved for the future. I had the outlines of a life, at least, if not the full, colored-in version. I'd been doing fine, and after everything, I considered fine a win.

But I couldn't leave it alone. Had never been able to, really. I'd never felt any comfort when Roy Mathews was arrested less than twenty-four hours after my sister's life ended. Everyone else in Ludlow had let out a collective sigh of relief. The madman was locked up; their lives could return to normal. But I'd looked at his expressionless face staring back at me from the front page of the local paper and thought: *You? How could it be you?* I'd asked Sheriff Baker if he was sure Roy had acted alone so many times that he'd eventually stopped answering my calls. Instead, he'd phoned my parents, told them I needed professional help. What followed was a string of therapists who chalked up the constant, always-there unease in my gut to post-traumatic stress disorder. But I knew it was something deeper. Eliza screaming in a frequency only I could hear. Now two more kids were dead, and I'd been right all along.

Finally, after all this time, I understood what had to happen. I was accepting a different invitation—*come back*—and I was heading home.

· · · ·

When I told my boss I needed to take an extended leave due to a family emergency, he didn't ask too many questions. Over the years I'd learned to deflect well enough that most people had stopped trying to get real answers. They figured I was private or had some horrible childhood I didn't want to disclose. Random guys I'd dated in college tried to guess what I was hiding like my past was a party game they could win through sheer perseverance. But even when they knew where I was from, it rarely triggered any sort of memory. Turned out Eliza's and Travis's deaths hadn't generated the frenzied headlines some murders received. I wasn't sure why exactly, but if I had to guess, I'd say it was because if we're going to pore over details of a murder, chat about it with our friends over coffee, and read the details online, we want something more gruesome. A bloody knife or a garrote of wire. A dungeon basement and a body-part trophy collection. Three bullets resulting in two bodies wasn't going to cut it. And then there was Roy Mathews himself. As a killer, he left a lot to be desired. He wasn't a jilted lover or a jealous stalker. He didn't even know Eliza or Travis, had never spoken so much as a word to either of them as far as anyone could remember. He wasn't charismatic or sly or even crazed. He was just an angry-at-the-world, not-too-bright eighteen-year-old with a bloodstream full of booze and a gun burning a hole in his pocket.

"Well," Mr. Goss said after I'd finished filling out the paperwork, "I hope everything turns out all right and you're back with us soon. The kids are going to miss you."

I'm a middle school guidance counselor, tasked with helping seventh and eighth graders navigate the choppy waters of adolescence. Trusted to steer them through potential emotional land mines and emerge safely on the other side, stronger and wiser, and hopefully with minimal lasting damage. Most days, though, I was simply treading water. Trying to save them from drowning when I could barely stay afloat myself.

It's okay to laugh at the irony. God knows I do.

. . . .

It didn't take me long to pack for my trip—no pets I had to farm out to willing neighbors, no plants to foist on friends while I was gone. For that matter, no friends I needed to leave with hugs and promises to keep them posted. No men consulting the calendar, eager for my return. Other than my colleagues, who I joined a few times a year for an after-work beer, I didn't have any attachments in Chicago. It was almost like deep down I'd been preparing for this moment, the day I would need to drop everything without a backward glance and rush home. And I knew, as much as I might want to pretend otherwise, that I couldn't go on the way I had been. Living a suspended half-life, waiting for something to change without taking a single concrete step to alter my course. Now, with the familiar lines of US-75 laid out in front of me, underneath the uncertainty and the fear, there was a pulsing vein of relief. Returning to Ludlow felt dangerous, like standing next to a powder keg with a lit match in my hand. But part of me longed for the oncoming explosion. Maybe I would find answers and this limbo could be over, one way or the other.

Most people are familiar with Kansas only from elementary school geography—the nondescript rectangle smack dab in the middle—and popular culture—Dorothy and her glittery red shoes; Truman Capote and a blood-splattered farmhouse. So if they ever actually visit, instead of flying over, they're armed with enough knowledge to expect the flatness, the fields of wheat and soybean, the tractors trundling across the earth like great metal beasts. But the sheer scope of the land has to be a surprise. How the flatness goes on and on in all directions, how the horizon melts into the sky, disorienting without any buildings to add scale or dimension. Out here, on the prairie, you feel as small as you ever have.

I used to love everything about this place. The sound of wind whispering through wheat, the metallic smell of a thunderstorm rolling in fast from the north, the thump of your car tires over the old brick streets running through the middle of town, a blue October sky so vast and cloudless you'd almost be forgiven for thinking it couldn't be real. The one place in the world where I'd felt like I could always be myself because everyone here knew me, knew exactly who Greer Dunning was, so there was no point pretending. I'd been the younger daughter, the borderline smart-ass, the one who'd walked right up to the line of too much spunk without stepping over. I'd talked fast and laughed loud, and nowadays I could barely lay hands on the ghost of that girl. She was as lost to me as Eliza was.

As I glided past the "Entering Ludlow, Est. 1871" sign and took a right on Main, it hit me that all those things I used to love were now tainted with Eliza's death. The bandstand in the town park was no longer the place where we'd listened to "The Star-Spangled Banner" before Fourth of July fireworks. It was where my dad, drunk and stumbling, crashed through a railing during a memorial service for Eliza and Travis and puked all over my sobbing mother. The library wasn't my favorite childhood spot to hole up on rainy afternoons with a stack of books and a contraband Hershey bar. It was the place where, on the Halloween after Eliza died, I ran into a group of girls each dressed up as my dead sister, rubber cement for the bullet hole in her forehead and dripping red slime for the blood. When Roy Mathews pulled that trigger, he took more than my sister away from me. He took all my best memories, too.

My parents still lived in the house where I grew up, where my father grew up also. After Eliza died, part of me had assumed we would move. If not away from Ludlow completely, then at least to a new house. Someplace where Eliza's absence didn't echo from every corner. Where every square inch wasn't a reminder of who we used to be. But my parents never even mentioned the possibility, my dad probably out of drunken inertia and my mom because on some level she still hoped Eliza was coming back. Like maybe if they stayed put, one day Eliza would scratch her way out of the coffin, come shambling up the front walk just in time for dinner.

We were never the richest family in town. That was the Parkers, who owned the now-defunct oil refinery but continued to live large on the profits decades later. And we weren't the most devout family, either. That was Preacher and Mrs. Frogue and their passel of pale, waiflike children whose eyes always focused somewhere above your head, like they were already looking to heaven. But we were the steadiest family in Ludlow. You could count on the Dunnings, no matter what. My father owned the grocery store, passed down from his father and grandfather before him. He knew more about most people in town than they knew about themselves. Who stocked up on too much wine, who snuck in for a pregnancy test squirreled away in a paper bag, who asked to buy their groceries on credit until they were back on their feet. My dad knew everyone's secrets and would have died before he revealed a single one. For her part, my mother kept the town's social circles running. Room mom at school, president of the PTA, head of the church bake sale, and the library fundraiser, and the food pantry collection drive. And Eliza and I were steady, too. Pretty enough, but not beautiful. Smart, but not gifted. Well-liked, but not the most popular. We rode that middle line of small-town solidness every day of our lives. So when it all fell out from under us, we had no idea where to land. We became Ludlow's sideshow, and the Dunnings weren't meant for the stage.

From the outside our house looked the same as it always had— whitewashed brick, pale gray shutters, a wraparound front porch my grandmother had added on a few years after marrying into the family. To soften the exterior, according to my dad. The better to spy on passersby, according to my mom. The front door was unlocked, a small-town habit my parents couldn't break even after the murder of their daughter. The house might have looked familiar, but it didn't smell the way it had during my childhood. Chocolate chip cookies, a roast in the oven, faint cigar smoke from my dad's Sunday afternoon guilty pleasure. The only scent now was bleach, strong enough to make my eyes water. After Eliza's funeral, my dad picked up a bottle of bourbon, and my mom picked up every cleaning product known to man. Now she spent her days scrubbing, wiping, scouring until her knuckles were raw.

"Mom?" I called. "Hello? Anybody home?"

"Oh, Greer, honey." My mom bustled out of the kitchen with a broom in her hand. "You're here! I can't believe it!"

I dropped my duffel on the floor. "I'm here." I avoided looking to my right, where I knew the giant framed portrait of Eliza and me still took pride of place on the foyer wall. Teenagers trapped under glass. Safe and alive and forever smiling. A constant, painful reminder of what we'd lost, like a splinter buried too deep for removal.

My mom took a step forward, gave me an awkward one-armed hug. My first instinct was to flinch backward; it had been years since she'd touched me this way. Before Eliza, she'd been a woman of kisses, shoulder rubs, hugs when we passed in the hall. It felt like I'd spent half my childhood shrugging her off of me. But after Eliza she avoided contact, never reaching for me, eyes always focused a little to the side of my face. As if looking at me, acknowledging me, would be tempting fate, her rejection of me a way to tell the universe there was nothing to see here; it could move along and torture someone else. And thus far it had, but my mother and I lost each other anyway.

"Where's Dad?" I asked, although I already knew the answer involved a closed door and an open bottle.

The broom swept past me, picking up invisible dirt I'd tracked in upon arrival. "Resting, I think. He'll be down for dinner. Why don't you go get settled. We'll eat in half an hour."

My room had been repainted since I'd last been here twelve years ago. Christmas of my freshman year in college, a short three days that had stretched on like eternity. The walls were a soft, pale pink now, more suited to an infant than a grown woman. Maybe my mother hoped, somehow, for a do-over. Honestly, I couldn't blame her. I stepped through the adjoining bathroom and into Eliza's room. It was no longer preserved as a shrine, which surprised me. Given my parents' reactions to Eliza's death, I'd expected this place to stay exactly as it had been the last time Eliza slept here. But it was sterile now, swept clean of my sister's life, and an unexpected wave of sorrow hit me right in the chest. No more track meet medals hanging from the mirror, no Leonardo DiCaprio smoldering from the wall, no shoes tossed haphazardly across the floor. The furniture was different, too. A matching set of generic pale wood that didn't look like it would hold up over time. Perfect for a guest room in a house that never had guests. Even Eliza's garbage wall was gone—a huge bulletin board covered with the kind of worthless greeting card inspiration that always made me want to barf. "A ship in a harbor is safe, but that is not what ships are built for" and "Life isn't about waiting for the storm to pass, it's about learning to dance in the rain."

Back in my room, I tossed my clothes into my dresser and then crossed to the closet, hanging my coat and stowing my shoes in the rack on the back of the door. Almost against my will, my eyes shifted upward, snagging on the worn shoebox tucked away on the high shelf. I hesitated, heart thumping an uneven rhythm in my chest, and then turned away, shut the closet door firmly behind me.

"It's okay," I whispered to myself, sliding my palms down my jean-clad thighs and back up again, concentrating on my breathing. The one thing of value I'd learned from the therapists I'd seen after Eliza's death. "You're okay." Slow and steady. In and out. Over and over until I heard my mom's voice calling me down for dinner.

Chapter Two

How many meals had I eaten at our front-porch table over the years? Hundreds? Maybe even thousands? Brunch after church, back when we still darkened Preacher Frogue's doorstep. Grilled cheese and tomato soup on rainy childhood Saturdays when Eliza and I would pretend we were in a lifeboat sailing over stormy seas. Too many family dinners to count: birthdays, holidays, random Tuesday nights. One of Eliza's first dates with Travis had been at this table, the two of them sharing a pizza while our moms peeked through the living room curtains and giggled over glasses of wine, thrilled their children had chosen each other. So I'd thought the motions of setting the round table, carrying out a pitcher of water and basket of bread, would come back to me. But turned out it wasn't like riding a bike, every movement now unfamiliar and strange. Should I pull away the empty fourth chair where Eliza would never sit again? Should I space out the remaining three spots so her absence wouldn't be as obvious? In the end, I left the table as it was, fourth chair and no place setting in front of it. Eliza was never coming back, but I didn't want to pretend like she'd never been here at all.

My mom had always been a good cook in a hearty Midwestern way. Family dinners revolved around a generous cut of meat and enough starchy sides to feed an army. Some type of condensed-soup-laden casserole was also a popular option, served alongside a salad made with iceberg lettuce and drenched in ranch or a Jell-O ring laced with canned fruit. In Kansas, we used the term "salad" loosely. And homemade dessert was an everyday occurrence rather than a special-occasion treat. But tonight's dinner consisted of a frozen lasagna heated up in its aluminum tin. Don't get me wrong, I wasn't complaining. The lasagna was hot and I didn't have to make it, but I wondered what my parents' meals were usually like now. The two of them in this big, old house. Did they even eat together anymore? I could more easily picture my mother hunched over the kitchen sink with a sad sandwich in her hand while my father ate dinner upstairs alone. My throat tightened at the image. It was one thing for me to eat most of my meals solo; it was another to know my parents did the same. As kids, Eliza and I had made gagging noises every time our parents kissed in front of us, rolled our eyes and squealed in disgust when they danced across the kitchen floor, our dad's big hand skating dangerously close to our mom's backside. Despite our protests over their public displays of affection, our parents' almost effortless connection had been something we secretly loved, a security blanket wrapped tight around our family. I'd hoped, after everything, my parents would at least still have each other. But the last time I was home, they'd moved around each other with stiff, impersonal politeness, their interactions so stilted I could hardly bear to watch. And I doubted things had improved in the years since.

Tonight my dad joined us at the porch table, though, five minutes late and already three sheets to the wind. He didn't so much sit as sink into his chair, eyes rheumy and glazed. I stared at him until he met my gaze. "Hey, Dad," I said, fork spearing a chunk of lasagna with a little too much force.

"Greer," he said, the word drawn out like he wasn't entirely sure of my name. He waved away my mother's attempt to serve him, settled back in his chair, and gave me a faraway smile. "It's nice to have you home. It's been a long time."

"It has," I agreed. I talked to my mother twice a month on the phone and saw her every spring when she visited me in Chicago for a long weekend. A trip that inevitably left me exhausted and depressed. I always picked a museum or landmark to take her to, a loud restaurant where our lack of conversation wouldn't be as obvious. I wanted to tell her she didn't need to bother coming, but wasn't sure if her face would register hurt or relief at the reprieve, and I didn't want to find out. And at least she made the effort. It had been more than seven years since my father had come along, and time had not been kind to him since last we'd seen each other. It wasn't only the drinking that had aged him. He'd lost something vital when Eliza died. Not just his firstborn child. Not just his beloved daughter. His belief in the fairness of the world. All my life he'd told me that if I did good, if I *was* good, then good would come to me. They weren't simply words he'd spoken; they were a creed he'd lived by. A fundamental truth he'd believed in. Until the day Roy Mathews had made a bloody mockery of every syllable, had spit in the face of every kind and selfless deed my father had ever done. My dad didn't believe in anything anymore. He was still breathing, but he was the definition of a man going through the motions. He'd given up—on life, on his family, on himself—and I would never forgive him for it.

"Are you staying through the weekend?" my mom asked. "Too bad you won't be here longer. The Fall Festival is coming up. You always loved it when you were younger." As if I was going to put on a costume and get a pumpkin painted on my face like in the good old days.

"Actually, I'm thinking of staying for a few weeks, if that's okay?"

My mom lowered her fork, surprise floating across her face. She'd stopped expecting me to come home years ago, had almost too readily accepted the list of excuses I'd come up with—*I have exams*; *Work is crazy*; *A friend invited me to her house for the holidays*—until both of us had simply ceased broaching the subject. "Of course it's all right. But what about your job?"

"I took a little time off," I said. "Nothing to worry about. I needed a break."

"And your boss doesn't have a problem with that?"

I shook my head, shoved a bite of lasagna into my mouth. "How's the store? Are the new owners taking care of it?"

My mom glanced at my dad, waiting to see if he'd answer, but he was busy staring off into the distance. "They've changed a few things. You'll have to stop by and see."

"Sure," I said. And I would, although I didn't want to. That store had been in the Dunning family for a hundred years. It was an institution in this town. Or at least it had been until my dad's drinking got in the way. Maybe he would have ended up selling even if Eliza hadn't died. Maybe neither Eliza nor I would've had any interest in staying in Ludlow and continuing the family business. But I liked to think that would've felt like something we decided together instead of one more thing that simply happened to us.

The rest of our dinner conversation consisted of the kind of surface small talk you engage in with strangers. It was worse, somehow, than silence would have been, each generic question and response landing like an anvil inside of me. I knew we wouldn't talk about the latest murders or Eliza or the gaping wound that was our family. We never talked about anything important anymore. I tried to imagine how this scene might've played out if I'd been the one to die instead. Would my parents be as broken? Would Eliza have stayed in Ludlow to help? Would the three of them have somehow found the right words to say to one another in the aftermath? I'd never believed my parents had a favorite child, and I still didn't. Eliza hadn't been the sun we all revolved around. She wasn't the gilded child. If I were the one in the town cemetery right now, I think our family would still have imploded. The difference would have been Eliza. She was always the softer sibling, the one more likely to apologize first or take the high road. Of the two of us, she was the bigger person. If our positions had been reversed, she would have found a way to talk to our dad, encouraged him to put down the bottle instead of sitting back and watching him stumble away from the table, a small, vicious part of her hoping he would trip and fall. She would have folded our mother's poor, abused fingers between her own and urged her to stop cleaning, to stop *doing*, and simply be. Eliza would have at least tried to make it better, understanding that the effort is sometimes worth more than the result. She would have managed to offer grace to our parents that I had never been able to find inside myself.

• • • •

After dinner I retreated to my room and finished unpacking, then sat on my bed, unsure what to do next. In Chicago I would have read a book, lost myself in a show I could binge without thinking. Gone for a walk on streets crowded with bodies, taking comfort in my anonymity. No one knew me and no one cared. But here my mind was buzzing, a low-level hum burrowing under my skin. I couldn't settle down, the house too empty and still around me. I grabbed my car keys off the dresser and raced down the stairs. I thought about calling to my mom on my way out the front door, but the kitchen was dark, so I eased out without a goodbye.

I drove down the main drag, where ninety percent of Ludlow's commerce was centered, and clocked the changes the last twelve years had wrought. In a lot of ways, Ludlow was like many small, middle-of-nowhere Midwestern towns. Barely hanging on, each generation hemorrhaging more and more residents, kids graduating high school and disappearing into the wider world, just as I had. Towns surviving on the old-timers who refused to let go, the folks who still managed to own farmland that hadn't been swooped up by big agriculture or the ones who couldn't imagine themselves leaving a place where their great-great-grandparents had put down roots more than a hundred years ago. The lucky few got jobs at the meatpacking plant twenty miles down the highway; the rest eked out a living any way they could. But all of it was just so much life support. Eventually the plug would be pulled, and Ludlow would fade away—vacant buildings and a distant memory out on the prairie. A whole way of life that was never coming back.

For now, the drugstore was still there, along with the credit union next door, and the hardware store on the far corner. The gas station looked the same as always, and I knew come morning the old-timers would gather in a ring of lawn chairs on the cracked pavement out front to shoot the shit. The boutique was gone, though, as was the electronics store and the deli. The beauty salon where I'd gotten an ill-advised asymmetrical bob in sixth grade now sported soaped-over windows and a faded "For Lease" sign tacked to the door. I slowed at a sad bouquet of balloons floating inches above the sidewalk, a couple of roses strewn underneath. Next to them, flapping between two parking meters, was a small banner announcing a vigil for Dylan Short and Addy Johnson, the latest gunshot lovers. Their photos were grainy and distorted, looking more like mugshots than memorials. *You waited too long*, their gazes accused. *You waited too long and now look what happened to us.* Even as I drove away, their eyes followed me, burning into the back of my neck.

I saved the grocery store for last, foot easing off the gas as I got closer, not quite ready to see. The hand-painted "Dunning General" sign had been replaced with a mass-produced IGA logo. They'd taken out the original front doors, too. Hundred-year-old wood and glass that always stuck in humid weather. Now people entered the IGA through automatic sliding doors. A hiss of air in greeting instead of the tiny golden bell that used to ring out whenever anyone stepped inside. Maybe my dad had the right idea after all. Much more of this and I'd be picking up a bottle myself.

I wasn't up to actually going inside the store yet, so I glided past, took a right at the corner, and continued on Elm toward the park. The year after Eliza and Travis died, the town put in a memorial bench in their honor. It wasn't placed in front of the parking spot where they died. Everyone agreed that would be tacky. The bench was across from the duck pond, and I'd never seen a single soul sitting on it. Like all of Eliza and Travis's bad luck had rubbed off on the wood and no one wanted to risk contamination.

I pulled over across from the pond, could make out the bench silhouette in the small spill of light from the streetlamp on the corner. I cracked my window, and the chill October night blew in the distant smell of burning leaves and the faint sound of laughter. Probably teenagers sneaking a few beers in the park shadows, ignoring their parents' pleas to stay home in the wake of the latest murders. I wondered if they'd do the obligatory pre-Halloween Ludlow murder tour later, half wasted and with no business driving, squished into the front cab of somebody's beat-to-shit pickup truck. It's an October tradition around here, a retrospective of all Ludlow's bad deeds. Proof that not even sleepy small towns are immune from the worst of human nature. First stop, the white bungalow on Locust where sixty years ago George Weathers chased his wife out of the house and gave her upwards of twenty hacks with an axe he kept next to the back door for splitting firewood. As a kid, whenever we drove down Locust, my mind conjured up a picture of Mrs. Weathers fleeing for her life, hearing the axe whistling through the air behind her, knowing what was coming but too slow to outrun the blade. Story I'd always heard was that George killed her because he was sick of her burning his bacon.

Next up was the historical marker out on Route 24, a two-lane highway with gravel sides and wildflowers growing right up to the edges of the pavement. The metal sign on the side of the road memorialized the Bloody Benders, a Kansas family of the late 1800s who'd lured weary travelers to their home with promises of food and lodging, only to bash their heads in or slit their throats before robbing them. Around here, we were weirdly proud of the Bloody Benders. They were practically a bedtime story.

Final stop was the hulking remains of the shuttered oil refinery, former lifeblood of Ludlow, now a dilapidated eyesore. By the time I left town, some of the walls were starting to cave in, so a chain-link fence topped with barbed wire had been erected around the perimeter. But that didn't stop us from sneaking inside to see the spot where the summer before I was born, Ludlow High's prom queen was found naked and strangled, dumped among the broken glass and chunks of concrete like one more piece of trash. People swore you could still see the outline of her body on the dirty floor if you looked close enough.

And now there was my sister and Travis, along with Dylan and Addy. Did the current high schoolers talk about how scary it must have been for Eliza, seeing Roy Mathews's hulking frame through the window, gun raised and pointed? Did they reenact the various murders from the front seat of the pickup, beer fumes fogging up the glass as they tried not to laugh? I could picture it so clearly only because it used to be us.

That's the thing about murder. It's all fun and games until it happens to you.

Chapter Three

By the time I returned home, the house was dark even though it was only eight thirty. I didn't like seeing firsthand how small and sad my parents' lives had become. How they probably marked off the minutes until they could turn out the lights and be done with another day. Of course, if I was being honest, my own life wasn't much better. My mom had left the porch light on for me, and it cast long shadows across the lawn. Living in Chicago, I'd forgotten how quiet Ludlow could be, no cars passing, no music playing, no voices raised in joy or anger. A rustle from the overgrown hydrangea bushes at the side of the house stopped me in my tracks, and I waited for a neighborhood cat or curious raccoon to make an appearance, but nothing moved. I stayed very still, the silence loaded with anticipation like the moment before the thunder booms or the door slams. A silence that lets you know, by its very emptiness, that you aren't alone.

"Is someone there?" I asked. I maneuvered my keys between my knuckles like I always did in Chicago parking garages.

"Greer," a low voice singsonged. It seemed to come from all the dark corners of the yard at once, and the tiny hairs on the back of my neck woke up. "Come out and play, Greer Dunning."

Recognition and relief flowed through me, and I lowered my

keys on a burst of laughter. "You assholes," I called into the darkness. "Get out here." Two shapes emerged from behind the hydrangea bushes, hands waving in frantic greeting.

"You should have seen your face," Cassie said, making a mock terrified expression as she enveloped me in a hug. I couldn't remember the last time someone had hugged me this way, and I clung onto her, breathing in the still-familiar scent of her coconut shampoo. That was Cassie; once she found something she liked, she never saw a reason to keep looking for anything better.

"Don't be an idiot," Ryan said, elbowing Cassie out of the way for his own hug. "She looked way more scared than that." He pulled back and gave me his trademark lopsided grin. Even now, as a full-grown adult, he still looked eighteen with his dirty-blond hair and bright blue eyes, a smatter of freckles across the bridge of his nose. "I feared momentarily that you might piss your pants. I thought all these years in the big city would've made you tougher."

"Shut up," I said. "You're both full of crap." This, right here, was one of the reasons these two had remained my closest friends even though we'd been separated by both time and distance. They didn't tiptoe around me after what happened. They were sympathetic, of course, and kind. But they still treated me the way they always had—teasing, giving me shit, reminding me there was a world outside my own head. Trusting that I could take it. And even when, at times, it felt like maybe I couldn't, I appreciated their faith in me.

"How did you know I was back?"

"My mom was out mowing the other day and got to chatting with your mom," Ryan said.

Cassie punched me in the upper arm, a little harder than necessary. "Why didn't we hear it from you?"

"I was going to call once I got settled in." Which was true. But being back in Ludlow, seeing my parents, sleeping in my old bed, reconnecting with the people I'd left behind, seemed like something it was wiser to ease myself into rather than jumping in all at once. I should have known Cassie wouldn't have the patience for that approach.

"Settling in," she said. "That sounds like more than a quick trip."

"Come on," Ryan said. "You can tell us all about it, but let's get comfortable first."

I nodded, and he led the way through my yard and into his mother's. When we were kids, before his parents split up, Ryan's dad built a gazebo in the back corner of their lot, screened from his house by bushes and from ours by a wooden fence. It's where Ryan's dad spent most of his time in the years before the divorce, going so far as to put in a propane firepit so it was usable space even when the temperature fell. Once he was gone, the three of us had claimed it as our own. Sleepovers, dance parties, drunken evenings planning our respective futures. It was beginning to rot on one side now, but still had a roof, dusty wicker furniture, and privacy. Which was all we really needed. And it was the place where we shared our biggest emotions, starting back when Ryan's dad left. I'd come home from school, assuming Ryan's absence that day was due to illness, and my mom had sat me down and told me Ryan's dad was gone. "Gone where?" I'd asked, munching on an oatmeal cookie. My seven-year-old brain imagined a trip to Kansas City or Wichita. Wondered if he'd bring back something cool. Last time he'd gone out of town, he'd returned with a badminton set we'd played with all summer. "No," my mom had said, mouth tightening. "He's gone for good. He's not coming back."

Later, after dinner, Cassie and I had knocked on Ryan's front door and his mom had directed us to the backyard. We'd found Ryan in the gazebo, curled up on the love seat. He'd taken one look at us and burst into tears, hiding his face in a throw pillow, sobs wracking his tiny shoulders. And Cassie and I had sat beside him, wrapped our arms around him, and hung on. We'd said nothing, not because we'd intuitively known that's what he wanted, but because we were seven and had no idea what words might help. After that, the gazebo had become our code—a message that we needed to share big feelings, and we didn't want reassurance or words of encouragement. We just wanted to be held and allowed to weep. Or to jump around like crazy and scream with happiness. Cassie had used it the first time she asked a girl out, her cheeks red with excitement, hands twirling through the air as she told us the details. I'd used it the night after Eliza's murder, sobbing on the floor with Cassie and Ryan tangled around me. Over the years, this place had soaked up so much pain and so much joy. Stepping inside it always made me feel lighter somehow, its splintered wood the unlikely foundation of a friendship that surpassed the usual limits. The three of us went to movies and traded confidences and laughed at inside jokes. We knew one another's pet peeves and bucket lists. But we held one another's hurt, too, like it was our own. Not a burden but a privilege, the kind that over time knits you together to form your own type of family.

"Man," Cassie said, sinking down onto the faded love seat. "I'd kill for a beer about now." She jabbed Ryan with her elbow. "Why didn't you tell me to pick some up on my way over?"

"Because I can't think of everything."

"Forget the beer," I said, digging around in my bag. "I have something better." I pulled out a joint I'd been saving for the right moment and held it aloft. "Courtesy of Luke Brown. Eighth-grade stoner."

Ryan laughed. "You stole that from one of your kids?"

"I think 'stole' is too strong a word. I prefer to think of it as relieving a minor of something that would have caused him a world of hurt if I'd reported it. Basically a win-win situation for both Luke and me."

Ryan snorted. "Whatever you say."

"You catch kids with drugs a lot?" Cassie asked, eyebrows raised.

I shrugged. "Often enough." People always seemed surprised by the stupid, no-thought-to-the-potential-consequences decisions that teenagers made. But I never was.

I lit the joint and sucked in a lungful of smoke, held it as long as I could before breathing out. Almost immediately I felt better, lighter, the tight fist in my chest easing. "Remind me to thank Luke when I get back to Chicago," I said, passing the joint to Ryan. "Kid knows his weed." I stuck my foot out and poked Cassie's knee. "Sorry I never texted you back. How are things going with you and the waitress?"

"Bartender," Cassie corrected. "And that ended last month."

"Jesus, Dunning," Ryan said. "At least try to keep up."

"Cut her some slack," Cassie said, taking her own puff off of the joint. "You know how hard it is to keep track of my relationships." She rolled her eyes. "What with all the eligible lesbians here in Verdigris County."

"True," Ryan said. "I think at this point you've dated all three of them. Twice."

Cassie laughed. "I would punch you. But, unfortunately, you speak the truth."

Growing up, Cassie's sexuality had never really been a secret between the three of us, and by our sophomore year of high school everyone knew, although many a boy had tried to talk her out of it. Took one look at her curves and waves of auburn hair and felt sure his magical dick would be the one to change her tune. I'd always thought she might move away once we graduated. Not because people treated her badly, but because I'd figured somewhere bigger might give her more opportunity to find someone to spend her life with. But Cassie had chosen to stay. Her family had lived in Ludlow for generations, same as mine. Ludlow was small, and it was dying, but it was home. It was fried chicken at the diner on

Sundays after church; cicadas in the town park and parades down Main Street; the cinnamon gum Mrs. Scudder, the librarian, always chewed, so you could smell her sneaking up on you in time to hide any books she'd deem inappropriate; the green sky right before the tornado sirens sounded and the fresh, clean tang of the air once the danger had passed. It was joy and shame and grief and longing. Ludlow was woven into every part of me, and we could never be untangled.

"What about you?" I asked Ryan. "Divorce final yet?" I was stalling, but I did genuinely want to catch up on their lives. I was shitty about responding to their texts and emails most of the time, lived with a low-grade guilt about letting them carry the heavy load of our friendship into adulthood. After Eliza died, I'd pulled away, needing both distance and solitude, but Cassie and Ryan hadn't allowed a full retreat. Showing up once a year in Chicago without fail, texting and calling and never letting my frequent silence deter them. They held on, tight and sure, my strong, steady anchors in a life that sometimes threatened to swamp me.

Ryan sighed, holding his hand out for the joint. "I'm going to need that before I talk about *that*. But yes, the divorce is basically done. I'm just waiting on the final papers."

I caught Cassie's eye for a second and then looked away. We'd both known Bethany and Ryan were never going to work. Cassie had sent me rapid-fire emails during the entire rushed engagement spitballing ways we might engineer a breakup, her penultimate suggestion being kidnapping Ryan and holding him for a ransom we doubted Bethany would ever pay. Ryan himself seemed to be the only one who couldn't see how wrong Bethany was for him. At the wedding, an overly stuffy affair held in a generic Kansas City hotel ballroom, Ryan's mother had leaned into me, eyes bright with too much wine, and whispered, "She's going to break his heart. Sooner rather than later." In the end, it took a bit longer than Joanne Sawtell had predicted, but her mother's instinct hadn't been wrong. And now Ryan was back in Ludlow, trying to pick up the pieces.

"Well, good fucking riddance," Cassie said. "She sucked."

"She really did," I told Ryan, thinking of Bethany's slightly pinched smile whenever she looked at him, like she was already cataloguing all the ways he was bound to disappoint. "You were way too good for her."

"Yeah, a thirty-year-old underemployed dude living with his mom. I'm a real catch."

"Stop," I said, reaching over and giving his elbow a shake. "If it makes you feel any better, Cassie and I aren't exactly setting the world on fire, either."

Cassie huffed out smoke. "Speak for yourself, loser. I make thirteen bucks an hour and have a line on a semi-attractive chick who works at the Dollar Store in Neosho."

We laughed, but only because we knew Cassie was content. She might bitch and moan about the lack of available potential mates or her going-nowhere job at the diner. But she was one of those people who was satisfied with the life she'd created, even if other people might think it lacked imagination. Cassie had never needed big dreams, huge accomplishments. She didn't light up at other people's approval or wilt under their disappointment. Her opinion of herself, and her life, was the only one that mattered. I had always envied her ease inside her own skin.

Through the trees I watched Joanne Sawtell's kitchen light go off, and I imagined her walking into the living room, settling on the floral armchair in the corner with a romance novel and a glass of wine. As a kid, I'd spent so much time in Ryan's house that I knew its rhythms and tics as well as my own. In the distance the nine o'clock train whistle blew, long and mournful. We used to dare one another to lie across the tracks, only moving when the train was close enough that the rails jumped under our bodies or Chet Majors came out of his house and screamed at us to stop acting like fools.

"You can still set your clock by that train," I said.

"Yep. Ludlow isn't big on surprises," Cassie said, then paused. "Except for you coming home. Ryan and I had a bet on how long it would be before you came back again." She pointed at Ryan. "You owe me twenty bucks, by the way."

"Nice try," he said. "It was ten bucks. And you'll get it when I win the lottery." He turned to me. "So what's the story? Why'd you decide to come home after all this time?"

"Not that we aren't thrilled," Cassie clarified. "But it was unexpected."

For a second, I thought about telling them the truth. But I didn't want to see their worried expressions, watch them exchange looks I wasn't meant to catch like in the weeks following Eliza's death when I'd cornered anyone who would listen to tell them I had a feeling we still didn't have the full story, despite Roy Mathews's arrest. That the who wasn't enough: We needed to figure out *why* Roy had killed Eliza and Travis. My dad had gone so far as to ban me from the store for a while, tired of me inserting myself into every conversation to ask if anyone shared my suspicions. I'd been borderline crazed; I could recognize that now. I'd just wanted to find one person, one single person, who would ask more questions. Who would push the way I needed them to. But I never had. And then came the shoebox hidden away inside my closet. After that, I'd never spoken my suspicions aloud again, and I wasn't going to start now.

I shrugged. "I was worried about my parents, with the new murders. My dad left me a message, drunk and crying. I figured I'd come home for a bit. And work has been a slog lately. I could use the break."

"Yeah," Ryan said. "The whole town's been pretty shook up about Dylan and Addy."

"Did you know them?" I asked. Dylan Short and Addy Johnson. Both eighteen. Both shot to death in the same parking lot where Eliza and Travis died fourteen years ago this month.

"Only to say hello to," Ryan said. "You know how it is around here. No one's a total stranger." His brow furrowed. "Did *you* know them?"

I shook my head. "Not really. I remember Addy's mom coming into the store sometimes. But I don't remember Addy. She would have barely been in elementary school when I left Ludlow. And Dylan's name doesn't ring a bell at all."

"Yeah, his family moved here a few years ago," Ryan said. "Dad got a job with the railroad, I think. Same as my dad, back in the day. From what I've heard, Dylan wasn't thrilled about the move."

"You know we'll always be here for you, right?" Cassie asked, leaning forward to snag my hand in hers. "Whatever you need, even if it's only for us to listen. It doesn't matter why you're back. We're just glad you are."

"Especially because it saves us a trip to Chicago. That's not exactly in the budget right now," Ryan said, shooting up his leg to block Cassie from smacking him. His face sobered, and he put his free hand on top of our joined ones and squeezed.

They were giving me an opening, and I almost came clean. Told them what I was really doing back in Ludlow now. About the nagging feeling I'd carried for fourteen years, like a claw in my gut, telling me this wouldn't be over until every dark secret had been dragged out into daylight. I knew they'd listen, like they always had. Humor me in the kindest possible way, even if they didn't truly believe. But even with my best and oldest friends, there were some things I couldn't risk talking about. So I smiled and kept my mouth shut. Old habits dying hard.

Chapter Four

Roy Mathews wasn't from Ludlow. He'd been raised by his grandmother in Neosho, about fifteen miles down the road. No one knew exactly what had brought him to Ludlow the night of the murders. Neosho was a bigger town, sporting not only a McDonald's but also five bars, a Mexican restaurant, and an ice cream shop. As far as the cops could gather after the fact, Roy hadn't had any friends in Ludlow. But something drew him to our town park. Or someone.

In the year after Eliza died, I drove by the house where Roy grew up a dozen times. I don't know what I thought it might reveal, why I found myself outside the tiny, run-down ranch house over and over again. But whatever I'd hoped to find never showed itself. This morning it looked even sadder than it had back then. Paint peeling off in long strips and the rusted chain-link fence now sagging at the corners of the yard. A battered "Beware of Dog" sign hung off the gate, but there was no snarling beast in sight.

I hadn't meant to actually stop. The plan was to drive by, give the house a look, before heading back to Ludlow for breakfast at the diner. Cassie was working the morning shift and had promised to save me one of Mabel's famous cinnamon rolls. But when I saw what looked like fresh graffiti splashed across the front of the Mathewses' tiny detached garage, I hit the brakes. "MURDRER" in dripping red paint. I assumed the vandal had been going for "murderer," but even with dubious spelling the intent was clear enough. I wondered how often Roy Mathews's grandma had to deal with things like this. Did it happen all the time, or had the execution started it up again?

As if my thoughts had summoned her, I watched as Virginia Mathews emerged from the house onto her tiny front stoop. She was wearing a pink velour tracksuit, her sparse white hair permed to within an inch of its life. She looked smaller and frailer than I remembered, as if a good strong wind might send her tumbling across the yard like a leaf. She paused when she saw my car idling at the end of her driveway, and raised one liver-spotted hand in a tentative wave.

I wasn't surprised that she didn't recognize me. It had been thirteen years since we'd sat in the same crowded courtroom. She'd tried to speak to us only once, stammering out the beginnings of a tearful apology before my mother had steered us around her and out the door. And while Eliza and I had shared a few things—our height, our long fingers, a smile that was a little too wide for our faces—we'd never looked particularly alike, at least in the ways most people compared appearance. Her hair had been coffee to my chestnut, her eyes brown to my hazel. It wasn't until they knew we were sisters that most people claimed to see a resemblance.

I was easing my foot off the brake when a man rounded the corner of the garage, paint can in one hand and roller in the other. He paused, shoulders tightening when he saw my car. Dean Mathews was taller and rangier than his younger brother, with the same mop of dark hair and straight brows. But unlike Roy's carefully neutral gaze, the look Dean gave me across the yard was quick and alive. His grandmother might not be able to place me, but Dean sure as hell could. During the trial, we'd sat on opposite sides of the courtroom for weeks—the only siblings of the victim and the accused, a macabre matched set. We'd never made eye contact. Had never spoken a single word. A sudden flash of memory barreled up from the depths: Dean Mathews sitting stoic and stone-faced through the entire trial, except during the endless closing arguments when the prosecutor had waxed poetic about Roy's elaborate fantasy of killing Eliza and Travis. Personally, I hadn't believed Roy Mathews bothered thinking much beyond his next meal or can of beer. For his part, Dean had shaken his head, slow and steady, unable to recognize his brother in the man the prosecutor was describing.

Dean Mathews set the paint can on the grass and took a step toward the street. I pushed down on the gas, kept my eyes on the rearview mirror. Watched him watching me as I drove away.

• • • •

Like most of Ludlow, the diner didn't look like it had undergone many upgrades in the years I'd been away, but somehow its interior came across as homey and nostalgic rather than depressing. The booths along the wall were still covered in mint green faux leather, worn at the edges, and milky white pendant globes that reminded me of my elementary school classrooms hung from the high tin ceiling on black chains. This had been one of our favorite places to gather after school, doing homework while nursing chocolate milkshakes and inhaling all-you-can-eat baskets of fries. We favored the two booths in the back, both roomy enough for a crowd. Cassie, Ryan, and I crammed into one, sometimes joined by Stella from my homeroom or whichever girl Ryan was dating. The other booth home to Eliza, Travis, and their crew. But every once in a while, when everyone else was busy, it was just Eliza and me huddled together while she helped me with geometry or I proofread her English paper. We had never been the type of sisters who competed with each other, but we weren't best friends the way some sisters are, either. Back then, I'd always hoped that would come later, when we were older. The years binding us tighter and tighter. I'd always pictured us going to the same college, maybe even living together in an off-campus apartment. Holding each other's hair back after drunken parties, helping each other through tough classes. Later, trading maid of honor duties at our weddings. Cradling newborn babies and talking on the phone every day during the hard early years of motherhood. Caring for our parents as they got older, then leaning on each other when we someday lost them. I'd always thought that, eventually, Eliza would be not just my sister but my friend as well. Sometimes I thought most of my grief over her death stemmed from the loss of what might have been rather than the loss of what actually was.

I tore my gaze away from the back booths, shaking off the sharp twinge in my chest, and waved at Cassie as she poured coffee for Chet Majors at the counter. Chet smiled when he saw me, shifting slightly on a counter stool that seemed too delicate for his considerable bulk.

"Well, goddamn," he said as I slid onto the stool next to him. "Look who the cat drug in." He put one arm around me and gave a gentle squeeze. "How you been, darlin'?"

"I've been doing okay," I told him, patted his free hand with my own. Chet had always been Ludlow's resident curmudgeon with a heaping side of busybody. The one who screamed at you for getting up to no good, who complained about the diner coffee being too bitter or the burned-out streetlight on the corner of Elm that needed replacing. The one who knew all the latest scuttlebutt and loved to share, even while he claimed to hate a gossip. People liked to complain about him behind his back, but I'd always loved Chet. Loved knowing he was watching out for me, for all of us, really. He'd been a fixture in my dad's store. Semiretired, even back then, he'd liked to sit on the extra stool next to the cash register and keep my dad company. "Talk my damn ear off's more like it" was my dad's version of it, but I'd known he secretly looked forward to Chet's appearance every morning the same way I had.

"How about you?" I asked. "Life treating you okay?"

"Eh," Chet said. "Got this bum hip makes it hard to walk. And these damn too-high stools don't help the situation." Given Cassie's eye roll, I guessed it wasn't the first time he had voiced that particular complaint. "And my grip is shot. Damn arthritis." He flexed swollen knuckles in my direction. "Never mind what anyone's told ya, Greer. All that rah-rah 'you're only as old as you feel' bullshit. Truth is, aging's a pain in the ass."

"I don't doubt it," I said.

Cassie slid a mug of coffee and a plate with a giant cinnamon roll across the counter toward me. "Enjoy," she said. "If you can manage it while listening to Chet."

Chet ignored her good-natured dig, picked up a fork, and helped himself to a bite of my roll. "Heard you're some kind of school counselor up there in Chicago."

"I am." I took a careful sip of coffee. The diner had always been known for liquids that could scald the skin clean off your tongue, and I doubted that had changed in my absence.

"Kind of surprised to hear it. Never pictured you working in a school. Always thought Eliza was the one who liked kids."

Goddamn Chet. For all his blabbing, he listened, too. Kept everything filed away. "She did," I said, and stuffed a piece of cinnamon roll in my mouth to avoid elaborating. He was right, though. Working with kids had been Eliza's goal, never mine. Unlike her, I'd had no real idea what I wanted my future to look like. I'd floundered in college, changed my major half a dozen times. Waited for advice or direction from my parents that never came. In the end, I'd decided to be a guidance counselor in some vain, pointless tribute to Eliza. Maybe I could fix what had been broken. My new career, my new life, proof that while Eliza was gone, her dreams weren't. And it turned out, I was good at my job, even if most of the time I wasn't sure whether I enjoyed it. Maybe that's why the kids trusted me, though, opened up to me in a way they didn't with most of the other adults in the school—because I didn't commit the cardinal sin of trying too hard. But, in some ways, that only made me feel like more of a fraud. Rather than giving something back to Eliza's memory, I'd ended up stealing from her future instead.

"Hmmm . . ." was all Chet said, for once keeping his abundant opinions under wraps.

"What's with all the ribbons?" I asked, pointing with my fork at the red and blue bows ringing the pickup window behind the counter. The second the question left my mouth, I already knew the answer.

Chet cleared his throat, eyes cutting away from mine. "Those are for Addy and Dylan. Their favorite colors. We've got 'em up all over town."

"They were purple and green for Eliza and Travis," I said, my appetite suddenly gone. I remembered seeing those ribbons on lampposts and doorknobs and wrapped around trees. A reminder—*your sister is dead*—everywhere I looked. "How's everybody doing?" I asked.

Chet huffed. "About like you'd expect. Sleeping with one eye open and a shotgun in their hands." He shook his head. "It's been rough, Greer. Brings back a lot of bad memories. Everybody's hoping they solve this one quick, too. But it's already taken longer than most people would like."

"You have any theories?"

He shook his head. "Not a one. Baker's been trying to keep people calm. Seems pretty set on the copycat theory, and most people don't want to think it was someone from around here. Not like last time. Although in some ways, that was better. Knowing who it was

and getting him locked up so quick. Made it easier to move on."
He paused. "Although not for you, I reckon."

"No," I said with a wince. "Not for me." I pushed away the last
of my cinnamon roll. "Did you know Roy Mathews back then?
Before what happened to Eliza and Travis, I mean?"

Chet furrowed his brow, but didn't seem particularly surprised
at my question. "Know him? Not to speak of. I'd seen him around,
but that's it."

"Around Ludlow?"

He nodded. "Not often. A few times that summer before. Driving that clunker of his. Probably wouldn't have even noticed him,
but that damn muffler sounded like a jet engine. 'Course, didn't
actually know that was him until after the fact."

My heart rate picked up, pulse thrumming in my neck. "What
was he doing here, do you know? Was he ever with anyone?"

"Not that I recall. Just driving down Main. Minding his own
business, far as I could tell."

"And you never saw where he went?"

"Assumed he was passing through." Chet clicked his tongue
against his teeth, concern radiating from underneath his bushy
brows. "You don't still have questions about Roy's guilt, do you,
darlin'?"

"No," I reassured him. "I never had questions about that." That
much, at least, was the truth.

Chet nodded, the sudden tightness in his shoulders easing away.
"Well, if it's any consolation, I'd still like to know why he picked
your sister and Travis, too." He shook his head. "Never made a
damn lick of sense."

In his confession, Roy Mathews had said he'd never seen Eliza
or Travis before the night of their murders, and I believed him. He
hadn't seemed clever enough to cover his tracks or lie convincingly.
If he'd been watching Eliza and Travis, keeping tabs on them, he

would've been spotted. But maybe someone else had been watching. Someone more cunning than Roy. Someone careful. Someone who knew how to kindle a thought in Roy's head and then nurture it into a flame.

. . . .

It was strange to actually walk into the Do Drop Inn, one of Ludlow's only bars and a place I'd glimpsed multiple times from the open doorway but never actually set foot inside. In the two years after Eliza died but before I left for college, I'd been forced to collect my dad from the Do more times than I could count. It was where he hung out back when he was attempting to hide his drinking from us. When he still had some shame. The call always came late, after closing time, my dad too sloshed to even be allowed to walk home along Ludlow's empty sidewalks, never mind drive. My mom stopped answering the phone after the first few times, waving a weary hand in my direction from the doorway of her bedroom. "I can't," she'd always say. "I just can't." I wanted to scream at her retreating back, "What makes you think I can?" But the answer was in the fact that I always, always did. Answered the phone, said I'd be right there, got into my mom's car with my newly minted driver's license, and drove the five blocks in the dead of night. Met Jim, the ever-patient owner of the bar, at the door, and together we'd steer my dad into the passenger seat. Some nights he was singing off tune, a stupid grin on his face I wanted to slap off. Most nights he was weeping, mumbling my sister's name like a record stuck on repeat.

But tonight I wasn't collecting a drunken parent; I was meeting Cassie and Ryan. Apparently they had a standing Thursday night meetup, and now that I was back in town, it was assumed I would join in. I'd been to plenty of bars over the years that worked hard for their dive-inspired interiors. But the Do appeared to come by its dive designation naturally after a lifetime of neglect. Warped wooden floor, cracked mirror behind the Formica-topped bar, dim lighting that was less the result of intent and more a function of shitty bulbs. Everything in the bar looked at risk of leaving behind a sticky residue on your fingers if you touched it. Of the dozen mismatched tables, only half were occupied, although most of the bar stools were taken. Out on the makeshift dance floor a lone couple swayed together to the faint twang of a country song.

"Good god," I said, pulling out a chair. "This place is even more depressing than I imagined. And what is that smell?"

"Beer and sweat. Maybe a little vomit," Ryan said, matter-of-fact. "You get used to it."

"We don't come for the ambiance," Cassie informed me. "We come for the shitty drinks."

"Don't forget the stale peanuts," Ryan said, holding up a small bowl of pale, pre-shelled nuts. He motioned for the server who was leaning against the far wall, picking at something under her nails.

I ordered a bottled beer, which seemed safe enough. "So," I said. "Thursday nights, huh? Getting the weekend started early?"

"Can't come on Fridays. It's eighties night and the place is packed. 'Hungry Like the Wolf' on repeat until you want to bash your brains in." Ryan palmed a handful of peanuts and tossed them into his mouth.

"Sounds delightful."

The waitress returned with my beer and I took a swig, wincing a little at the bitter aftertaste. From behind me, I heard a commotion by the door, the rowdy boom of men's voices.

"Great," Cassie said, voice dry. "The king of Ludlow has arrived. Guess the party can start now." She looked at me. "Hold onto your panties, Greer."

I glanced over my shoulder and saw a pack of guys about our age ambling inside. The one in the lead was Garrett Bloom. Undeserving recipient of my high school crush. Taker of my virginity in the backseat of his car at his senior prom. Me, drunk and crying over Eliza. Him, humping away and telling me he was about to make me feel so good. Which, by the way, turned out to be false advertising. Afterward, we barely spoke again.

"Oh, Jesus," I said, swinging back to face the table.

"He's a cop now," Ryan informed me. "Maybe he can get his handcuffs out."

"Yeah," Cassie chimed in. "Tell you what a bad girl you've been."

I snorted out a laugh, and a heavy hand landed on my shoulder.

"Hey now, is that Greer Dunning I spy?"

I caught Cassie's eye, and her shit-eating grin, as I looked up. "Hey, Garrett. How's it going?"

"Going great, going great." Garrett pulled out a chair without being invited, spun it around and straddled it, arms propped on the back. I tried very hard not to roll my eyes. He was still objectively good-looking—light brown hair, green eyes, dimpled chin—but I had a hard time remembering what it was I'd ever found fascinating about him. He looked generic to me now, interchangeable with a thousand other guys who've never had to work for a woman's attention a day in their lives, so grow to think they're entitled to it.

"Glad to hear it," I said, ignoring Ryan's foot pressing against mine under the table.

"I'm in law enforcement," Garrett told me. "Been with the sheriff's department for almost ten years. Dating a gal teaches third grade here in town."

"Wow," I said. "Sounds like you've done well for yourself." *Be nice*, I cautioned. An inside track with a local cop might come in handy, if I played my cards right.

Garrett nodded, flashed me the grin that used to make my stomach give birth to a whole net of butterflies. "May have to dump the girlfriend, though, seeing as how you're back and looking good." He stretched the last word out to twice its normal length, capped it off with a wink and a click of his mouth.

"Charming," Cassie muttered, and I smiled around my upturned beer bottle.

"Well, I don't want to keep you from your friends," I said, glancing at the table behind me. I recognized the same crew of guys Garrett had hung out with back in high school—Eric, Tag, Connor—and returned their waves with a half-hearted one of my own. Looking at their faces triggered a quick, queasy flash of déjà vu, as if we were all teenagers again, Travis and Eliza hovering on the edges of the party, just out of sight. I took a deep breath, blinking against the strangeness, forcing reality back into focus. Behind Garrett's friends, the door to the bar opened again and a man walked in. It took me a second to place him, only because he was the last person I'd expected to see in the Do. Dean Mathews. My breath stuttered in my chest, and I sucked in a little whooping gasp.

"Aw, hell, no," Garrett said. "What's that shit stain doing here?"

I watched as Dean took an empty stool at the far end of the bar, gestured for the bartender with an upturned hand. The air in the room had turned thick with anticipation, everyone eyeing Dean and waiting for what might happen next.

"Want me to get rid of him?" Garrett asked, chair legs scraping as he started to stand. I had a sudden vision of him making a scene, grabbing Dean by the scruff of the neck and the seat of his jeans and giving him the old heave-ho through the front door. Or at least trying to. Something about Dean Mathews told me he'd probably learned the hard way how to hold his own against guys like Garrett.

"Leave him alone. It's fine." I looked around the table. "Who's ready for another round?" I was up and walking to the bar before anyone could answer. The space next to Dean was open and I slid into it, leaned forward and rested my elbows on the bar top without making eye contact. I had no idea what I was doing, what I was hoping for. A conversation? An explanation? An apology? I'd spent years hating Roy Mathews, and by extension his entire family. My wrath always felt too large to rest on a single person. I'd blamed his grandmother for raising him wrong. I'd blamed his brother for not stopping him. I'd blamed them both for the violence Roy had unleashed into the world. But now, with one of my targets right in front of me, my anger was taking an ill-timed vacation. And I desperately needed to hold onto it, terrified of the other rawer emotions buried behind my fury.

Next to me, Dean was cupping a glass of amber liquid, remnants of white paint on his fingers. I glanced up, and our eyes met in the mirror behind the bar. Dean took a swallow of his drink. "Spelling's not a strong suit around here," he said, flexing his free hand, where more white paint lined his knuckles. "But they get their point across." His voice was deeper than I'd expected, his southern Kansas twang less pronounced than his brother's.

"Does that happen a lot?" I asked. "People vandalizing your grandma's house?" I felt suspended outside my body, listening to myself speak but not really believing I was actually having a conversation with Roy's brother after all these years.

He shrugged. "Often enough." I watched as he took another slug of his drink, set the glass back down with a sharp tap.

I turned slightly away from him, signaled the bartender.

"You weren't at the execution," Dean said.

"No." For so long, as I watched my family crumble and couldn't do a damn thing to stop it, I'd longed for the day when Roy Mathews would take his last breath. But in the end, I hadn't been brave enough to witness it. And Roy dying hadn't changed a damn thing. I looked at Dean. "You were there, I'm guessing?"

"Yeah. Didn't want to be." He slid off the bar stool, slapped a ten-dollar bill on the counter. "But he was my brother. I couldn't let him die alone."

And there it was, just in time. Resentment boiled up from the pit of my stomach, bile rising in my throat. Eliza might have been in Travis's arms when Roy pulled the trigger, but she'd still died alone, scared, and without her family. My hand knotted on the bar top. "Are you seriously asking me to feel sorry for you right now?"

Dean shook his head. "Believe me, Greer," he said, voice weary as he turned away. "I'm not asking you for anything at all."

Chapter Five

Sheriff Wayne Baker looked like a lawman. Not a cop in a patrolman's uniform. Not a detective with a suit and tie. An honest-to-god lawman, like someone out of an old Western with the star pinned front and center on his chest and his narrow, weather-beaten, no-bullshit face. He always came across as laconic, body relaxed and voice a lazy drawl, leaning against the counter at the grocery store back in the day, shooting the shit with my dad and Chet Majors. But I knew it would be a mistake to underestimate him. I'd always suspected he could have his gun drawn and a shot fired before you'd even realized he'd moved. Seeing him again after all this time, it was a bit of a shock to find him eating scrambled eggs out of a styrofoam cup with his legs crossed at the ankle and propped on the desk in front of him.

"Hey, Sheriff," I said, pushing through the low swinging gate that separated the lobby from the area where he was seated. As far as I could tell, we were the only people at the police station, the front counter unmanned and the other desks empty even though it was already late morning. Given the recent murders, most of the deputies were probably out asking questions and reassuring anxious residents.

He forked in another mouthful of egg before setting the cup aside, then swung his legs slowly off the desk. "Heard you were back in town. Been years. I bet your parents are glad to see you home after such a long time."

My stomach clenched, but it was a gentle enough rebuke, considering. "They are," I said, although whether it was true, I had no real idea.

"What can I do for you?" Baker asked, and I didn't think I was imagining the slight hesitation in his voice. He was probably worried I was going to start vomiting conspiracy theories all over the place.

"Nothing, actually," I said. "I wanted to talk to Garrett. He around?"

Baker gave me a long look and pointed toward the rear of the station. "Out back." I nodded, picked my way around the desks. "Word is you've got a whole life for yourself up in Chicago," he said as I reached the back door.

"A whole life" might be pushing it, but I understood what he was getting at. I paused and looked back at him, confident he had more to say. "Be a shame to see you get all turned around again, Greer. It took a toll last time. On everyone. Sometimes it's best to let things lie."

I wondered if he was remembering the morning he'd come to work and found me sitting on the sidewalk outside the door, waiting for him. Already asking questions and spouting theories before he'd even gotten his key in the lock. I'd peppered Baker with questions whenever I'd seen him—at the funeral, at the store, outside the police station when he was getting out of his patrol car. At first he'd been patient, but as the days wore on, his patience gave way to aggravation and then to pity—that final confrontation burned into my mind like it had happened only yesterday.

He'd let me into the station with a sigh and then called my parents. Hadn't even been able to look me in the eye as he led me out to my mother's car idling at the curb. Later that same afternoon I was in Wichita sitting across from a therapist who spoke in soothing tones that made me want to scream. No one believed me. No one heard what I was saying, my insistence that everyone was missing an essential piece of the puzzle ascribed to my grief. I'd never mentioned the murders to Baker again.

"Good talk," I said, shoving the door open with my shoulder.

I found Garrett outside, leaning against the cinder block wall with one leg cocked. He looked like someone on a smoke break, but he was clutching a tin of Altoids instead of a cigarette. "Hey there," he said, shielding his eyes with one hand against the glare of the sun. "What brings you here?" In the light of day he seemed less full of bravado, even decked out in his uniform, than he had last night in the bar.

"I didn't get a chance at the Do, but I wanted to ask you about the murders. The recent ones like Eliza and Travis."

Garrett held out the mints as I took up a position next to him leaning against the wall. "These things clear out your sinuses like a blowtorch, but I got myself addicted to them when I was quitting smoking last year."

"No, thanks," I said.

He pocketed the tin and leaned his head back. "Don't know how much I can tell you that you probably don't already know. Addy and Dylan were both seniors at Ludlow High. Like your sister and Travis. He was on the baseball team. She was involved in the-ater. Been dating about a year. Each killed with a single shot to the head."

"What kind of gun?"

"A .44 Magnum."

"Same as Eliza and Travis."

"Not the same gun, though, obviously," he said. The gun that had killed Eliza and Travis had been recovered from Roy Mathews's house. Hidden under his mattress and covered with his finger-prints. Purchased from a private dealer a week before the murders.

Roy hadn't been old enough to buy a six-pack of beer, but getting his hands on a gun hadn't been a problem.

"And copycat is what you're thinking?" I asked.

Garrett shrugged. "I suppose it could be a complete coincidence. But seems unlikely. Same type of gun. Same time of year. Same MO, sneaking up on a couple of teenagers dry humping in a car at the town park. Like shooting fish in a barrel." He glanced at me. "Sorry."

"Don't worry about it." Over the years I'd heard a hundred worse things. That my sister'd been killed with her boobs hanging out. That Travis had died mid-orgasm. That any hunter worth a shit should have been able to take them both out with a single shot. That Eliza was a slut who'd deserved it. Each one an arrow I'd taken as a direct hit until, eventually, the barbs barely registered. By now, when it came to how Eliza had died, I had skin so thick it felt impenetrable.

"At this point, we're figuring it was someone passing through," Garrett said. "Some crazy who came to town wanting to re-create what happened with your sister and Travis and then kept right on moving."

His words sounded rote, like something he'd memorized in the bathroom mirror, and I raised my eyebrows at him, but he kept his gaze fixed straight ahead. "Have you found any evidence of that?" I asked. "Like online? Maybe someone making threats beforehand?"

"Not yet," Garrett admitted. "But we're still looking."

"Was there anything different this time? Anything that stood out?"

Garrett shook his head. "I can't give you any more details, Greer. Some things aren't for just anybody to know."

"I'm not just anybody," I pointed out. His casual dismissal sliced through the tender parts of me, making it hard to catch my breath. *Just anybody?* As if Eliza hadn't died the same way. As if I hadn't stood in the funeral parlor and gazed down at her misshapen head, the shattered pieces of her skull the mortician had tried in vain to reconfigure into someone resembling my sister.

"You know what I mean." Garrett pushed off from the wall. "Better get back inside before Baker has a stroke." He paused at the door. "It's really good to see you again. We had fun at prom, didn't we?"

Of all the adjectives I might have used to describe that night—"drunken," "sweaty," "painful," "humiliating," "stupid"—"fun" wasn't even on my list. "Yeah, sure," I said, voice flat.

"Maybe we could try it again sometime."

"What about the third-grade teacher you're dating?"

He grinned. "What about her?"

I blew out a groan. "You're not nearly as charming as you think you are, Garrett."

That only made him grin wider. "As I recall, you were pretty charmed back in high school."

"Yeah, well, I was young and dumb."

He laughed, threw me an exaggerated wink. "Just how I like 'em."

I smiled despite myself, shaking my head. What had Eliza always said about Garrett? *You can't keep that guy down. He's twenty pounds of confidence in a ten-pound bag.* "Are you going to the vigil tonight?"

"Yeah," he said, grin fading. "I'll be there. You?"

I nodded, stayed leaning against the wall after Garrett went back into the station. Tonight would be my first real test. Ludlow out in force and eager to judge. I could already hear the words, innocuous on the surface, but full of teeth down below. *We thought you'd never come back! Look at you, it's been so long! We figured you'd forgotten all about us!* A big part of me wanted to skip the vigil, stay home and hide. But I owed it to Addy and Dylan to be there, to bear witness. Because if I had been braver, they might still be alive.

. . . .

I was sprawled across my bed, trying to decide if I had the energy for another stilted dinner with my parents, when my mom knocked on my doorjamb. "You awake?"

"Yeah," I said, propping myself up on my elbows. "What's up?"

"Nothing, really." She hesitated in the doorway "I wanted to talk to you."

I sat all the way up, swinging my legs off the side of the bed. "Okay." My voice was reluctant, but inside I couldn't stifle the stupid, never-gonna-learn part of me that hoped after all these years we were finally going to have a real conversation again. That for even a few minutes she might resemble the mom who used to scratch my back when I couldn't sleep, who let me try to teach her every new dance craze and never got mad when I laughed at her attempts, who always marked even the most minor of occasions with cupcakes or a card, who sometimes talked to me so much I prayed she'd leave me alone. That maybe, finally, I'd be able to open my mouth and tell her all the things I didn't know how to say.

"I just . . . I . . ." She gave her head a small shake, wrung her hands together. "Does chicken and rice casserole sound all right for dinner?"

I looked away from her. Outside, an airplane cut across the sky, its fluffy white contrail the only mark on an otherwise crystalline blue canvas. "Yeah, that's fine." I flopped back onto my bed, covered my face with both hands. "Whatever you want."

Chapter Six

The vigil for Dylan and Addy was held at the town park, the most picturesque spot in Ludlow and its central point, the rest of the town fanning outward from its green interior. It was almost dark by the time Ryan and I arrived, and although we hung back on the edges of the crowd, whispers started almost immediately. I kept my head up, my eyes forward, but I wished Cassie hadn't had to work. I missed her larger-than-life presence pressed to my other side.

"Hey," Ryan said, slinging an arm across my shoulder and giving me a squeeze. "You good?"

"Yeah," I said with a grateful nod. "I'm okay." I wasn't really. My eyes kept pulling toward the oversized photos of Addy and Dylan propped on easels in the grass, bouquets and stuffed animals scattered at their bases. Red and blue ribbons fluttering in the breeze. They were the same pictures I'd seen on the banner announcing the vigil, but these versions were clear and in screaming Technicolor. A blond girl with ocean-blue eyes, a sliver of a gap between her front teeth. A boy with brown hair that fell in a swoop over his forehead, his mouth ticking up on one side with the promise of a grin. They looked impossibly young and beautiful, and I blinked frantically against the burning in my eyes as I looked away.

Pete Jenkins, the owner of the gas station, handed Ryan a box filled with long tapers pushed through cardboard circles meant to catch the wax as they melted. Ryan took two, holding them toward Pete's lighter, while I cupped the flames against the breeze. I turned to pass the box to the woman on my right, distracted as I reached for my lit candle with my other hand.

"I thought that was you," Mrs. Allard said, leaning forward a little to capture my attention. A smile on her lips, but not in her eyes. "I was starting to worry you'd forgotten your way back to Ludlow."

Well, that didn't take long. One quick sucker punch to my gut she could tell herself later had been only a joke, even as I still nursed the bruise she left behind. "Nope, I didn't forget," I said, working to keep my voice light. "How have you been?"

"I've been all right," she said. "This has been hard." She gestured toward the crowd with her candle. "They were good kids. Both of them."

"Were they in your class?" Mrs. Allard was a staple at Ludlow High, patrolling the halls with a ruler in her hand that she whacked against lockers when kids were in danger of missing the bell. Her domain was honors English, and she had a love affair with *Wuthering Heights* so intense that Eliza had been convinced she probably spent her free time writing Heathcliff erotica. The memory brought an inappropriate laugh bubbling up, and I swallowed it with a cough. I'd almost forgotten how funny Eliza could be sometimes, her humor always sneaking up on you.

"I retired before Addy started high school," Mrs. Allard told me, her tone laced with another reminder about everything I'd missed by staying away so long. "And Dylan just moved here his sophomore year. But you know how it is in Ludlow, no one's a stranger."

I turned back to Ryan, leaning into his side with a shiver. I was grateful I'd thought to throw on a sweater as I left the house. With darkness descending, the air had bite. We were far enough from the center of the vigil that I only got the outlines of what was happening. Someone speaking into the microphone, voice still too soft to make out; a remembrance read in a monotone; hymns sung off-key with most of us mumbling the words.

"Are the parents here?" I whispered to Ryan between songs.

He shook his head. "I don't think so."

I couldn't blame them for not coming, for not being willing to put their grief on display for the entire town. It was theirs, but somehow everyone felt entitled to a piece of it. In the days after Eliza died, when people showed up at our door with casseroles or gathered around us in knots at the burial, their concern, well-meaning as it might have been, came at a price. We'd been spared a vigil, at least, because Roy had been caught so quickly. Once he was behind bars, everyone wanted to move on, not dwell in the horror. There'd only been the memorial, held months after the funerals, to dedicate the bench, and that had been painful enough.

As the evening grew darker, faces glowing in the ring of candlelight, I let my gaze wander. Clumps of teenagers wearing red or blue T-shirts, arms around one another as they cried. Parents with drawn faces, imagining their own children's pictures on display. I saw Baker near the microphone, his gaze sweeping the crowd. Garrett was on the other side of the circle, his eyes ticking back and forth, just like Baker's. And across from him, another deputy, body still and watchful. They weren't here as supportive members of this community, mourning the dead, I realized suddenly. They were hunting, looking for what didn't belong. An overabundance of tears, a misplaced smile, a stare that lingered. Ice flowed along my limbs, pooling in my stomach. No matter what they said to the press, what they tried to make everyone believe, the cops thought the same thing I did. The killer was still here in Ludlow. One of us.

A movement on the far side of the gathering caught my attention—a man standing alone, backed up almost to the edge of the tree line, candle held so low I couldn't get a good look at him. I squinted, peering into the shadows, taking a step closer until I almost collided with the couple in front of me. "Sorry," I murmured, eyes still searching. In the distance, the man's candle lifted, illuminating his face. My skin tingled, a breath hitching in my chest. Dean Mathews. All around us people lowered their heads in prayer, but I kept my eyes raised until he looked at me, our gazes locked. In the candlelight his face looked almost gaunt, mouth drawn tight. His eyes burned. Even from where I stood, his pain reached out to mine—a recognition passing between us. I was carrying the weight of so many dead. But maybe I wasn't carrying it alone.

. . . .

After only a few days at home, I'd fallen right back into the routine I'd established before I'd left. Resenting my parents, avoiding my friends, fixating on Eliza's death, driving around in the evenings, aimless and alone, trying very hard not to think beyond the next mile in front of me. Already I could feel this place working at me, long fingers of memory reaching into the dark, neglected recesses of my mind, trying to unravel the careful stories I told myself. Tonight I stopped at the park again, pulled into the tiny lot as the sun was beginning to slip away. In the distance, I could see Eliza and Travis's bench. But for the first time I could recall, there was someone sitting on it. I fumbled with my seat belt, practically tumbling out of the car in my rush. I knew it was stupid to think the person sitting there had anything to do with Eliza's death, but I wanted to see for myself. Who in this town would choose that spot to take a load off, sit back and relax on a bench marked for the dead?

But when I got closer, I saw it wasn't a Ludlow local. And Dean Mathews wasn't relaxed. He was hunched over, his forearms resting on his knees, hands clasped, shoulders bunched tight. I slowed, started to pivot back toward my car, when he turned his head to the side and saw me. We stared at each other the way we had in the bar mirror. The way we had across the crowd at the vigil just a few days ago. Assessing, challenging, but also strangely companionable. Like maybe our hells weren't the same, but we'd both been living there.

"Hey," I said, voice quiet.

He didn't answer, but he scooted down the bench, leaving room for plenty of space between us if I chose to take the offering.

I slid in next to him, watching the long shadows of evening turn the grass a dark, mossy green. The crisp edges of fall nipped at my skin, and I pulled down the sleeves of my sweater, tucked my hands inside. "Do you come here a lot?"

"Every once in a while. It's a good thinking spot. What about you?"

"No. Never. Not to actually sit." I realized how stiffly I was holding my body and forced myself to sink back against the bench.

"I've always wanted to talk to you," he said after a minute of silence.

"Okay," I said, careful.

"I feel like I owe you an explanation. Or something." He spread his hands, let them fall back to his thighs. "All my life, it was my job to watch over Roy. Make sure he went to school, make sure he didn't get in fights, make sure he got to work on time. But that summer before the murders, I just . . . stopped." He sighed. "Talk about falling down on the job at the worst possible moment. Jesus."

"Weren't you only a year older than Roy?" I asked. "Why was any of that your responsibility?"

"Our mom walked out when we were kids. Never called, never sent a card. She disappeared in search of her next high, her habit more important than we were. And my grandma did her best, but we were a lot to handle. If I didn't try, there wasn't anyone else."

I remembered that from the sentencing phase of the trial. Roy's attorney arguing that his shitty childhood and absent mother had warped him, making him no longer responsible for his actions.

"Roy was acting weird before the murders. Or weirder than usual," Dean continued. "On edge. Some days happy, others angry and withdrawn. I should have paid more attention. Done *something.*"

Dean was accusing himself of the very things I'd already convicted him of inside my own head. Here, finally, was my chance to rub salt in his wounds, but I couldn't quite bring myself to do it. Somehow his easy acceptance of blame made me less eager to dish out condemnation of my own. It was a neat party trick, and the cynical side of me wondered if he knew exactly what reaction he'd draw out of me with his sad eyes and hangdog expression. "What could you have done? You couldn't have watched him every second," I pointed out.

"I don't know. Pushed him harder about what was going on. Forced him to talk to me." Dean threw up a helpless hand. "But I was tired. Sick of worrying about him. Sick of my life. I know it doesn't help, but I wish all the time I could go back and do it differently."

"But we can't." He had no idea how many nights I'd lain awake wishing for the exact same thing.

"Nope." He gave me a forced half smile. "We can't."

A fat goose waddled in front of us, inching our way in search of food, and Dean stuck out his foot to keep it from getting too close. I took the opportunity to really look at him, a little disconcerted by how much he actually had in common with his brother. Same sharp jaw and straight nose. Blue eyes and dark brows. But Roy was forever a teenager in my mind, skin unblemished by time and age. Dean's face told a very specific story of sun and wind and hard labor. Fine lines and weather-browned skin. The years working away at him the same way they had at me. It was like sitting next to a Roy who'd gotten away with it instead of being executed, and something dark and heavy walked over my grave.

"Do you think they'll put a bench for Dylan and Addy right there?" Dean pointed to the empty patch of grass to his left, pulling me out of my own head. "Or tack another plaque onto this one?"

I turned to glance at the plaque on the back of the bench. "Dunning and Pratt. Gone too soon." Generic would be an understatement. "This makes them sound like a law firm. If they add two more last names, it'll really seal the deal."

Dean laughed, his eyebrows shooting up. "I'm guessing the engraver charged by the letter." He'd returned to his earlier position, bent forward, arms on knees, but his gaze was on me.

"It's weird, isn't it?" I said. "The new murders. After all this time." I knew what I was doing, poking around the edges of what I really wanted to say. Hoping if I gave him an opening, he might walk through.

"Yeah," he said. "It's weird. Doesn't feel random to me."

The tiny hairs on my arms stood up; a chill tiptoed up my spine. "What do you mean?" I asked, while inside a little voice chanted: *Please please please.*

He shrugged. "It's why I come here. To think about Roy and what happened." He closed his eyes. "You are not the person I should be talking to about this."

"We'd probably give the entire town of Ludlow a collective heart attack if they saw us sitting here together," I agreed. "But I don't care. Not anymore. I wouldn't have asked if I didn't want an answer." And he was the one person I could ask, I realized. The one person to whom I didn't owe a single thing, who expected nothing of me. The one person in this entire town I couldn't hurt or disappoint.

"Okay, then." He rubbed the back of his neck with one hand,

opened his eyes. "I know my brother killed your sister and Travis. Not a doubt in my mind. Hell, he told me he did it right to my face, and he was a terrible liar. I would have known if he was bullshitting me. Truth is, Roy was volatile and violent and capable of a lot of bad shit. But he was also unmotivated and definitely not the sharpest tool in the shed. He was the kind of guy who might get provoked into a fistfight and end it with a knife. Something like that wouldn't have surprised me. But sneaking up on two people he didn't even know? Shooting them for fun? That wasn't Roy. If nothing else, it took too much effort. Roy reacted. He didn't act." Dean leaned back against the bench again. "Does that make any sense at all?"

"Yes," I said and paused. Then took a chance. "You don't think it was his idea, do you?"

"No. But that could be my own wishful thinking. Maybe I want there to be another person to shoulder some of the blame. Maybe—"

"I don't think he came up with it alone, either," I said before Dean could talk himself out of his own conviction. Before he could try to talk me out of mine. It was the first time in years I'd spoken these words out loud, and there was a relief in expressing them again.

"Which would mean," Dean said, holding my gaze, "if there was someone else involved, then Dylan and Addy are probably part of it, too."

"Yes," I said in a rush. "I don't know how or why. But yes."

He blew out a long breath. "Is that what brought you back here?"

"I'm in Ludlow because I felt like I had to be." *Come back.* "Ever since Eliza's murder, it's like I've been waiting for the other shoe to drop. My whole life just . . . paused." Sometimes my life since Eliza's death felt like a blank canvas, years sliding past with nothing of substance to mark them. Just a pale, sad imitation of living that left no permanent imprint behind. "There were times I could almost convince myself it was all in my head. But now, with the new murders . . ." I trailed off, and Dean didn't need to say a word for me to know he understood. That what had happened here on a chilly October night more than a decade ago followed him, too. A specter he couldn't outrun.

"You know it won't change anything," he said. "Even if we're right. It all still happened." He paused. "They'll always be gone." He meant more than Eliza and Travis, more than Addy and Dylan. He meant his brother, too.

"I know that," I said. And I did, better than anyone. But it would never end for me until I uncovered the whole story. I would look at every face in this town I used to love and ask myself, *Was it you?* If there was ever any hope of moving forward, I had to go back. "But I want to try. For all of them, and for myself, too." And maybe it would be less terrifying with someone beside me, someone who listened to my theories and didn't look at me with pity or disbelief. The irony wasn't lost on me—the one person I could finally talk to about this was also the last person I'd ever expected to confide in.

"The police are already investigating," Dean pointed out. "They've come to talk to me and my grandma, trying to find a link between Roy and the new murders beyond the obvious. If there's anything to be found, don't you think they'll find it?"

"Maybe," I said. "But that doesn't mean we can't look, too."

He paused, staring down at his hands like he was weighing the pros and cons in his palms. "All right," he said finally, with a small shake of his head, like he couldn't quite believe the words coming out of his mouth. "I'm in."

I pictured what Ryan and Cassie would say if they were here to witness this. Not to mention my parents or Sheriff Baker. A laugh cracked out of me before I could stop it. "Where do we start?"

"The only place we can," Dean said. "At the beginning."

Chapter Seven

t turned out "the beginning" was a relative term. Dean and I agreed pretty quickly that there wasn't much benefit in going all the way back to the day Roy was born or re-creating Eliza's life from kindergarten forward. The summer before the murders felt like the key. That was when Roy had started acting differently and, given the fact that Dean and I had no actual idea what in the hell we were doing, it presented a manageable chunk of time to delve into.

We'd decided that if we were going to do this, there was no point wasting time. Maybe both of us were worried the other would change their mind if we didn't get cracking. So we'd agreed to meet first thing the next morning. I'd woken up before my alarm and was filling a small thermos with coffee when my mom bustled into the kitchen, a laundry basket perched on her hip. "You're up early," she said to me.

"Hmmm . . . yeah."

"I can make you some eggs, if you like. Or pancakes."

"Don't worry about it. I'll grab a granola bar."

She set the basket on the kitchen table and pulled out a clean dish towel, folded it into a neat square with a snap. "Are you going somewhere?"

"Meeting a friend," I said. I scooted out of the kitchen and

down the hall before she could ask any more questions. I knew my
hanging out with Dean was going to get back to her eventually—it
wasn't the sort of thing you could hide for long in a town Ludlow's
size, not when we were going to be out in public, asking questions
and making nuisances of ourselves—but I wasn't prepared to have
that conversation yet. It had been bad enough right after Eliza died,
when I'd insisted there was more to the story. Every time I'd said
the words, my mother had burst into tears as she pleaded with me
to stop, and my father's eyes had taken on a faraway look, like he
was retreating to a place I could never reach. I'd stayed away so long
in part because I wasn't quite ready to watch my unrelenting need
to know butt right up against my parents' pain and press hard on
their open wound. We'd barely survived it the last time.

Dean and I had agreed to meet on the corner of Locust and
Elm, and I tried not to scurry down the street like a fugitive. He
was already at the corner when I got there, idling in a rust-speckled
white SUV.

"Hey," I said, hauling myself inside.

"Mornin'. You have to give that door a hard slam to get it shut."

I yanked on the door as instructed, hit the manual lock for good
measure. "I was a little worried you might not show up. Leave me
hanging."

He glanced at me. "I wouldn't do that."

I took a swig of coffee from the thermos and then held it out,
but he shook his head. "Where we headed?" I asked. We'd decided
to start by digging into Roy's life, and I'd left it up to Dean to figure
out our first steps.

"Stafford's," he said, drumming his fingers against the cracked
steering wheel. "Piece-of-shit auto graveyard out on 47. It's where
Roy worked the couple years before the murders. He dropped out
of high school after his junior year and went to work for Merl."

I had a vague notion of where Dean was taking us—the auto-salvage eyesore glimpsed off in the distance every time you drove between Ludlow and Neosho. But I'd never actually turned down the gravel road and visited the place. Which turned out to have been a smart move considering the number of tire-swallowing potholes Dean had to navigate around just to get us there. If your car wasn't shot to shit before you arrived at Stafford's, it would be by the time you braved the narrow gravel driveway and pulled up in the weed-infested front lot. The entire patch of land was covered in junked cars as far as the eye could see. Some there long enough they appeared to be growing out of the ground, flat tires melting into the dirt, green shoots of plants weaving out of shattered windshields and wrapping around the rusting frames. The wind gusted in off the prairie, moaning and sighing as it swept through the metal husks.

"Word of warning," Dean said as I reached to unbuckle my seat belt. "Merl Stafford is kind of a dick. Try not to take it personally."

Before I could ask any follow-up questions, an overweight man of indeterminate age wearing dirty overalls and a pit-stained wife-beater appeared from the dark doorway of the garage nearest our car. He had long gray hair tied in a ponytail at the nape of his neck, and despite his size, he moved gracefully, quicker than you'd expect at first glance. He wiped his hands on a grease-encrusted rag and glared at us.

"Hi there, Merl," Dean said, exiting the car and motioning for me to follow.

"What the fuck you want?" Merl said. "And who's she?"

"She's local. From Ludlow."

Merl ran his gaze from me back to Dean. "Didn't ask where she was from. Asked who the fuck she was."

I stepped forward. "My name's Greer. I'm a friend of Dean's."

Merl stared at me, hawked up a brownish loogie, and spit it at my feet, then turned and disappeared into the dank garage.

"*Kind of* a dick?" I whispered to Dean, and he elbowed me gently in the ribs.

"Well, you coming or not?" Merl bellowed. "I ain't got all fucking day."

I followed Dean into the garage, stepping around abandoned car parts and puddles of oil. Merl was already back to work, systematically ripping apart a sad little Honda that had seen better days even before Merl got his hands on it.

"Won't keep you long," Dean said, leaning back against a cluttered workbench. "We wanted to ask you a few questions about Roy."

"'We'?" Merl asked, turning his gaze to me. "What fucking business is it of hers?" He stared at me with flat eyes, and my stomach dropped to somewhere in the vicinity of my toes. I suspected people might call Merl a lot of things, but a dog with no bite wasn't ever going to be one of them.

"Don't worry about her," Dean said, voice even.

Slowly, Merl turned his gaze back to Dean. "Last I heard, your lazy, thieving brother was dead. What's the point of asking questions now?"

I watched Dean's jaw tighten up and then release, and I admired his self-control. I suspected over the last decade he'd had lots of practice. "Roy never did tell the cops why he did it. Never told me, either. I'd rest easier if I knew."

Merl stepped away from the car, fished a tin of tobacco from his pocket, and tucked a healthy wad into his gum, using his tongue to work it into position. "Don't like what your brother did," he said. "But don't like what happened to him, neither. Government ain't got no business killing people. Not with how often they screw up everything else." He twisted his head, spat onto the concrete floor. "What you wanna know?"

Dean pushed himself away from the workbench, moved a little closer to Merl. I stayed where I was, tried to melt into the background. I had a feeling the less Merl saw of me, a stranger he didn't trust, the looser his lips might be. "How was Roy that summer? Did you notice anything different about him?"

Merl grunted. "Not really. Only thing stood out was he started helping himself to my till. Been working here for almost two years and all of a sudden starts stealing. Only a little at a time. Five dollars here, ten dollars there. That's why it took me so long to notice. Fired his ass the day I figured it out. Should have beat his ass while I was at it."

"How long before the murders did the stealing start?" Dean asked.

"Let me check my calendar," Merl said, rolling his eyes. "Hell, I don't know. But not more than a month or two. Maybe three."

"Did he say what he needed the money for?"

"Nope, and I didn't bother asking. Don't care if he was using it to save a dying orphan. Wasn't his goddamn money to take."

"Did you notice anyone hanging around here that summer? Was Roy spending time with anyone new?"

Merl snorted, sucking phlegm down his throat, and turned back to the Honda. "I never paid any attention to what Roy was doing that didn't involve work. He coulda rolled up here with the goddamn Dallas Cowboy Cheerleaders in his car and I wouldn'ta paid no mind so long as he did his job."

"That's a no, then?" Dean pressed.

Merl was bent over at the waist, working under the hood, and he shook his head back and forth, slow, letting out a long stream of air. He reminded me of a bull, one wrong move away from a full-on charge. "That's a no," he said finally. "Now get the fuck outta here and let me work."

I didn't speak until we were safely back in the car and headed down the drive. "Well," I said, "he seemed great. Real charmer."

Dean snorted out a laugh. "He's worse than I remembered."

"Do you think he was telling the truth?"

"With Merl it's hard to say. He'd have no problem lying, for any reason or no reason at all. But I also don't know why he'd bother. I seriously doubt he's covering up some big secret about Roy. Like he said, all he cared about was the work getting done."

"Did you know Roy was stealing from him?"

Dean shook his head. "No, I hadn't heard that before. I've got no idea what Roy was doing. What's the point of stealing ten bucks here and there? Especially from a guy like Merl. That's risking your life for a pretty measly reward."

"Could he have been saving up for the gun?"

"I don't think so. Merl would have noticed sooner if he'd taken that much, even over time. And after Roy was arrested, my grandma realized her engagement ring was missing. She'd had to stop wearing it when her arthritis got too bad. Pretty sure Roy hocked it to pay for the gun." He sighed, rubbed the back of his neck with his free hand. "I spent two years looking for that ring. Probably hit every pawnshop in a hundred-mile radius."

"No luck?"

"No luck. At the end of the day, it was just one more shitty thing Roy did to our grandma."

I watched browning stalks of wheat whip by, the sky bright and enormous after the dark of Merl's garage. "How did Roy last working at that place for two years?"

Dean's hands tightened on the wheel. "He didn't have a lot of choice. He was good with his hands, but not with people. He got frustrated easily and lost his temper. Merl might be a grade A asshole, but he mainly left Roy alone."

"What about you?" I asked.

"What about me?"

"Where do you work?" I realized I knew next to nothing about Dean. Not how he usually spent his days or where he lived or who his friends were. All of this should have felt awkward, spending time with a virtual stranger, especially one connected to Roy. But Dean was easy to be around in a way I hadn't anticipated after all my years of resenting him from a distance.

"I help Jack Steadman farm his land. His wife, Mary Ellen, was my history teacher in high school. I think she probably felt sorry for me, if I'm being honest. I wasn't a total dumbass, but school was never my strong suit. Pretty clear I wasn't going away to college even if I could have afforded it. And Jack was getting older, their kids had all up and moved away, and he needed help. When Mary Ellen asked me if I wanted a job after graduation, I couldn't think of any good reason to say no."

"Do you like it?"

"I didn't at first. People think farming is just throwing some seeds in the ground and waiting, but it's more complicated than that. It's hard, thankless work a lot of the time. You're at the mercy of the weather, and there's nothing worse than depending on something you can't control. But I got used to it. Got better at it. Now I can't imagine doing anything else. Start to get a little claustrophobic when I spend too much time indoors. I work the line at the meatpacking plant during the winters, and I practically count down the hours until I can get back to the fields again." He gave his head a little shake. "Sorry, I'm talking too much."

"No, you're not," I said. "What are we going to do? Ride around in silence?"

"Fair point," Dean said. "Heard you're a school counselor?"

"Yeah, I am. But where'd you hear that?"

He took one hand off the steering wheel, flapped it through the air. "I don't know. Around." He paused. "Makes sense."

I jerked my head back a little in surprise. I'd never thought it made sense. Had never heard anyone else who knew me say it did, either. "How's that?"

"You're a good listener."

"Huh," I said. "Maybe." Although personally I didn't think not wanting to talk was the same thing as being a skilled listener.

"Hungry?" Dean pointed up ahead to the Sonic on the side of the road.

"They serve breakfast now?" As teenagers, Eliza and I had made countless trips to Sonic for cheeseburgers and onion rings, Vanilla Cokes and root beer floats. Our dad always muttering that he didn't understand why we had to drive five miles down the road for the same food they served at the diner right up the street in Ludlow.

"Oh, yeah," Dean said. "You haven't lived until you've tried their breakfast burrito."

"Okay, I'm game."

We pulled into one of the stalls at Sonic, and I told Dean to order me whatever he usually got, which turned out to be a breakfast burrito and a side of tater tots. "Remember when they used to bring out your food wearing roller skates?" I asked.

"I can't believe they never got sued by their employees. I swear, somebody used to go ass over teakettle at least once a week."

"Food flying everywhere. We used to rank the likelihood someone would fall based on how much the tray wobbled when they skated out the door." I laughed at the memory, thankful that Dean had reminded me of one that wasn't marred by what came later.

When our server approached the car, it was on very practical tennis shoes. I hadn't thought I was hungry, but as soon as the smell hit my nose, I all but inhaled my first tater tot. "Oh, my god," I said. "What do they put in these?"

"Grease and carbs. The two best food groups."

"These were always Eliza's favorite. She could eat a large order in about ten seconds flat." Dean didn't respond, and I glanced at him. "Does it bother you when I talk about her?" I hadn't realized until that moment how long it had been since I'd actually spoken about Eliza. I'd thought that here, in this car with Dean, I didn't have to worry about hurting anyone but myself by bringing her up. But maybe I'd been wrong.

Dean shook his head. "No. It doesn't bother me. We're going to have to talk about all three of them, if we're serious about trying to figure this out."

I took a big bite of burrito, using a mouthful of cheese and egg to avoid engaging. It was one thing to wander around town asking questions about Roy. It was another to sit next to his brother and hear personal stories, to acknowledge that Dean had lost someone, too.

"I've already told you Roy was acting weird that summer," he said. "But what about Eliza? Or Travis? How did they seem?"

"Normal, from what I can remember. Totally devoted to each other. Busy with their summer jobs. They were talking about applying to college. Eliza was excited about her eighteenth birthday coming up in September. Regular summer-before-senior-year stuff. Nothing stands out."

"What about right before the murders? Did anything change?"

I picked a jalapeño out of my burrito and flicked it onto my napkin. "Not really." I tore off a piece of tortilla and rolled it into a tiny ball, dropped it next to the jalapeño.

"What are you not saying?" he asked.

"Nothing," I responded, too quickly.

"This is only going to work if we tell each other the truth."

"How do you know I'm not telling you something?"

He pointed at my napkin. "You get fidgety."

Huh. It was always strange when someone figured out something about you that you barely knew yourself. Like maybe all your private, not-for-public-consumption quirks weren't hidden after all. That after so many years of keeping people at a distance, it really only took one observant person to pry open a lid I'd thought was permanently locked. The idea was both horrifying and strangely comforting.

"It's probably nothing," I said. "I mean, I told Sheriff Baker about it at the time and he didn't seem too concerned."

"Yeah, well, he would probably say we're insane to be doing this. Who cares what he thinks?" Dean had a point there. "What was it?" he asked again, voice gentle, like he was coaxing a skittish animal out of hiding.

This was what I'd always wanted, wasn't it? Someone to ask the right questions, to sit next to me and really listen to the answers. But I'd been silent for so long, it was harder than I'd imagined to find my voice again. "It was the night of the murders," I said finally. "Eliza was getting ready for her date with Travis, and I was running out the door to meet my friends when she stopped me. Said she had something to talk to me about and it was important. But I told her I was late, and she'd have to tell me the next day. I left before she could say anything else."

"That's it?" Dean said. "Did she give you any clue as to what it was about?"

I shook my head. "She didn't seem upset, really. And she wasn't like grabbing my arm or trying to force me to stay. But I could tell it was something important from the look on her face. She always got a crease right here when she was serious." I lifted a finger between my brows, my heart squeezing when I brushed it over my skin. "It was definitely something she wanted me to hear."

Dean leaned his head back on the headrest, looked out the windshield. "Could it have been about her and Travis? Planning to elope or something?"

"No way. That wasn't Eliza's style. Not getting married at eighteen and not running away to do it, either." I paused. "I definitely got the feeling it had to do with me."

Dean swung his head in my direction without lifting it from the headrest. "Why do you say that?"

I shrugged. "No reason, really. Just a hunch." I thought about Eliza's face, in those last minutes I'd spent with her. There had been concern in her eyes, but not fear. A little sadness, maybe. Reluctance tempered with resolve. Whatever she'd been going to tell me, she knew I wouldn't like it, but she was going to say it anyway. And I had no idea, even all these years later, what it might have been.

Dean sighed, scrubbed a hand across his jaw. "Who knew everybody would be so good at keeping secrets?"

"We were teenagers," I reminded him. "Secrets were all we had."

Eliza

Things she loved: the diner's famous chicken with homemade noodles; Greer's smile; seeing a whole field of ripe wheat spread across the prairie; the scar on her dad's left pointer finger from a dog bite when he was a kid; the sound of cicadas on a hot summer night; watching Travis throw a perfect pass; the musty sweet smell of her family's grocery store; decorating the Christmas tree and knowing the story of each ornament; listening to her mom hum while she folded laundry; sliding down the banister instead of taking the steps; Ludlow.

Things she hated: meatloaf; mosquitoes; stocking the freezer section of the store; algebra homework; the smell in the house when her mom made pickles from scratch; Travis cracking his knuckles; the look on her dad's face when she did something to disappoint him; turtlenecks; when people didn't close their mouths all the way while they chewed; hurting Greer, even when it was for her own good.

Chapter Eight

Because a morning spent in Merl's company hadn't been shitty enough, I asked Dean to drop me off within walking distance of the grocery store instead of down the street from my house. I figured now was as good of a time as any to get it over with, but I still wasn't fully prepared when I stepped into the "new and improved" store for the first time. Growing up, we'd spent the summers bitching endlessly about the lack of air-conditioning in the store, dragging ourselves around the aisles like we were being tortured and standing dramatically in front of the box fans our dad kept whirring in the corners. According to him, the lack of air-conditioning built character, but I'd always suspected his resistance had more to do with not wanting to change the fabric of the building, a need to keep things as they always had been, even as Ludlow slowly withered away around us. The new owners had no such qualms, apparently. There was no real need for air-conditioning in October, even on an unseasonably warm day, but even so, the second I walked through the sliding doors, artificial cold slapped me in the face.

I'd known from my quick drive by that things were different now. But I hadn't expected it to be virtually unrecognizable. I stopped in my tracks, a tiny "Oh" gusting out of me. Gone were the old, chipped black and white porcelain floor tiles where Eliza and I had played endless rounds of hopscotch. Gone were the built-in wooden shelves that had lined the far wall, hand-carved by our great-grandfather and stained and restained through the generations until they had taken on the patina of old leather. Gone was the single checkout line sans conveyor belt, behind which our dad had perched on a swivel stool and chatted up each and every customer who came through the door. I'd always loved our house, but this store, more than anyplace else, had been where my childhood lived. And now it was a stranger to me. Everything was shiny and new and clean and horrible. I could have been anywhere. Or nowhere at all.

I forced myself to walk forward, down an aisle full of cereal boxes, prices neatly computer-generated and stuck to the shelves. There was more variety, but less of what people in Ludlow probably wanted. No Honey Smacks, specially ordered for Laverne Wells, who swore she couldn't start the day without a bowl. I wondered what she did for breakfast now. Made do with Cheerios or Frosted Flakes, I guessed.

At the end of the aisle, I took a right, walked over to the frozen food section, eyes already searching the tiny sliver of wall between the last freezer and the swinging doors that led into the storeroom. It had been repainted, of course it had, the moss green replaced with a more suitable cream. I ran my fingers over the spot anyway, imagined I could feel the slight depressions where Eliza and I had carved our names with our dad's Swiss Army knife the summer she was twelve and I was ten. Eliza had been reluctant, a rule-follower to her core. So I'd gone first, carving out the letters with a heavy hand, giddy with laughter as the plaster scraped away. "Dad won't care. It's *our* store," I'd said when I was done, holding the knife out to her. She'd given in, like she usually did when I wanted something, but her name had been cramped, the letters uneven in her rush to finish. As it turned out, our dad had cared—extra freezer-stocking duty and an afternoon of the silent treatment—but not enough to paint over our vandalism. It had taken the new owners for that final erasure. I pressed harder, knowing we were long gone but telling myself I could still feel us there, right below the surface.

. . . .

When it came to entertainment around Ludlow, there weren't a lot of choices for teenagers. If you were sick of the diner and the town park, you were left with illegally scaling the fence at the abandoned refinery for a night of vandalism and cheap beer, a game of mini golf on the neglected course behind the library, or paying fifteen dollars a carload to watch decades-out-of-date movies at the drive-in. The only other choice, drag racing out on Poplar Lane, had been sadly curtailed with the addition of speed tables my senior year of high school. Now that we were adults, we could add a night at the Do to the list, but I wasn't sure I could handle another round of stale peanuts and questionable company so soon after the first.

The drive-in was the winner this evening, and the three of us had made ourselves comfortable in the bed of Cassie's pickup, leaning back against pillows propped up behind us. Me in the middle, Cassie on my left clutching an industrial-sized vat of popcorn, and Ryan on my right holding a bottle of whiskey, a blanket pilfered from his mom's sofa spread across our legs. We'd assumed our regular spots like no time had passed. Did people who grew up in bigger, more populated places have friends like these? Ones to whom they were bound so tightly it felt like nothing could undo the tethers, your lives interwoven through every nook and hidden-away cranny? Maybe in those places friends drifted in and out, old faces replaced with new ones as the years scrolled by. But in Ludlow, the kids you met the first day of kindergarten were the same ones you graduated next to years later. Hardly ever a new face in the crowd. So if you were lucky enough to find one or two who understood you, accepted you, loved you through all your various flaws and questionable phases? You hung on, as hard and as long as you could. Until, eventually, you would no longer be you without them.

"Let me guess," I said, reaching for a handful of popcorn. *"Back to the Future?"*

Ryan made a buzzing sound. "Wrong. *Halloween.* The new owners like a theme, and nothing says October like a bloody knife."

Or a loaded gun, I thought, but didn't say.

"Tomorrow they're showing *Friday the 13th,*" Cassie said. "We figured Michael Myers beat out Jason."

"Solid choice," I said, talking around a mouthful of popcorn. "They show a different horror movie every night of October?" The former owners, sticklers about their offerings being family friendly, hadn't allowed horror movies at the drive-in at all.

Ryan shook his head. "No, only the two movies in rotation for an entire month. They wouldn't want to dazzle anyone with too much variety. This is Ludlow, after all. We're easily overwhelmed."

Cassie held out her hand for the whiskey, and Ryan passed it to her. "No, thanks," I said when she offered me a swig.

"Suit yourself. But alcohol may be the only way we survive this." She adjusted her pillow, then crammed the popcorn bucket between our outstretched legs.

On the drive here, I'd considered telling them about what Dean and I were doing, but I couldn't find a way to make it sound less insane than it probably was. But while I might not be ready to come clean, that didn't mean I couldn't pick their brains a bit. "Hey," I said, "did you guys think anything was going on with Eliza the summer before she died?"

The whiskey bottle stilled on the way to Cassie's mouth. "Wow, that came out of nowhere. You never talk about Eliza. Or what happened." She paused. "Not anymore."

"That's not an answer."

"It's not an answer," Ryan said. "But it's a fact. What's going on?"

"Nothing, really," I said.

"I smell bullshit." Ryan kicked my foot with his. "Cassie?"

"Yes," she said. "I, too, smell manure of some kind."

"Okay, you assholes," I said, laughing. "I think being back here, it's all front and center again. I can't stop thinking about that summer before." That wasn't a lie. Every face I saw, every familiar scent and sound, dragged me backward. I knew it was where I needed to go, but some part of me still resisted. Scared of what would be revealed.

"What about it?" Cassie asked, brow furrowed.

"I don't know. Whether I missed something. Whether Eliza was acting different."

"I don't know about Eliza," Ryan said. "But you were off your game."

I turned to look at him. "What? No, I wasn't."

"You totally were. You ghosted the shit out of us that summer."

Heat climbed up my neck into my cheeks. "I did not. And ghosting wasn't even a thing back then."

Ryan rolled his eyes. "I'm pretty sure the concept was alive and well."

I glanced at Cassie, eyebrows raised. "Correct me if I'm wrong, but I think it was you who was MIA that summer, not me."

"What are you talking about?" Cassie said, throwing a handful of popcorn at me.

"No," Ryan said. "Don't pelt her with our food. She's not wrong. Now that I think about it, both of you pulled a disappearing act that summer. Left me by my lonesome where I was forced to hook up with Hope Turner at the pool just for something to do."

"God," Cassie said. "Your standards have always been shit. And for the record, that was the summer I was dating Samantha Leary on the sly. That's why I wasn't around as much, remember?"

"How could we forget?" Ryan groaned.

"Hey," Cassie protested. "The drama was her, not me!"

"I think it was both of you," I said. Back then, Cassie had been a fan of the kind of relationship that swung between true love and pure hatred. No middle ground. She never ended anything gracefully. There were always tears and fights and doomed second chances. And she always picked girls who had the same penchant for excessive feeling.

"Maybe," Cassie said. "She took it a step too far, though, when she accused me of slashing her tires. Crazy-ass bitch. But in answer to your earlier question, Greer, I think Eliza was the same as always that summer."

"Yeah," Ryan agreed. "I don't remember anything unusual." He paused, giving me a quick glance before he continued, like he was worried about my reaction. "Remember the night we all came here, at the end of that summer? Our last hurrah before school started again?"

"Oh, my god, I'd forgotten about that," Cassie said.

I had, too, until Ryan reminded me. We'd come to watch *Grease*. Ryan, Cassie, and me in one car. Eliza, Travis, and a few of Travis's friends in another. Halfway through the movie, Eliza had clambered out of Travis's car and come over to ours. "Too many boys. They talk over the music," she'd said by way of explanation, hauling herself up and landing between Ryan and me, settling in the way she had when we were younger and she'd crashed our sleepovers.

"She sang every song," Ryan said, wincing. "Right into my ear. Her voice was so fucking bad."

"So bad," Cassie agreed with a small smile. "But she didn't let it stop her."

Their tone was quiet, careful. Like they were stepping over land mines. Not because it was hard for them to talk about Eliza, but because they were worried about me. It made me wonder how often they talked about her when I wasn't around, and I felt strangely jealous about missing out on memories I could hardly stand to hear.

"Okay, everybody, shut up," Cassie instructed. "The movie's starting."

I settled back against my pillow, leaned my head on Ryan's shoulder. "Don't mind me," he said. "Make yourself comfortable." But he scooted a little closer so I didn't tweak my neck.

I zoned out as Michael Myers started his reign of terror on the screen and Ryan and Cassie passed the bottle back and forth across my lap. The drive-in was only half full, and I let my eyes skate over the cars. A lot of pickup trucks, an older-model minivan stuffed with kids way too young to be watching this movie, a white SUV with rust on the passenger door. I raised my head, peered through the gathering gloom. Was that Dean's car? As I watched, the driver's door opened and the man of the hour hopped out, threading his way through the cars toward the cinder block building that housed the concession stand and the restrooms.

"I'll be right back." I pushed myself forward to slide off the end of the pickup bed. "Gotta use the bathroom," I said at Cassie's questioning look.

"Grab some Twizzlers while you're over there," she yelled as I walked away, and I waved my hand over my head to let her know I'd heard.

When I got to the concession line, Dean was the only one there, leaning on the counter and waiting for the kid behind it to hand him a hot dog.

"Hey," I said, sidling into the space next to him. "If I didn't know better, I'd say you were following me."

Dean glanced at me, surprise written all over his face, and before he could respond, I held up both hands. "I have no idea why I said that. That was dumb. God, sorry. Ignore me."

"I promise I'm not following you," he said. "Although it might be worth it to listen to you stumble over your sentences."

"Ha ha." I pointed at the Twizzlers and pushed some cash across the counter. "You're a fan of the drive-in?"

"Not really. Some nights I need to get out of the house, and this is somewhere cheap to go where no one will bother me." He took a bite of his hot dog. "Gourmet food is only a side benefit."

Without discussing it, we'd started walking on the path that wound behind the last row of cars. For anyone to notice us, they'd have to turn around, take their eyes off the movie, where currently Jamie Lee Curtis was blissfully getting ready for a night of babysitting with no idea what awaited her in the dark.

"People bother you?" I asked, although I already knew the answer, remembering the Do and how the air turned thick with malice the second Dean walked through the door.

He sighed. "The usual bullshit. I'm sure you can imagine. Guys getting in my face, wanting to fight me. And girls are either scared of me or all over me. It's bizarre as shit, and I don't know which reaction is worse." He ran a hand through his hair. "The whole world looks at me and all they see is my brother."

"Do you ever think about leaving?" I asked. "Going someplace where nobody knows you?" Although I understood as well as anyone that leaving a place behind didn't always mean you escaped it.

He gave me a grim smile. "All the time."

We walked in silence for a few seconds, the light from the movie screen drifting over our faces. "If you're free tomorrow, I had an idea of someone else we could talk to," Dean said as we neared the last row of cars. "Roy's girlfriend, Libby."

I stopped walking. "Roy had a girlfriend?"

Dean nodded, slowed to stop beside me, and held up a finger

while he finished chewing his last bite. "So to speak. They were off and on the six months before the murders."

"I don't remember her from the trial. She didn't testify, did she?"

"Nope. And I doubt she knows anything, but figure it's worth a try. If she'll even talk to us. She's not my biggest fan."

"Why's that?" I asked, distracted, still trying to wrap my head around the idea of Roy Mathews and a girlfriend.

"I dated her first. Not for long, but it didn't end well. When she hooked up with Roy, I always suspected it was to get back at me. I couldn't have cared less except I didn't like her using him. He was so glad a girl was paying attention to him that he couldn't see what bad news Libby was."

"First Merl, now Libby," I said. "You're going to spoil me."

Dean smiled, flash of white, here and then gone. He tossed his hot dog wrapper into a nearby trash can, shoved his hands into the front pockets of his jeans.

"Okay, well, I'm over there," I said.

He nodded. "I'll see you tomorrow, then."

"Yeah," I said, turning toward Cassie's truck. "Tomorrow." I took a few steps, looked over my shoulder, but Dean had already melted away into the darkness.

• • • •

I'd expected my parents to be tucked away upstairs by the time I got home from the drive-in, but a dim light was burning from the living room window, and when I climbed the front steps, I was greeted by the shape of my father slumped on the porch swing.

"Dad?" I said, not really expecting a response. He was snoring lightly, his mouth hanging open. I had a sudden urge to kick the swing, startle him into wakefulness. Instead, I sat down next to him, leaned my head back on the swing with a sigh. Out on the lawn, the first brittle fall leaves pinwheeled across the grass, blown by a sharp October breeze. Nothing else moved. Everything was silent and bathed in darkness. It should have felt peaceful. Serene. But tension nestled at the base of my spine, a hot rock of watchfulness I couldn't ease.

"I went to the store," I said. "They've changed everything. It used to be my favorite place in the whole world and it's just . . . gone." My voice broke, and I blinked rapidly until my eyes stopped stinging. "Remember when we used to be happy?" I looked at my father, his prematurely old, haggard face, and wondered how much more he could endure.

I would have given anything to have one more Father's Day with him, back when Eliza and I would pool our money and take him out for lunch at the diner, the three of us lined up at the counter. Me on his left, Eliza on his right. Every year, we'd order more than we could possibly eat. Fried chicken, loaded baked potatoes, milkshakes, three of Mabel's cinnamon rolls. Afterward, we'd walk home clutching our stomachs, swearing the next year we'd show some restraint. And even though it was Father's Day, and we were meant to be celebrating him, our dad would always end the outing by listing all the ways he was lucky to have us for his daughters— Eliza's reliability and tender heart, my stubbornness and reckless enthusiasm. No matter what he'd said, I'd known that Eliza and I were really the lucky ones. I could never have imagined back then that someday he would sit next to me and feel like a stranger. "I'm sorry, Daddy," I whispered. "I wish I could undo it. Make things how they used to be."

At the corner a patrol car appeared, idling even though there wasn't a stop sign. It was too dark for me to see who was driving, but I pictured Garrett behind the wheel. Checking up on me. Tiny goose bumps prickled my arms for no reason I could name, and I leaned back, hiding in the shadows of the porch. I watched as the patrol car turned left, away from our house, engine a low purr in the night.

Next to me, my dad stirred, pulling my attention as he made a snuffling exhale. "Greer?" he rasped. "What time is it?"

"I don't know. After midnight."

He squinted at me. "Where's your sister? Is she home yet? I told Travis not to keep her out too late."

I inhaled sharply, strangely jealous that even for a moment he got to believe Eliza was alive and nothing had changed. "She's dead, remember?" My voice was flat and hard.

My dad didn't respond. His eyes fluttered closed, and he sank back into oblivion. And out on the street the patrol car cruised quietly by.

Chapter Nine

Growing up, Eliza and I had always been early risers. It was hard to sleep in when your father got up at the crack of dawn, slamming drawers and whistling his way down the stairs, hollering that the coffee was ready in a voice meant to carry. Waking before my alarm was a habit that had stuck, and it served me well in a profession where I was expected at work when a lot of people were still hitting the snooze button. But back here, in my childhood home, my dad no longer rose with the sun. I could hear his deep snores every morning as I made my way downstairs to start the coffee.

Today I was a little bleary-eyed, even after my first cup of coffee. I hadn't slept well, a hazard of returning to Ludlow, I'd discovered, and I was hoping caffeine might help clear my mind. Dean and I had plans to meet up, and I was eager to get moving, wondering if today might be the day we made some progress. I threw on jeans and a T-shirt, reached into my closet for a hoodie and stopped. Eyes rising to the shoebox on the high shelf. Blood whooshed in my ears, my heartbeat hard and heavy in my throat. I knew I couldn't avoid it forever, so this time I forced myself to reach up and pull the box down. I sat on the edge of my bed and took off the lid, fingers sifting through paper.

After the murders, I'd received emails and cards, a few actual letters. Many from people I knew, some from strangers outside of

Ludlow. Most were kind, wishing my family well, expressing con-
dolences, hoping for justice. But some were nasty and cruel, saying
Eliza and Travis deserved what happened to them, or suggesting
that perhaps my fucking the random author of the missive might
help heal my pain. I'd printed out most of the emails, even the
horrible ones, folded them carefully, and put them in this box.
Same with the cards and letters. I didn't know why, but it had felt
important to keep them. On bad days in the months after Eliza
died, when I could hardly force myself out of bed, I reread the
most hateful ones, a necessary twisting of the knife. The pain offering a strange type of release.

I thumbed through the pile, eyes catching a word here and
there—"sorry," "great girl," "nice ass," "anything we can do,"
"whore," "much love"—but I didn't stop to read. I was looking for
something in particular, and my fingers slowed when I glimpsed a
flash of red. I pulled it out pinched between my thumb and pointer
finger, stomach doing a slow forward roll. It was a heart cut from
red construction paper, uneven, like a child might craft in grade
school, and backed with a white doily, clumps of dried glue oozing
from the edges. In the center, block letters written with thick black
marker. "I DID IT." I turned the heart over already knowing what
was on the back. Same lettering, same marker. "FOR YOU."

My palms were slick and greasy suddenly, and I dropped the
heart, let it flutter onto the bedspread next to me. All these years
later, I had still been able to close my eyes and visualize it from
memory, every detail seared into my brain, but it was something
else to touch it again, to feel the glide of paper against my skin. I
remembered clearly the moment I'd first seen it, stumbling downstairs before dawn, unable to sleep. A splash of red on the wood
floor by the front door. Someone had shoved it through our mail
slot in the night, exactly one month after Eliza's death. I'd stood

there in the foyer flipping it back and forth, back and forth, trying to decipher what should have been five simple words: *I did it for you.*

The heart had confirmed my worst suspicions, the ones that had kept me up at night and landed me in a therapist's office. When the heart had been pushed through our mail slot, Roy had been miles away, locked up tight in prison. He couldn't have delivered the heart, which meant he hadn't acted alone. Someone else had been involved in the murders. But the heart had also stopped my questions, quieted my voice just when I finally had some proof that I wasn't crazy. It hadn't been the therapists, my parents' tears and pleading, or Baker's pity. It hadn't been Cassie and Ryan's loyal, careful understanding that was almost more painful than disbelief. No, it had been the message on the heart that had finally rendered me mute. The knowledge that somehow Eliza's death was my fault, even if I didn't fully understand how or why. Guilt a muzzle that kept me silent all these years.

I picked up the heart, smoothed it between my fingers. *I did it for you.* It sat coiled and alive in my hand. I swore I could almost feel it beating.

• • • •

Dean had texted me early, when my hands were still shaking around my cup of coffee, and asked if I could pick him up this time because his SUV had a flat. I'd responded that I didn't mind, glad to have a task, something to focus on instead of the heart tucked back into the shoebox inside my closet, seething in the darkness. But when I'd told Dean I could drive, I hadn't pictured actually having to walk up his grandma's cracked front sidewalk and knock on her door. I'd envisioned something more clandestine, but clearly Dean wasn't as worried about being seen together as I was.

I was surprised again when it was Virginia Mathews who answered the front door at my knock. She was still dressed in her housecoat and slippers, her permed hair flat to her skull on one side.

"Hi," I said, giving a tentative wave. "Is Dean here?"

"Yes, yes," she said, shuffling back and motioning me inside. "Come in. Let me pour you an orange juice."

"Oh, no, that's okay," I said. "I can wait—" But she was already walking away from me, one hand out to steady herself against the narrow hallway wall, and I didn't have much choice but to follow.

She led me into the kitchen, a small, cramped room that caught all the late-morning sunshine, making it feel warm and close even though the air outside was mild. The entire space felt like a dollhouse, way too petite to have once housed two teenage boys. I wondered if all the rooms were like this, pictured Dean growing up in a bedroom where he could stand in the middle and touch two walls with outstretched arms, had to hunch over to keep his head from hitting the ceiling. His grandma had already put a pitcher of orange juice on the tiny table tucked against the wall, three flower-painted glasses at the ready next to it. She motioned for me to have a seat and then poured me a drink with a shaky hand.

I took a sip, expecting her to sit next to me, but she remained standing, her gnarled fingers clasped in front of her. "When Dean told me you two had run into each other and finally talked, I was so glad, especially when he said you'd be coming by this morning. I've always wanted to tell you how sorry I am," she said, voice quiet. "All these years I've wanted to say it."

I set down my glass, pressed my hands flat on the worn wooden tabletop. I hadn't been sure she knew who I was, even with an up-close look this time. I would have been happier if she hadn't recognized me, if we could have left it alone.

"Thank you," I managed.

She wrung her hands together, as if my acknowledgment of her words had somehow upset her. "I should have written a note, but Roy's lawyer told me I couldn't. After the trial, I started to write a hundred times. But I'd think about you and your poor parents and I'd freeze up, couldn't think of a single word that came out right."

"It's okay," I said. "I know it wasn't your fault." These were the words I was supposed to say. The ones that would bring an old woman some comfort.

She sat down across from me, finally, let out a weary sigh. "You're kind to say that. But I think it probably was at least partly my fault. I raised him, didn't I? Somewhere along the line, I did wrong by him. Didn't teach him how to treat people." Tears gathered in her rheumy eyes and she swiped at them with trembling fingers.

"That's not true," Dean said from the doorway, and at the sound of his voice his grandma's face broke into a rueful smile. "You raised me, didn't you?" he went on, coming up behind her and resting his hands gently on her shoulders. "And I've turned out okay."

Virginia let out a little laugh, reached up and patted his hand. "You've turned out just fine." But it was clear from the look on her face that Dean had done more than turn out fine; he'd hung the moon and stars. "Here," she said, pointing at the empty chair, "sit down and have some orange juice with us."

Dean looked at me, mouthed "Sorry" over his grandma's head before he took a seat as instructed.

"What are you two getting up to today?" Virginia asked. "I still don't like the sound of this."

I glanced at Dean, surprised he'd told her what we were doing, and he gave me a minuscule shake of his head. "I told my grandma how we were retracing Roy's steps that last summer. To try and get a better idea of what he was thinking." He'd told her some of the truth, but not all of it.

"Just don't stick your nose where it doesn't belong," Virginia said. "Leave the policing to the police." She paused, laid a hand on top of Dean's. "What happened to those kids, Dylan and Addy, had nothing to do with Roy, not directly." The gentle tone of her voice told me this wasn't the first time they'd had this conversation.

Dean slid his hand out from under his grandma's, avoiding eye contact with both of us. "Don't worry," he told her. "We're just going to talk to Libby."

Virginia made a dismissive cluck. "Nothing but trouble, that one. You'd be wise to steer clear." She looked at me. "Did I offer you a drink?"

"Yes," I said, hoisting my glass a little. "You did, thanks."

She blinked at me, her face wiped clean for the span of a few seconds before she came back to herself. "I'm sorry," she said. "I forget things these days."

"It's okay, Gram," Dean said, standing and reaching for her hand. "Why don't you go take a rest. I'll be back this afternoon, and I can help you make the grocery list."

I watched Dean lead her toward the doorway, one hand resting carefully on her back, and marveled at his patience. "Oh, wait," Virginia said, putting a hand out against the doorjamb as she turned to look at both of us. "If you're trying to figure out what Roy was thinking those last months, you might want to talk to that girl he was seeing."

Dean sighed. "Yeah, Libby. We're going to talk to her today."

Virginia shook her head. "No, not her. The other one."

"What other one?" I asked, my heart suddenly beating double time.

Virginia's face tightened with effort and she closed her eyes. "I never met her. Saw her in his truck once. Or maybe twice." She opened her eyes. "She had a ponytail."

"That was Libby, Gram."

The confusion on Virginia's face was heartbreaking, the look of a child who doesn't understand what's happening to her. "It was?"

"Pretty sure," Dean said. "Now let's get you to bed."

I followed them back down the hall and let myself out onto the front porch to wait, desperate to be free of that too-small space. I leaned back against the side of the house and closed my eyes, took a deep breath of fresh air, and willed my mind to quiet.

"Ready?" Dean asked a few minutes later, the screen door closing gently behind him, and I opened my eyes, gave him a nod.

"Sorry about that," he said once we were buckled into my car and easing down the driveway. "She gets confused nowadays. I worry about leaving her alone, but we can't afford anyone to take care of her."

I put my foot on the brake and turned to look at him. "Have you always lived here, with her?"

"I moved out for a few years after I graduated. Had a little apartment. Shithole, really, but it was a space that was all mine. After the murders, when people started harassing her and driving by at all hours throwing crap at the house, I moved back. Been here ever since. Thirty-three years old and still living at home. How pathetic is that?"

"You're good to her," I said.

Dean shook his head. "I think about leaving at least once a day. Imagine packing up my shit, getting in my car, and driving away. Making her somebody else's problem. Doing the exact same thing my mom did to us all those years ago. I've hated my mom for it every day since she left, and lately all I feel is envious." When he glanced at me, his eyes were exhausted, and I wondered how long it had been since Dean Mathews had given himself a break.

"But you don't leave," I reminded him quietly. "You stay."

"Yeah." He sighed. "I stay."

I started to lift my foot off the brake and paused. "What did she mean about Dylan and Addy?"

Dean turned his head away from me to look out the passenger

window, and I thought he might not answer. When he finally spoke, his voice was low. "I used to ask Roy why he did it. Especially at the beginning, right after he was arrested. Practically beg him to tell me why, how, what had been going through his head. Anything to make sense of it. But all he would say was that he'd pulled the trigger. It had been him. Beyond that there was a steel door, and no matter how hard I banged on it, he wouldn't let me in." He paused. "I wish for Addy's and Dylan's sakes that I'd pushed him harder."

I stared at Dean, and just like at the vigil, pain breached the space between us. Our shared guilt like a third body in the car, resting heavy hands on our shoulders. I was looking for answers. But Dean, I realized, was searching for absolution.

"If it helps," I said, "I wish I'd stayed and listened to what Eliza wanted to tell me the night she died. I wish for that every single day."

Dean scrubbed at his face with one hand, letting out a frustrated growl. "My grandma is wrong. Addy's and Dylan's deaths have everything to do with Roy."

I nodded without speaking, the heart hidden away in my closet beating in my throat.

"It keeps me up at night, you know?" he went on. "Thinking I could have stopped it somehow." He paused, let out a shuddering breath. "Worrying about whether it's going to happen again."

My hands clenched the steering wheel, tentacles of ice twining around my stomach and lungs, as my gaze flew to Dean's. "You think it's going to happen again?"

"I don't know," he said, somber eyes on mine. "I don't know anything. And that's what scares me."

• • • •

It took us a little longer to find Libby than we'd originally anticipated. Turned out she no longer worked at the Mexican restaurant where Dean had run into her last. And no one answered our repeated knocks at her last-known address, a run-down motel converted into apartments on the edge of Neosho.

We were about to give up when the door to the apartment next door opened and a woman in a bikini top and cutoff jean shorts leaned out. Just looking at her made me shiver. "Jesus Christ," she said. "You gonna keep up that racket all fucking day? Haven't you got the message yet? She's not home."

"Know where she is?" Dean asked.

"If I did, wouldn't be any business of yours, would it?" The woman smirked at him, gave me a dismissive glance. "What you want her for anyway?"

"Need to talk to her. We're not looking to cause her any trouble."

"Can't help you. Sorry," she said, sounding anything but.

Dean took a step closer, pulled off his sunglasses, and put on a grin instead. "Aw, come on now," he said, working his drawl in a way I'd never heard before. "This is Neosho, not New York City. I can track her down easy enough, but are you really gonna make me work that hard?"

Dean's smile apparently did the trick because the woman's arms uncrossed and her body loosened, one hip jutting forward. "Oh, I don't know," she said. "You look like you can handle it."

I could tell the laugh Dean let out was fake, even if she couldn't. It was jarring how quickly he could put on this new persona, like slipping into a familiar skin. He leaned a little closer, shoulder balanced on her doorjamb. "You gonna help me out, or what?"

"Okay, fine, but you didn't hear it from me," the woman said around her grin. "She's working at the laundromat over off Wilson. The eight-to-five shift."

"My lips are sealed," Dean said. "Thanks."

"No problem," the woman said, lingering where before she'd been ready to slam her door in our faces. "Maybe I'll see you around."

"Maybe." Dean gave her a little salute with two fingers. He waited until we were halfway across the parking lot before he glanced at me. "What?"

"Nothing," I said, shaking my head. "You just knew exactly how to get to her, didn't you?"

"It wasn't any special trick." He moved away from me to the passenger side of my car. "I'm pretty sure everybody knows how to play nice to get what they need."

I slowed, watched him open the door and slide into my car. Through the glare of the sun off the windshield I could no longer see his face, only the outline of his body, the impatient tap of his fingers against his knee. Playing nice to get what he wanted. Was that what we were both doing right now, with each other? Maybe. Because I knew that underneath all my recent bullshit about forgiving Roy's family, a pocket of resentment and anger and misplaced blame still lived no matter how hard I tried to stomp it flat. I had to assume Dean carried the same hidden pocket inside himself, one that looked at me and my family and imagined us celebrating the death of his brother, high-fiving and popping champagne while Roy's heart stopped under the glare of fluorescent lights. I couldn't fault Dean. And maybe it didn't matter. Maybe none of it mattered, so long as we both got what we needed in the end.

Chapter Ten

ibby Harris was not what I'd expected. After Virginia's warning that Libby was trouble, I'd pictured someone hard-looking, a cloud of danger and bad choices swirling around her. But Libby looked exhausted and not much else. We found her in back of the laundromat, hauling huge cloth sacks of dirty laundry out of a beat-up van. She was petite, with honey-blond hair in a high ponytail that made her look younger from a distance. But up close the fine lines around her eyes gave her age away. She was pretty in a worn-down way, like a vase that had lost its shine. The bones were still good, but the sparkle that made it worth a second glance had faded away.

Libby took one look at us and huffed out a laugh. "You've got to be shitting me."

"Hey, Libby," Dean said, easy. "How you been?"

"Fucking great, as you can see. Soon as I'm done here, I'm running off to my yacht for a trip around the world."

Dean reached out and grabbed one of the heavy sacks from her hand, carried it over to the pile by the laundromat's back door.

"Hi," I said, squinting against the sun. "I'm Greer."

Libby looked at me. "You seem normal enough. What in the hell are you doing hanging around with him?"

"Thanks," Dean said, voice dry.

"Suit yourself," Libby said with a shrug in my direction. "But don't say I didn't warn you when he starts lying to you, then dumps your ass without a second glance."

I thought about correcting her, but didn't think she cared that much about my relationship status with Dean. She was more concerned with getting her shots in, even after all this time. To prove my point, she threw another bag toward him, a little force behind it. "What do you want?"

"Couple questions, that's it," he said. "Then we're out of your hair."

Libby paused in her work, ran the back of her hand across her sweaty forehead. "Get on with it then."

"When you and Roy were dating, was he seeing anyone else?" Dean asked.

"Dating?" Libby smirked. "That's what you're calling it? We went out for cheap food and fucked in the back of his truck." She raised her eyebrows. "He didn't have your finesse, but the guy had stamina, I'll give him that. And Roy was lucky to have landed me for as long as he did. I seriously doubt there were two of us dumb enough to hang out with him."

Dean's jaw tightened in a way that I was starting to find familiar. It reminded me of a pressure valve, a way for him to ease out some steam so he didn't blow. "What about anyone new he might have been hanging around with that summer before the murders, guy or girl? We talked to Merl and he was no help at all."

"Well, guess this ain't your lucky day," Libby said. "Because I sure as hell don't remember your brother making any new friends."

"What about the money he was stealing from Merl at work?" Dean asked, surprising me. "What was going on there?"

"I have no fucking idea what you're talking about," Libby said, hands on her hips. "Are we done?"

"Yeah, we're done," Dean said. "You've been a big help. Really." He was already turning to leave, but I stayed put.

"What about people who were out of place that summer?" I asked. "Anyone lurking around?"

"What, like a stalker?" Libby snorted.

"Come on," Dean said, face tight with frustration. "Let's get out of here."

I turned to follow him, but Libby's voice stopped us. "Wait," she said. "There was a guy I saw a couple of times. At least I'm pretty sure it was a guy. Could have been a chick, I suppose. He was never that close to us, just hanging around on the edges of wherever we happened to be, if that makes sense. It was probably nothing. But I remember noticing him once or twice."

"What did he look like?" I asked, pivoting to face her again.

Libby scrunched up her brow, like she was trying to conjure a decade-old face out of thin air. "Honestly, I don't really remember. He was always wearing a ball cap, I'm pretty sure. He was average. Nothing stands out."

"Age?" Dean asked.

"How the fuck should I know?" Libby said. "Not old. White. No facial hair, I don't think." She threw up her hands. "That's all I've got."

"What made you think he was watching Roy?" I asked.

Libby sighed, her patience with us and this topic wearing thin. "I have no idea. He probably wasn't. He could have been watching me. Or maybe it was all coincidence. You asked if I noticed anyone out of place or who was hanging around, and he came to mind. I remember getting that feeling before I would actually see him, the one where the back of your neck prickles? Know what I'm talking about?"

I nodded, unable to speak. I did know what she was talking about. I'd had that feeling myself off and on that summer before Eliza died and had ignored it. Had felt it again when I'd first held the paper heart in my hand.

"Would you recognize him if you saw him?" Dean asked.

"Not a chance," Libby said. "He could walk up here and shake my hand and I'd be none the wiser." She paused. "You know how it is, Dean. Some people aren't that memorable."

. . . .

"Holy shit," I said to Dean's profile. "What did you do to her? She hates your guts."

He blew out a breath as I pulled back out onto Wilson Street. "I honestly don't know. I mean, I probably didn't handle the breakup well, but I was nineteen years old, for fuck's sake. I didn't handle anything well back then. And when she started dating Roy right after, I was pretty shitty about it."

"Because you were jealous?"

"Because I didn't like her playing with him."

"Maybe you had it wrong. Maybe she genuinely liked him."

Dean shot me a look. "We both know that wasn't why she was seeing him. You heard her."

"You don't think she had anything to do with the murders, do you? She could have wanted your brother punished for some reason and talked him into doing something horrible so she could sit back and watch him suffer. Or maybe it was all about making you suffer." Either way, it seemed ridiculously extreme and would do nothing to explain the heart I'd been given. But I was willing to consider any possibility, determined not to count anyone out too soon.

Dean shook his head. "Nah. Libby's the right-in-your face type when she's pissed. She's not sneaky. She'll kick you in the nuts and be done with it. And besides, what possible beef could she have with your sister or Travis? Or Addy and Dylan, for that matter?"

"Maybe they were collateral damage," I said.

"Maybe," Dean said, but he didn't sound convinced. "But that would be one coldhearted bastard. Like I said, Libby runs hot."

"Yeah, she looked like she wouldn't mind taking a couple swings at your head with one of those laundry sacks. When was the last time you saw her?"

He bit his bottom lip as I glanced at him and then back to the road. "I hooked up with her once or twice over the years. Nights we ran into each other when we'd both had a little too much whiskey and I didn't want to go home. Not for a long time now, but every time it happened, it only made things worse."

"Oh, I bet it did," I said. "Now her being pissed makes a little more sense. Nobody likes being used."

"I didn't think of it like that. I wasn't trying to hurt her, and I knew I was playing with fire. We were oil and water from the word 'go.' But she was the last taste of normal I ever had. After we broke up, everything went to complete shit like a snowball rolling downhill. Sometimes, when I was a few shots in, I could convince myself that maybe she was the secret. Like if I could make it work with Libby, then magically things would go back to how they used to be." He shook his head. "Which was goddamn stupid because things weren't even that great before it all went to hell."

I watched my hand reach out, my fingers closing over his. "I get it," I said.

His hand turned over under mine, giving me a gentle press of his fingers, and warmth surged up my arm, settling heavy in my rib cage. His touch was comforting, but the look he shot me was dubious. "It's okay," he said. "You don't need to try and make me feel better. I know you had the life everyone wants. At least until my brother up and destroyed it."

"My life wasn't perfect before Eliza's murder. I know it might seem that way to you. Hell, it probably seemed that way to a lot of people. But it wasn't."

Dean let go of my hand and I pulled it back, left it lying pale and limp on the console between us. I took a deep breath, wondering how far my honesty was going to take me. "My dad's a drunk now." From the corner of my eye, I saw Dean's head snap in my direction, but I kept my gaze on the road. "And all my mom does is clean. You could eat dinner off any surface of our house at any time. If you don't mind the bleach aftertaste." My smile tasted bitter on my lips. "For a long time after Eliza died, I tried to pretend that her death caused all of it, but that's not completely true. Because my dad always liked a drink in his hand. Looking back, once five o'clock hit, he was rarely without his trusty glass of bourbon. And my mom was one of those people who had to be busy every second of every day. Bake sales and volunteering and decorating for every stupid holiday. Like if she slowed down, the world might end. But despite those things, I always thought we were solid, you know? Not perfect, not happy all the time, but solid."

Solid. That's how life had felt to me back then. I used to walk through the front door of our house every day after school and peace settled over me like a gentle wave. It never mattered how shitty my day had been or how much homework I had waiting for me; once I stood in our foyer, I was *home* and everything was better. I knew there would be something good to eat for dinner, that my parents would ask about our days and listen to our answers, that Eliza and I would handle after-dinner cleanup and fall into a familiar, comfortable rhythm even on nights we barely spoke. Back then I never doubted the power of our family, the idea that our connection to one another would overcome any obstacle. I'd been so stupidly naive; I'd had no idea how fast it could all be ripped away.

I cleared my throat against the knot lodged in my windpipe. "I thought we could weather most anything. But the very first time we were tested, we fell apart and never managed to pick up a single piece." I risked a glance at him. "I'm not telling you this to make you feel worse about what Roy did. He's the reason Eliza's dead, but he's not the only reason for the rest of it. Eliza died, and we stopped living." I gave a sad little wave at nothing. "So long, Dunnings."

"You're still here," he said, voice quiet.

"Am I?" I asked on a broken laugh. "Sometimes it doesn't seem like it."

"You're still here," Dean repeated, firmer this time. He reached down and took my hand again, squeezed in time with his words. "You're. Still. Here."

And for the first time in a long time, it felt like I was.

. . . .

I was tasked with bringing the booze, which, considering where I lived, was an easy job. All I had to do was grab one of my dad's bourbon bottles and an armful of beers from his stash in the basement fridge, and I was all set. Ryan was in charge of the pizza and was already biting into a slice when I climbed the steps to the gazebo.

"You better not have eaten half of it already," I warned. "I'm hungry."

"Don't worry, first piece, I swear." Ryan wound an errant strand of mozzarella around his finger. "I have to try and get my fair share in before Cassie shows up. She'll hoover the entire thing in two minutes flat."

"She's not coming," I said, dropping the bottle of bourbon and a blanket onto an empty chair. "Apparently the clerk at the Dollar Store came through and we got bumped."

"Not surprised," Ryan said. "Can't say I fault her priorities. Pass me that bourbon. I need a drink."

"Hard day?"

"Yes, god help me. I have got to find a new job." I handed over the bourbon and set the beers on the battered coffee table as I lowered myself onto the ground across from him. I angled my body toward the glowing firepit, warmth racing up my side.

"How's that going anyway?" I'd been surprised when Cassie texted and told me Ryan had agreed to help Chet renovate his house while he was back in Ludlow. I loved Chet, but even an hour in his company usually felt like too much. I couldn't fathom spending all day with the guy.

"About like you'd imagine. Some days it's all I can do not to duct-tape his mouth shut for five minutes of peace."

I laughed. "How did you end up agreeing to help him anyway?"

"There's not a lot of demand for a middle manager type in Ludlow. And I spent all the summers in college doing remodeling work, remember? I figured I could put that knowledge to good use and keep myself busy, make some money while I'm here. But damn, I never figured Chet would be micromanaging me the entire time. He's wearing me out."

"I bet he is." I gestured to the pizza box, dark grease stains leaking through the cardboard. "Gas station?"

"But of course," Ryan said in his best British accent. "Dig in."

There had never been a pizza joint in Ludlow, so when we were kids, the local gas station started selling pizza from an ancient set of ovens in their dinky kitchen. It was surprisingly good, especially when you didn't have anything to compare it to.

Ryan grabbed a second piece and leaned back against the sofa, stretching his legs out in front of him. "Goddamn, did you ever think we'd be sitting here at our age, living with our parents again?"

"Speak for yourself," I said around a mouthful of pepperoni. "I'm only visiting."

"Technically, so am I. But when I moved in four months ago, I said it was for a couple of weeks and look how that's turned out."

"I'm kind of surprised you're back after the divorce." I passed him a beer, watched as he popped the top on the side of the table.

Cassie and I had roots in this town. Our parents were born here. Our grandparents, too. I never thought about whether I liked Ludlow because my love for it was so strong. It was where the Dunnings belonged. But Ryan was a transplant. His parents had moved here when he was five, when his dad got a job with the railroad. His arrival—*There's a new kid moving in!*—had elicited a wild excitement in me. Poor Ryan never stood a chance. From the minute I'd spied him from my backyard, he'd been stuck with Cassie and me whether he liked it or not. Stuck with Ludlow, too, even after his parents divorced and his father moved away.

He took a long swig of beer before he answered me. "This town sucks in a lot of ways, but it's also easy to get comfortable here. It starts feeling like too much trouble to go anywhere else. Bottom line is, it doesn't really matter whether I like it or not, it's home."

"You were happy in Kansas City, though, weren't you? Have you thought about going back?"

"Oh, god, who the fuck knows? I thought I was happy there. For a while, at least. But the whole time things with Bethany were unraveling, and the harder I tried to fix them, the faster they went to shit. At least here I have family, friends. It could be worse." He gave me a rueful smile. "And really, who in the hell is actually happy?"

"Cassie," I said without hesitation, plucking a black olive off my pizza and flicking it at him.

"Yes, well, Cassandra is a rare and magical creature. Us mere mortals can't compare ourselves to her."

"That is true." I pointed at a beer and waited for Ryan to pop the top and hand it to me.

"I saw your dad today, told him I'd be over this weekend to rake the leaves."

I set down my newly acquired beer and made a time-out motion with my hands. "First of all, since when are you my parents' lawn boy? And second, you saw my dad? Where?"

"In the backyard. I talked to him over the fence. And I wouldn't classify myself as their lawn boy, but I help out with the yard when I can."

"Was my dad upright when you saw him?" I tried to keep my tone light, as if my dad's drunkenness were a quirky personality trait like wearing socks with sandals or littering his conversations with bad puns.

"He was walking and talking just fine, as far as I could tell."

"Huh, must have been before noon then."

Ryan leaned forward and tapped the neck of his beer bottle against my wrist. "Since you've been back, have you talked to him about his drinking?"

"Nope," I said. "Wasn't aware that was my job."

"Well, it's not your *job*. But he's your father. I know my mom has tried once or twice over the years. Maybe he'd be able to hear it if it came from you."

I hated when Ryan started dispensing advice I'd never asked for and didn't want. The wise-older-brother mode he went into with Cassie and me even though we were all the same age and had made all the same dumb decisions over the years. He'd been notorious for it when we were teenagers, so often the voice of reason that Cassie had taken to calling him Dear Abby our freshman year. The fact that it was solid advice, coming from a good place, only made it that much more unwelcome. Cassie usually managed to blow it off, but it always made my hackles rise. "He took a leave of absence from being my father more than ten years ago," I said. "And as far as I can tell, he doesn't have any plans to resume the position. I've got better things to do with my time than lecture him on drinking and then watch him go right back to the bottle."

"Okay, okay." Ryan held up both hands in the universal gesture of backing off. "Forget I said anything. Although, for the record, I wasn't suggesting a lecture. More a loving nudge."

"What would the point be anyway? It's not like he has much of a life left now that the store is gone." I jerked a piece of pizza out of the box, half the cheese slipping sideways. "I still can't believe he sold it."

"From what I hear, he held on as long as he could. The store was in trouble, Greer. It had been for years. The insurance money he got after Eliza died was only a Band-Aid."

I lowered my piece of pizza. "What insurance money? Where'd you hear that?"

Ryan shrugged. "From Chet. He sold your dad the policy right before he retired."

An insurance policy on his teenage daughter? We'd never been poor, but money had always been tight. My mom clipped coupons, and our family vacations were usually a weekend somewhere within driving distance. It didn't seem like my dad to spend money on something as unlikely to be necessary as an insurance policy on Eliza. Except it had been necessary after all. "Was there one on me, too?"

"I've got no idea. You'll have to ask somebody with more knowledge than me. Chet mentioned it in passing one day when he was waxing poetic about his insurance days. And yes, it was exactly as riveting as it sounds."

We didn't talk too much after that. Sat together and watched the back-porch lights come on as the sky darkened. Worked our way through the pizza and a beer or two. If Ryan's inclination for unsolicited advice was one of the things I didn't like about him, his ability to be comfortable with silence was one of the things I did. He'd always been the comedian among us, quick with a laugh, easy with people and new situations. But that didn't mean he was always "on." He knew, in a way very few people ever master, how to be still.

There'd been a brief time our freshman year of high school

when I'd wondered if maybe Ryan and I were destined to be more than friends. An idea planted by a girl in my math class who'd seen us hanging out and made an assumption I couldn't stop rolling around and around in my head afterward, wondering if it had merit. Then an afternoon up in my bedroom, both of us sprawled across my bed listening to music, when I'd leaned into his body and pressed my mouth to his. Pushed my tongue tentatively between his lips. It hadn't been horrible, but it hadn't caused my stomach to knot or my breath to come faster, either. When I'd pulled away, scared I'd ruined everything, not sure how to even begin to backtrack, Ryan had smiled at me, tucked a piece of hair behind my ear. "I love you, Greer," he'd said. "So much. But not like that." And then he'd hit play on the next song. He'd understood, with a maturity way beyond my own, that our love wasn't the physical kind, and we didn't need to try to force it to be just to make our relationship easier for other people to understand. He'd made my misstep practically painless, a stubbed toe instead of a shattered leg. Something we could move past without permanent injury.

Ryan reached down and tweaked my foot, capturing my attention. "Hey," he said, voice gentle. "I know you're back here for a reason." He went on quickly before I could interrupt or disagree. "It's fine that you're not ready to tell us about it yet. But whatever you're searching for, whatever it is you need, you're going to find it, Greer." He gave me a small smile. "And everything is going to be okay."

He had no idea what he was talking about, but I had to give him credit for his conviction. His gaze never shifted. His voice never wavered. That's more than half the battle with a lie—believing it's the truth.

Chapter Eleven

There was a clump of boys kneeling around something in the dirt when I turned the corner toward Cassie's apartment. They were too engrossed to notice my approach, and I probably would have left them to it if I hadn't heard the telltale click of a lighter as I walked past. They didn't look much older than ten, definitely not old enough to be getting up to no good with something flammable.

"Hey," I said, voice a little louder than necessary. "What're you guys doing?" They all shot backward like I'd fired a gun, the one nearest to me banging into my legs and coming down hard on my toes. "Ow, Jesus," I said.

"Sorry," the kid mumbled.

"I asked what you're doing," I repeated.

They all stared at me. The one I would have labeled the hard case of the group if he'd shown up in my guidance counselor office back in Chicago gave me a dismissive once-over. "Nothing," he said, his eyes daring the rest of them to say something different.

"What's in the box?"

Hard Case shifted his weight, his face registering surprise before he could clamp down on it. "What box?"

"The one you're hiding behind your back." I made a rolling motion with my hand. "Come on, what are you guys up to?"

"We don't have to tell you," Hard Case informed me, but the

rest of his crew looked about to shit their pants. These were kids still young enough, and sweet enough, to be scared of adults. It was almost endearing.

"It's just a frog," one of the smaller boys blurted out. "In the box."

"Yeah? What else is in the box?"

Hard Case heaved out a long-suffering sigh and set the box on the ground, lifted one end of the lid. I crouched down and took a peek inside.

"Firecrackers?" I looked at the ring of faces above me. "Seriously? Get out of here before I tell your moms you're torturing animals."

"Frogs aren't animals," one of them said.

"Come on," another boy chimed in. "Let's go." They shuffled off in a pack toward the park, giving me baleful looks over their shoulders.

"Crazy bitch," one of them said, loud enough to carry.

"Crazy *old* bitch," Hard Case supplied before they turned the corner. I had to hand it to the kid, he knew how to hit where it hurt.

I took the lid off and turned the shoebox onto its side. "Better get while the getting's good," I told the frog, but he stayed motionless, blinking in the sudden sunshine. I left him there, probably contemplating his mortality, and climbed the rickety wooden steps up to Cassie's apartment. I didn't bother knocking, simply let myself in through a front door I knew would be unlocked. Cassie was sitting at her kitchen table, feet propped up on the chair across from her. She barely looked up from her sudoku as I came through the door.

"You need to start locking this," I told her. "It's not safe, and you have a pack of preteen delinquents roaming the neighborhood. I caught them out there about to blow a frog to smithereens with a handful of firecrackers."

Cassie took a bite of toast, crumbs flying as she spoke. "Eh, rite of passage. We sent a few frogs to their maker back in the day, too."

"We did not," I said, genuinely shocked.

"We sure as shit did," Cassie said, swinging her legs off the chair. She held out the rest of her toast to me, but I waved her off. "Down by the creek. We were probably like twelve-ish. I had leftover firecrackers from the Fourth of July. You and Ryan got covered in mud catching the frogs."

"I don't remember that at all." I opened up my mind, sure Cassie was mistaken and there was nothing to find. But almost immediately I was hit with a swift, sudden flash—the smell of gunpowder, ringing ears, frog guts smeared across bright green grass. Guilt mixed with sick excitement. *So this is how it feels to be bad.* It made me think about what else was hiding there, crouched in the neglected recesses of my brain. Not forgotten, simply tucked away where I didn't have to see. But I wasn't ready to look yet, and I steered my mind away so fast I could almost hear the screech of tires as I forced a course correction.

Cassie bumped me out of the way with her hip, edging into the kitchen with her plate, mug, and juice glass clutched in one hand. Waitress skills at the ready even in her own apartment. "What brings you by?" she asked. "Not that you need a reason. Mi casa es su casa and all that jazz."

"I wanted to see your place. Ryan told me you moved in not that long ago."

"Yeah, I'd been bunking with Jeff after I left my old apartment. But my god, between the kids and the dogs and Becca, who never fucking shuts up, I couldn't take it anymore."

Jeff was Cassie's younger brother. He'd gotten married at nineteen and now, less than a decade later, had already produced five kids. His wife, Becca, was a nice woman, but she'd give Chet a run for his money in the chatterbox division; I could see why Cassie had wanted out. Not to mention that this little apartment above the hardware store was a lot cuter than it looked from the outside.

The place was small—a living-and-dining-room combo with a tiny galley kitchen tucked off to the side. But the bedroom I'd glimpsed through the open doorway was large and sunny, with a sliding glass door that led to a balcony overlooking the park. And Cassie had decorated in her own eclectic style. So many colors it sort of hurt your eyes, but also made you want to settle in and never leave.

"This place is great," I told Cassie. "It's totally you." I took a seat at one of the bar stools at her kitchen counter and watched her rinse her dishes at the sink.

She gave her apartment an appraising glance over her shoulder. "Yeah, I like it. Feels like home."

Which was more than I could say for my nondescript studio in a run-down neighborhood of Chicago. I'd lived there for five years and the walls were still painted stark white, with not a single thing hung on them. Not for lack of time, more lack of caring. I already knew that no matter how hard I tried, it was never going to feel like home, so why bother trying at all?

"How'd things go with Miss Dollar Store the other night?" I asked.

"There's potential for a fling," Cassie said. "Not much more. But right now a fling is fine by me."

"Amen to that."

Cassie turned, leaned back against the sink. "I'm guessing you don't have anything serious going back in Chicago?"

"When have I ever had anything serious going?" I tried to make it sound like a joke, but I couldn't hold Cassie's gaze. Every time she visited me in Chicago, I could feel her worry without her even opening her mouth. The bland apartment, the lack of friends, the men I hooked up with and never spoke to again. She'd confronted me about it once, a few years ago, and it had led to the worst fight we'd ever had. She'd accused me of giving up on life after Eliza died, going through the motions without any joy or purpose behind them. The same sin I couldn't forgive my father for committing. She hadn't been wrong, but her anger hadn't pushed me to change, either. I didn't know how to explain it to her, that after Eliza died it seemed wrong to have a life of my own. Not when Eliza never would. Not when her being gone rested at my feet, even if I wasn't sure how or why.

Cassie crossed her arms, gave me her vintage stop-fucking-around look. "What are you really doing back here, Greer?"

I ran my fingers over the fake-granite countertop, picked up a toast crumb, and smashed it between my fingers. My heart thumped crazily, and I had to force myself to meet her gaze. "I need to put some things to bed."

Cassie raised her eyebrows. "That's all I'm going to get?"

"Please, Cassie," I said. "Don't push." This had always been our way. We asked the questions that needed asking, but backed off when space was required, even when the patience necessary for such an approach about killed Cassie. It had worked in the months after Eliza's death. It had worked when Cassie was struggling with coming out. I had to hope that it would work again now, that whatever damage I'd done to our friendship by my absence over the years, this one fundamental thing remained intact.

"Okay," she said, hands held up in surrender. "I won't ask again. But you'll tell me if you need help, right? Or someone to talk to?"

"Of course," I said. But I knew I wouldn't. At least not yet. *I did it for you.* Even after all this time, that message was still doing its worst to me. Keeping me silent. Keeping me scared. Every passing year solidifying my guilt into a wall I couldn't find a way to breach. But I wasn't going to give up this time, run away in a futile hope of leaving it all behind me. I was back, and I was going to push forward, even if that meant eventually it all came tumbling down.

When I left Cassie's apartment, the shoebox and firecrackers were gone. I pictured the boys I'd run off earlier slipping through the mud in search of a new frog—high, bright voices floating on the breeze as they tracked down the perfect victim.

· · · ·

"Well, that was a colossal waste of time," I groaned as I climbed into Dean's SUV.

"Oh, I don't know," Dean said. "I kind of enjoyed being mistaken for a cop. Made me feel like a badass."

I laughed, shaking my head. We'd spent most of the afternoon hunting down Will Quaid, a guy Roy had hung out with occasionally back in high school. It had felt fruitless before we'd even started and had turned out to be exactly that. We'd learned that Will hadn't spoken to Roy since long before the murders and barely recollected their sad excuse for a friendship. Mainly vandalizing houses and skipping school, according to Dean. Will was squirrely and shifty the entire time we talked to him, as if we were looming over him in an interrogation room playing good cop/bad cop instead of chatting him up over the soda we'd bought him. At first I'd thought his unease was because he knew something, but quickly determined that the track marks on his arm and his mistaken belief that we were undercover cops were the source of his distress.

"Would you mind if we made a quick pit stop at the farm?" Dean asked as we roared down the highway toward Ludlow. "Mrs. Steadman asked if I could move some hay bales, and it won't take long. Twenty minutes, tops. They're too heavy for Mr. Steadman these days, but if I don't get it done, he'll go out and start trying to lift them himself. Probably end up in the hospital with a hernia."

"Sure." I shrugged. "I don't have anywhere else I need to be." I doubted my parents would even notice my absence at the dinner table.

Dean took a right off the highway onto a deserted country road, straight and flat as far as the eye could see.

"This is where my dad taught me to drive," I told him. "Summer I was fifteen."

Dean made a humming sound in his throat. "Good spot. Can't remember last time I saw another car along here."

There hadn't been any cars back then, either. But one August day, we'd turned onto the road and been confronted with a bull, escaped from a nearby pasture and blocking the narrow road, head lowered at the front of our car. Before my dad could stop me, I'd lain on the horn, the sound piercing the lazy, late-summer heat. "Oh, shit," my dad had said at the same moment the bull pawed the ground, surging forward toward our car. "Reverse, reverse!" my dad had yelled. We'd careened backward, me frantically trying to keep one eye on the advancing bull and another out the rear window to make sure we didn't veer off the road and into the shallow ditch. I remember cackling crazily while fear unspooled in my gut. After what felt like a mile, but was probably a quarter of that, the bull lost interest and stopped to investigate the weeds on the side of the road. "Well, holy hell," my dad had said, leaning his head back against the seat. "Guess we can check reversing from an angry bull off the list of defensive-driving techniques I need to teach you." I missed that Dad, the one who always made me feel safe and protected. Who made me laugh. I missed being someone's daughter.

About a mile later, Dean turned down a long driveway, and we bumped along past a sprawling farmhouse and out to a huge weather-beaten barn with a couple of trucks already parked in front. Two sleeping dogs roused themselves at our arrival, padding over to circle the SUV, tails wagging.

"Hey, guys," Dean said as we hopped out. He pointed to the black Lab. "This is Hamilton and that mutt over there is Napoleon." At my expression, he laughed. "Mrs. Steadman was a history teacher, remember?"

I gave both of the dogs friendly pats as I rounded the front fender, using my knee to keep them from jumping up and shoving me backward. I followed Dean over to the barn, standing back as he slid the door open, releasing the scent of hay and dust. He grabbed a pair of work gloves from a bin inside and slipped them on. The barn was huge and ancient, with a suspicious leftward lean that made me worry it wouldn't survive the next tornado whipping off the prairie, but it was as organized and spotlessly clean as a barn could be, the dirt floor swept and every farming implement carefully stored. Someone took pride in this place. Probably Dean and Mr. Steadman both. Dean pointed toward a stack of hay bales. "Take a load off, if you want."

I lowered myself onto a bale, hay poking into my legs through my jeans, and Napoleon clambered up next to me, licking my face.

"Are you almost done for the season?" I asked.

"Almost." He pointed out the barn doors to the long furrows of fresh dirt crisscrossing the fields. "We just finished planting the winter wheat. Come spring, this whole place will be nothing but waving gold." I could hear the satisfaction in his voice, the love of the land and what he would coax from it.

"I bet that's beautiful," I said. "Standing out in the middle of it right before harvest."

"It is." He gestured outside again, this time with a pitchfork clutched in his hand. "Speaking of beautiful, in a little while you're in for a show."

I raised my eyebrows at him.

"The sunset," he said. "It's going to be a good one."

"How can you tell?"

"Not sure, exactly. You're out here enough, you start being able to feel it." He ducked his head a little. "That sounds crazy, right?"

"No, not at all." I could see why he liked this place, this work. The stillness, the sense of accomplishment at the end of every season, the scent of fresh dirt in the air. "Did Roy ever think about working here with you? Instead of at Merl's?"

"I don't know," Dean said. "But I never offered it. I liked that this was the one place I could get away from him. From my grandma, too. A spot that's just for me. I can be a selfish prick sometimes. And I wasn't a very good brother." He heaved a hay bale like it was nothing, grunting a little under his breath as he tossed it into an open stall.

"I doubt that's true."

"It's true. When we were kids, after our mom took off, I used to pick on Roy. I wanted so badly for it to be someone's fault that she left. Not hers, though. And definitely not mine." He barked out a brittle laugh. "So I made it his instead. Thinking to myself that if he wasn't such a pain in the ass she wouldn't have gotten fed up and left. I'd start in on him, call him names, shove him, tear up whatever he was working on for school. Because I knew eventually he'd lose his cool. He didn't know how to handle his emotions, and I'd push and push until he'd take a swing at me. And then I'd have what I needed, an excuse to pummel him." Dean turned his face away, breathing hard.

His pain plucked at a string inside me, the beginning notes of a familiar song. I knew how it felt to regret without the possibility of fixing what had been broken. The horrible gnawing ache that kind of loss left behind. Eliza and I had never fought like Dean and Roy. We'd never purposely hurt each other. But as teenagers, we'd somehow turned into two bodies existing in the same space with hardly a connection between us, so that by the time Eliza died, Cassie and Ryan felt more like my siblings than she did. Our paths had diverged, and it had barely registered. I'd thought all we'd had in front of us was time; it never occurred to me that we wouldn't someday wind our way back to each other. But while I understood

Dean's pain, it didn't mean I knew what to say to him, had no words that might ease the hurt. I couldn't possibly sit here and fill him up with platitudes that weren't worth the effort it took to speak them. "I can't imagine anyone pummeling Roy," I said finally, picturing Roy's broad shoulders in the courtroom, the way his lawyer had looked like a child next to him.

Dean laughed again, an easier one this time. "Believe me, it didn't last long. By the time he was twelve, he was giving as good as he got."

In front of us, the sun was sinking fast, lighting up the sky with pink and purple, a splash of fiery orange across the horizon. "See?" he said. "Told you."

We were silent for a few minutes, watching the sun put on its nightly farewell show.

"You said Roy couldn't handle his emotions very well." I kept my gaze on the darkening sky, and Dean gave a faint hum in response. "Was he like that from the beginning?"

"I can't tell you how he was as an infant or a toddler, but my grandma said he was always hard to console. A screamer. In my mind I always pictured him as one of those red-faced, pissed-off babies." I glanced at Dean, watched him toss another hay bale. "But maybe if he'd had a mom who wasn't doing drugs while she was pregnant, or who bothered to give a shit once he was born, things would have been different for him."

"He had trouble in school, right?" I asked, remembering bits and pieces from the defense attorney's closing arguments. Talk of bullying and fights. Detentions that gave way to suspensions and ultimately to expulsion.

"Yeah." Dean sighed. He took off his work gloves and shoved them in his back pocket. "Neither one of us was a rocket scientist, but I knew enough to keep my head down, do the work, not draw attention to myself. But Roy couldn't manage even that much, and so he got the reputation as a troublemaker pretty quick. After that, the other kids piled on. Talked him into doing dumb shit, poking at him the way I used to just to get a reaction. I must have told him a thousand times not to let them get to him, but he never listened." He paused. "Maybe he couldn't listen."

I'd asked the questions, but I didn't particularly like hearing about this version of Roy. The human one who suffered from things he couldn't control, just like all the rest of us. I hopped off the hay bale and zipped up my jacket against the oncoming chill.

"I'm about done," Dean told me. "Five more minutes."

"Okay," I said. "Thanks for the sunset, by the way."

He smiled. "No problem. I can't exactly take credit." As he spoke he bent his head, wiped his face with the sleeve of his T-shirt. I saw a flash of something red on his left bicep, jagged and pointy. My stomach dropped to my feet and kept on plummeting right through the floor.

"What's that?" I asked. My voice was breathy and weak, and I had to suck in a lungful of air before I could say anything more. "On your arm?"

His brow furrowed. "What? This?" He pulled up his sleeve, and the heart on his arm blared back at me. No smooth edges or symmetrical sides. It was misshapen, like it had been drawn by a child. He moved toward me, still holding up his sleeve, and I took a step back, my legs bumping up against the hay bale behind me. "It's a tattoo." He raised his eyebrows. "A really, really bad one."

"Where did you . . ." I scooted away from him, edging toward the open barn door. "Why do you have it?"

He laughed, the sound hitting me like a smack. "Hell if I know. Some guy who grew up down the street from me decided he was going to be a tattoo artist one summer. And Roy and I were dumb enough to be his guinea pigs. Thought it would be cool, if you can believe that shit." He glanced down at the tattoo with a shake of his head. "Guy couldn't draw to save his own ass. I have no idea what I was thinking letting him put something permanent on me."

"Roy had one, too?" I managed. "A heart?"

Dean dropped his sleeve. "Yeah. I should have known it was a bad idea when the guy only gave us the one option. Roy's was even more fucked up than mine, but at least it was on his back. My grandma about killed us when she found out." He peered at me. "Hey, are you okay?"

"Uh-huh," I said, gulping air. "I'll wait for you in the car."

I could feel him watching me as I walked away. My hands were shaking, and it took me two tries to get the passenger door of his SUV open, the handle slipping between my sweaty fingers. I wished I had my own car, that I could drive away and not look back. I slid into the passenger seat and closed my eyes, still breathing hard. I winced a little, imagining what Dean probably thought of me. How nuts I'd just acted for no good reason. My head knew how irrational I was being, but the rest of me wasn't quite getting the memo. The heart on Dean's arm had sent me reeling, not because I necessarily thought it had anything to do with the one I'd received, but because seeing it had reinforced the fact that he was a virtual stranger to me. What did I really know about him, his past, his motivations, his desires? Not much. And yet I was trusting him. Maybe not completely, but certainly more than I was trusting anyone else in my life. And I probably wouldn't know if I was making a horrible mistake until it was too late.

• • • •

The Ludlow United Methodist Church was only half full for its nine a.m. Sunday service. Ludlow had always been a God-fearing place. If you were Methodist or Presbyterian, you were considered normal. It meant you went to church on Sunday and tried not to cuss in front of company. Baptists were what the rest of us would call religious, singing the praises of the Lord and lamenting the perils of Satan to whoever would stay still long enough to listen. And as for atheists, well, Ludlow didn't believe in those. So I suspected the lack of full pews was more a case of people wanting to sleep in and hit church a little later in the day rather than a sudden lack of faith.

Prior to this morning, I hadn't been inside a church since Eliza's funeral. Frankly, I didn't think I was missing much. Belief in a higher power never seemed to spare anyone from the same suffering and sin as nonbelievers. But I stood dutifully to sing from the hymn book, lowered my head in an approximation of piousness when Preacher Frogue said the opening prayer. Most of his sermon focused on Dylan's and Addy's murders and how we all needed to band together to fight the evil that had pervaded Ludlow. The subtext being that someone from the outside had done this, no acknowledgment that perhaps the rot had been coming from inside Ludlow all along. Even as I tried to follow along, half of my attention was fixed on an older woman near the front—broad shoulders, neat cap of graying brown hair, sensible navy pantsuit. Travis's mom, Lydia Pratt. She'd always been a churchgoer and, unlike my parents, hadn't given it up in the years since the murders. I hoped it brought her some comfort.

After the service, I lingered on the stone steps outside the church, pretending to admire the stained glass windows but really waiting for Lydia to emerge. When she came through the double doors and saw me standing there, she gave me a look I couldn't read.

"Do you have a minute?" I asked.

She jerked her head in a quick nod, marched past me down the steps and toward a wooden bench on the church lawn. "Come over here, there's things need saying that I don't want the Lord to hear."

I'd always been under the assumption that if the Lord was real, he could hear what was said regardless of how close to a church you were standing when you spoke, but I did as she asked and took a seat next to her on the bench. I could see the resemblance between her and Travis—same oversized nose and squared-off jaw—that I hadn't really noticed in my youth. Features that worked on a man's face transforming into something a little too rough on a woman's. She surprised me by opening up her purse and pulling out a pack of cigarettes. She held it out to me, and when I shook my head, she extracted one and lit it up, took a fortifying puff. "You're back."

It wasn't a question, but I nodded anyway.

"How are your parents?" She took another drag from her cigarette.

"They're okay," I said. "Have you seen my mom lately?"

Lydia shook her head. "No, not really. We pass each other in the grocery once in a while. Give a nod and keep on moving. Sometimes it's hard to believe we used to be good friends."

"What happened between the two of you, if you don't mind me asking?" In the first months after Eliza's death, it hadn't really registered that Lydia was missing from our lives. We were all struggling through each day; anything beyond our basic needs fell by the wayside. And when I finally did notice, all my mom said was that they'd grown apart. Which shouldn't have surprised me. People on the outside always assumed that grief bound people together. But in my experience, all it did was maroon you on your own little island, the effort it would take to reach out more than you could spare.

Lydia waved her cigarette through the air. "We'd both lost children, but it wasn't the same. Travis was my only one. And without a husband, I didn't have anything left. Everyone acted as if your family's loss was worse because Eliza was a girl. Poor Eliza. Such a sweet girl. Such a pretty girl. Such a shame. Like Travis wasn't shot to death, too."

Heat rose into my cheeks, and I fought against the urge to bite back. Because at least no one had slut-shamed Travis in the aftermath. No one blamed him for his own murder, suggested that if he'd just kept his dick in his pants he might still be alive. In death, he'd at least been afforded some dignity. But she wasn't necessarily wrong about the rest of it. Dead girls always captured our attention more than dead boys. We liked to picture them sprawled out on the ground, hair flowing and skin pale. There was something almost romantic about a dead girl. A dead boy wasn't the same. "That must have been hard," I said finally.

"You've got no idea." She turned her face away. She was silent for a minute, the sound of the church choir floating across the lawn. Something about God and glory. "I know it wasn't your mother's fault. But it was easier to keep my distance. And it's not like your mother made much effort, either." She tapped ash from the end of her cigarette, glanced at me. "What did you want to talk to me about?"

I hesitated, wanting to tread lightly but needing to ask the question. "Before the murders, did Travis mention anything that might have been bothering Eliza?"

Lydia's brow furrowed. "Like what?"

"I have no idea. That's why I'm asking."

She shook her head. "Nothing comes to mind. They were as happy as ever, far as I could tell. Travis's whole life was your sister." A shade of bitterness in her voice she didn't bother trying to disguise. When Travis and Eliza had first gotten together, both Lydia and my mom were thrilled. What was better than your child picking your good friend's? But while Lydia hadn't exactly soured on Eliza after she and Travis got serious, there had been tension between them. Lydia realizing a little too late that Travis falling in love meant his mother was no longer the most important woman in his life.

"Okay," I said on a sigh. It was the answer I'd been expecting, but defeat hit me hard in the chest anyway.

Lydia puffed on her cigarette, shot out a cloud of smoke. "I looked for you at the execution."

"You went?"

"Of course I went." She sounded disgusted by the mere suggestion that she might have skipped it. "Best day I'd had in years. I only wish I could have been the one to kill him." Her eyes shifted to the church and she muttered, "Forgive me, Jesus," under her breath. Her hand shook slightly as she raised her cigarette again. "Your parents weren't there." It was impossible to miss the accusation in her voice.

"No."

She made a tsking noise. "What's your excuse?"

I thought of watching Roy's last moments, meeting his eyes through the glass, and my stomach shriveled, my nails digging into my palms. "I didn't see what good it would do, to watch him die."

Lydia's back stiffened. She dropped her cigarette and ground it out underneath the toe of her sensible shoe. "I tried to talk to that brother of his, after. But it wasn't allowed. Had deputies that kept us apart."

"What did you want to say to him?" I had a pretty good idea already and was glad, for Dean's sake, that the deputies had done their jobs. Doubly glad that I'd told him it was best if he didn't come with me today. Lydia didn't seem filled with the spirit of forgiveness.

She stood, hoisted her purse onto her shoulder. "I wanted to look him in the face, tell him I hope Roy suffered. Tell him I hope he never has a single second of peace, the same way I never will." She turned and marched away from me.

Well, so much for Jesus.

. . . .

Ryan was wasted. With a golf club in his hand. Not the smartest combo. "Hey, whoa, watch out," Cassie said, catching the club before Ryan could swing. "You're going to take someone's head off with that thing. I'd rather it wasn't mine."

"I'm fine," Ryan said, but he relinquished his grip on the club.

"Why don't you keep score and leave the hitting of golf balls to us?" I suggested.

"Okay," he muttered. "Whatever." He slumped down on a bench and rested his forehead in his hand. "I'm drunk," he informed us a second later, like he was imparting breaking news.

"No shit," Cassie said, rolling her eyes in my direction.

I stepped up to the sixth hole of the miniature golf course and lined up my shot. It was one of the difficult ones, trying to hit the ball through the bottom of a windmill between the spinning wooden blades. Cassie had sent me an SOS text right after dinner, letting me know that Ryan had gotten his final divorce papers in the mail and was already halfway to shit-faced. This outing had been our attempt to cheer him up and keep him from passing out drunk in his mom's living room. Not a good look for a grown man. "Whoo-hoo," I yelled when I got my ball through on the first try, listening to the satisfying clink as it dropped right into the metal cup on the other side. "Hole in one! Eat my dust, suckers!"

The mini golf course had undergone a bit of an upgrade since I was home last. It was technically on land owned by the library, but the course itself was the property of the Parker family. They'd spent years neglecting it, but according to Cassie, they'd finally decided to use some of their refinery riches to spruce up the joint. When we were teenagers, you could only play during daylight hours, but now there were floodlights, and all the artificial turf was a bright, glossy green. The obstacles at each hole were still original—the windmill, the moat, the castle—but they'd benefited from a new coat of paint. I imagined it was quite the draw come summer, but on a chilly fall night we had the run of the place.

Cassie dropped her ball carelessly, hacking away at it like she always did, too impatient to make a good shot. She watched dispassionately as her ball bounced off the side of the windmill and rolled right back to where it had started. "Fuck," she muttered. "I hate this game."

Ryan groaned behind me, and I took pity on him, passing him the bag of pretzels I'd brought. "Here. Eat some of these." Luckily, there wasn't another group behind us, because between Ryan's alcohol content and Cassie's ball handling we'd be lucky to be done by midnight. I sank down on the ground next to Ryan, held out my hand for a few pretzels.

"Hey, is Faith O'Neal still around?" I asked.

Cassie paused in her swing and looked at me. "Yeah. Why?"

Faith had been a friend of Eliza's, probably the closest girlfriend she'd had. But I still doubted Eliza had confided anything to her, or at least nothing earth-shattering. In the last few years of her life, Eliza had saved her secrets for Travis. But Dean's worry—*What if it happens again?*—wouldn't stop echoing in my head. We needed to move faster, and we weren't getting very far looking into Roy's life; it was past time to branch out into Eliza's.

"No reason," I said, trying to keep my voice casual. "I was just thinking about her the other day. Wondered what ever happened to her."

"Eric Carlson happened to her," Ryan said. "Haven't they had like five kids already?"

"Four," Cassie corrected. "But you're not wrong. I hope she never had any plans beyond making Eric happy because from what I hear, that's a full-time job."

Eric had run in the same pack as Travis and Garrett, all of them on the football team, although only Travis had any lasting talent. Eric had always been my least favorite of that group. Smug and dismissive, even of Eliza, which I knew had caused more than a few fights between Travis and him. I didn't remember Faith and Eric ever expressing an interest in each other, and I wondered how they'd ended up together. It could have been simply proximity and familiarity, which is how a lot of marriages happened in Ludlow's shallow dating pool.

Cassie tossed down her ball for the fifth time and drew back her club. I sighed. "We gonna be here all night?"

"We might be if you keep interrupting me," she said. "You just made me miss my shot. Again."

I snorted. "Yeah, I don't think that had anything to do with me."

"I love you guys," Ryan announced suddenly, his voice a couple of notches too loud.

Cassie and I exchanged an amused glance, and I patted Ryan's foot before standing. "We love you, too. Even if you're a sloppy drunk."

I was a little surprised at how hard the arrival of the divorce papers had hit him. To my mind, he was dodging a bullet, getting out of a shitty marriage before he had kids or wasted thirty years of his life. But when I mentioned that to Cassie while we were waiting for Ryan to stumble out of his house earlier tonight, she'd reminded me that we never really know what goes on inside a marriage, or any relationship, for that matter. What looked like an escape hatch to me probably felt like abject failure to Ryan, especially after the way his parents' marriage had blown up. He'd always sworn that when he got married someday it was going to stick. He'd had a wife, a decent job, a life outside of Ludlow. And now here he was, right back where he'd started.

"No, I mean it," he said, standing up and slinging a heavy arm around my neck. "This is good, right? The three of us. Here together again? It's good." His voice sounded a little desperate, like he was trying to convince not only us but himself, too.

"It's perfect," Cassie said. "I've been trying to get both of you home for years. Ludlow wasn't the same without you."

Come back. My gaze shifted between Cassie and Ryan, my oldest friends, my only friends, really, and a whisper of dread unspooled in my gut. I knew that's not what they'd meant. But I couldn't help the unease their words stirred inside of me. The same way I couldn't help my reaction to Dean's tattoo. The whole world appeared double-edged to me now. A warped funhouse mirror. Benign and innocent at first glance, but the longer I looked, the more distorted the image became—something dark and malignant taking shape right before my eyes.

Travis

Travis loved football. The feel of the ball in his hand, the way his muscles screamed after a game, the roar of the crowd in the stands, the smell of sweat and victory when he and the rest of his team kicked ass on the field. And he was good. He knew it, and everybody else in Ludlow knew it, too. Wherever he went in town, people slapped him on the back, gave him high fives, bought him beers he was too young to drink but did anyway.

The thing was, though, he wasn't great, no matter what his mom or his coach tried to tell him. He understood his limits. More and more every day, actually. The tiny twinge in his knee whenever he stepped backward for a pass. It wasn't going to stay tiny for long. For a different guy, that might have been a gut punch. The oncoming end to the only dream he had. But as much as Travis loved football, he loved something else more. Eliza Dunning.

It hadn't been love at first sight or anything. Hell, he'd known Eliza since birth, couldn't even remember the first time he'd seen her. She'd just been Eliza, whose dad owned the grocery store. And then one day in ninth grade they'd been put together for a group science project. And "just Eliza" had become something more. Turned out Eliza was smart, and she was kind, and when she smiled, she got a tiny dimple in her left cheek. Her skin always smelled like roses and her hands had calluses from lifting boxes in her dad's store. She wasn't scared of hard work, and she wasn't afraid to call him out when he was being stupid or selfish. After games she fussed over him, rubbing Bengay into his sore muscles. And she could do this thing with her hips when they fucked that made his brain feel like it was going to shoot right out of the top of his skull.

They already had a plan for the future. College, although any football scholarship he got would only last as long as his soon-to-be-busted knee. Maybe he'd stick it out for four years, or maybe he'd come back to Ludlow and wait for Eliza. Either way, once she was done, they'd get married. Twenty-two was young to tie the knot these days, but around here it was also normal. Nobody would bat an eye. He'd start helping Mr. Dunning at the store and Eliza would get a job at the middle school. But eventually she'd join him at the grocery, and they'd take over when Mr. Dunning retired. Along the way they'd have a couple of kids, and years from now, on a chilly October night like this one, they'd go watch their son play football for Ludlow High or join their daughter to cheer on the team from the sidelines.

So Travis wasn't all that broken up knowing that his football days were going to end sooner rather than later. Because he had Eliza. And they were going to last forever.

Chapter Twelve

Ludlow wasn't big enough, or prosperous enough, to be split into distinct neighborhoods. No rigid stratification based on income level like in so much of the rest of the world. Sure, there were a handful of well-off folks with the houses to match, the biggest being the Parkers' gray stone three-story perched on the corner of Elm and Maple that took up almost a third of the block. But right next to it was a run-down ranch and behind it stood a squat apartment block built in the seventies when "ugly" seemed to be the primary goal of architecture. All over town larger, more well-maintained houses butted up against modest bungalows or outright dumps. It was like when houses were being built everyone figured what they had in common—being stuck in the middle of nowhere—trumped any potential differences in bank account balance.

Even so, I guessed that the state of the house next door to Eric Carlson's tidy airplane bungalow had to be killing him. It was basically a glorified double-wide, and it looked like no one had bothered to mow the lawn in months; broken kids' toys lay scattered across the grass, and a mangy-looking pit bull was chained up next to a rotting doghouse placed right on the edge of the property line. Bushes had been planted between the houses, down the entire length of the driveway separating the properties, but it was going to be a few years before they were big enough to do much to block the view. If Eric was still anything like the guy I'd known in high school, he probably made his displeasure known to the neighbors every time they stepped outside. "You catch more flies with honey" had never been Eric Carlson's mantra.

When Faith opened her front door, painted a cheery yellow that clashed against the orange-and-black Halloween wreath hanging from a hook above the peephole, it took her a second to place me. "Oh, my good lord," she said when it finally clicked, one pale hand fluttering up to her neck before drifting back down. "Is that you, Greer?"

"It's me," I said, forcing a smile.

"I'd heard you were back in town, but I wasn't expecting you to drop by. And you're all grown up now." She stepped back and ushered me inside. "I guess we all are." Her laugh was light and easy. A perfect hostess. Which didn't surprise me. Faith had always been the bright, bubbly girl, the one you counted on for a smile and a hug. A ridiculously generic pep talk. I'd never seen her sad or upset; she wore her happiness like armor, and god forbid she ever set it down.

From what I could see of the inside of the house, it was as meticulously cared for as the exterior. The air smelled of furniture polish and roasting meat. No sign at all that four small children lived here. Faith offered me a drink, which I declined, then pointed me toward a faux-leather sectional. I perched on the edge, too many patterned throw pillows behind me for any attempt at actually getting comfortable.

"Eric said you're in Chicago," Faith said, taking a seat across from me. "That must be so exciting."

"Sometimes," I said. She'd be disappointed to know just how boring and quiet my life was. She was picturing late nights and fancy dinners, short dresses and too many cocktails. Truth was, her life was probably more exciting than mine. "And I heard you have four kids," I said after a pause that had gone on a little too long.

"Yep." She smiled, holding up her fingers as she ticked off their stats. "Emma is eight, Lily is six, Harper is three, and the baby, Hudson, is one. Thank god we finally got a boy. Eric might have left me if we'd had another girl." She laughed again, this one not quite so easy. "They're at their grandma's this afternoon. Eric'll be back with them soon. We don't let them out of our sight right now, not with everything that's happened." Her fingers moved to a tiny red-and-blue braided ribbon pinned to her collar that I hadn't noticed before, the colors lost among the flower pattern on her blouse.

"I'm sorry to drop by without calling first, I know you probably have tons to do, but I wanted to ask you about Eliza."

Faith cocked her head, her mouth drawing down. "What about her?"

"I'm not sure," I said, honestly. "This is probably going to sound crazy, coming out of the blue." I leaned forward a little. "But the night of the murders she wanted to tell me something, and I was in too much of a hurry to listen. Do you know what it might have been?"

Faith shook her head. "She never said anything to me." She paused, looked away.

"What?"

"There was something . . ." Her brow scrunched up. "But Eliza swore me to secrecy."

I bit back an impatient sound. "It's not like she's here to object, Faith."

"I think she may have been seeing someone on the side." Faith lowered her voice to a whisper even though we were alone in the house. "I think she was cheating on Travis."

I reared back a little, sending a flurry of throw pillows toppling to the floor. Cheating on Travis? I'd never seen Eliza even glance at another guy, let alone covet one. "Did she tell you she was cheating?"

"Oh, lord, no," Faith said, voice back to regular volume.

"Then what made you think that?"

"Okay, so, we were up in Eliza's room after school, and I was sitting at her desk. This was just a few days before the murders." She tightened her sandy blond ponytail with a quick tug and tucked her bare feet up underneath her in her chair, getting comfortable, warming to her story. I remembered this about her suddenly, how she could stretch a one-minute tale into ten, always heavy-handed with details that made no difference to the point. Eliza seemed to take it in stride, but I recalled a lot of rolling hand motions from the rest of their friends whenever Faith held the floor.

"It was the day before the game against Neosho South. I remember that because I'd asked Eliza if she'd put some temporary tattoos on my cheeks before the game. I'd ordered blue glitter comet ones online, and I couldn't wait to try them out. Turned out they were a waste of money because they peeled off within an hour. I tried to return them after the game and never got my money back."

I shifted slightly, sliding my hands under my thighs to keep from doing my own version of hurrying her story along. I made an encouraging humming noise in my throat instead.

"Anyway, I was sitting at her desk and just kind of half listening to some story she was telling me about Travis, and I saw this photograph, under a bunch of stuff."

"A photograph of what?" I asked, and Faith tossed me an annoyed look. "Sorry," I backtracked. "I'll let you tell it."

"I could only see like a third of the photo. It looked like it had been printed out, you know, like on printer paper? The color was kind of grainy. Anyway, I could tell it was a guy. He was wearing a T-shirt and sitting in a truck and all I could see was his arm out of the window. But it wasn't Travis. I knew that much."

"How could you tell?"

She pursed her lips and scrunched up her brow like she was re-creating the photo in her mind. "It was his left arm, because he was in the driver's seat, and he wasn't wearing that leather bracelet thing Travis always wore. But I wasn't one hundred percent sure until I asked Eliza about it. I remember I started to pull the photo out from under the junk on top of it, and Eliza practically flew across the room. She slammed her hand down so fast on top of the photo that she crushed my fingers." The corner of Faith's mouth kicked up in time with her eyebrows. "Whoever it was, she really didn't want me to see him."

"Did you ask her any more about it?"

"Believe me, I tried. But she wouldn't tell me anything. She got all shifty and weird and hid the photo away. And you know Eliza, she wasn't really the secretive type. So I knew it meant something big when she wouldn't let me see the photo or even tell me who it was a picture of."

"And you never saw the photo again?"

"Nope." She shook her head. "I tried to bring it up with her one more time, teasing her a little, and she about bit my head off. Told me to mind my own business. Which wasn't like Eliza, either. Something was going on there, but I never figured out what it was."

"You said the guy in the photo was sitting in a truck?"

Faith paused, closing her eyes for a second. "You know, I can't swear to anything anymore. It could have been a truck, a car, an SUV. I don't really know."

"Could you see anything besides his arm?"

"No. Just his arm, hand, and part of his shoulder. He was wearing a T-shirt, I remember that. The rest of the photo was hidden, and I never got a better look before Eliza grabbed it."

"What color was the truck? Or the car?" I pressed.

Faith sighed. "I don't know that, either, not anymore. Most of the time, I'd swear it was red. But sometimes I think it might have been white. Or blue. Or black. I know how that sounds, like I'm making all this up or something. But it's been years. And I only got to see the photo for a couple of seconds. I feel like after all this time I'm getting the color of his T-shirt mixed up with the color of his truck." She shook her head again. "I can't be sure about anything other than it was a guy. And Eliza didn't want me to know who he was."

"And that's what made you think she was cheating?"

"I mean, it was just weird, you know? Her reaction. It seemed over the top. And she'd been kind of off for a while right before the murders. Short with me and with Travis, too, which was unusual. She was keeping a secret," Faith finished. "That's all I'm sure about. Anything beyond that is only a guess."

"I know you didn't see the photo, but if she was messing around with someone, do you have any idea who it might have been?"

"No." Her answer came quickly, but it sounded wobbly and red splotches bloomed in her cheeks as I stared at her. I thought I might have to pry harder, but I'd underestimated Faith's love of telling a story, even if it came at her own expense. "Back then, I thought it might have been Eric," she said, not meeting my eyes.

"Eric?" I asked after a pause. "Like your husband, Eric?"

Faith breathed out a laugh, flapped her hand at me like I'd told a joke. "Well, he wasn't my husband back then. But yes, my Eric."

"Why would you assume that?" I couldn't imagine a scenario where Eliza would have looked at Eric with anything approaching desire. Eric had always had borderline bully tendencies, and that wasn't something Eliza tolerated. Once, at the diner after school, he'd been pushing around some younger kid, calling him names, stealing his food. Eliza had told him to stop, and he'd ignored her. When Travis had failed to step in fast enough for Eliza's liking, she'd given him the cold shoulder for a week. As for Eric, he'd gone straight to Eliza's permanent shit list.

Faith raised her eyebrows at me like I'd just asked the world's dumbest question. "Because Eric had a thing for Eliza. He tried to hide it, covered it up by being a jerk to her half the time. But if you were paying attention, it was pretty obvious." And clearly she had been paying attention. Watching Eric look at her best friend instead of at her.

"Did you ever ask Eric about the photo? Or if he and Eliza had been screwing around?"

"I did, yeah, after we started dating. He said he'd never messed around with Eliza. And he didn't know anything about the photograph."

"Did you believe him?" From outside, the sound of a car rumbled up the drive, then the harsh barking of the neighbor's dog and the clatter of children's voices.

Faith stood quickly, smoothing down her shirt. "I believe him," she said, looking out the front window. "He wouldn't have done that to Travis. Bro code and all that."

The front door of the house burst open and kids spilled inside, careening off one another and their mother like human pinballs. Shouts of "Mom!" and "Guess what?" and "Who's she?" blistering the air.

"Settle down, settle down," Faith said, smiling. Her laughter seemed genuine for the first time, her face lit up with maternal pride. "This is Greer. She's an old friend from high school."

"Where do you live?" the oldest girl asked me. All of the kids had Eric's dark hair and eyes. His chin and nose. Like Faith had nothing at all to do with their creation, a fact I bet Eric took as proof of his genetic superiority.

"Chicago," I told her, standing from the couch and moving toward the door.

"Chicago," the girl repeated. "That's a big city, right?"

"Pretty big," I agreed.

"Yep," Eric said from the doorway, the baby in his arms. "Miss

Greer up and moved to the big city. Thinks she's fancy now." He made wide eyes at his daughters, laughed like it was a joke, but there wasn't a smile on his face. "Hey, Greer," he said, turning his gaze to me. "What brings you by?" I'd only gotten a glimpse of him that first night at the Do, but he hadn't changed much. Still sporting a buzz cut and the kind of muscles you only got from too many hours at the gym. Although a ring of belly fat was just starting to make an appearance above his belt. That had to be killing him.

Faith hurried over and scooped the baby onto her hip, planted a kiss on Eric's cheek. "She just wanted to say hi. Catch up a bit."

"Huh," Eric said, jiggling his keys in his hand.

I pointed to his blue polo shirt, "Ludlow High" emblazoned on the breast, "Coach" right below. "You at the high school?" I asked.

"Yep. Teach history. And I'm the head football coach." His chest puffed out a bit on the last three words.

"Nice. I bet you're good at it," I said, meaning it. I could picture him with a whistle around his neck, yelling kids through drills and passing out high fives. Relishing the power, but taking it seriously, too. "Well, I'd better take off. Leave you to it."

"Let me walk you out," Eric said. He glanced at Faith. "Dinner when I come back in, yeah?" He lifted his voice like it was a question, but there was no missing the demand in his tone.

"Sure," Faith said, smiling. "It's almost ready." She turned, ushering the kids in front of her toward the kitchen, calling a goodbye to me over her shoulder. She liked it, I realized—the certainty of her place in her family's hierarchy. She never had to wonder exactly where she stood or what was expected of her. Dinner on the table, a clean house, a pretty smile. If Eliza had lived and married Travis, would she have ended up the same way? I hoped not. I hoped Travis would have been happy with less. I hoped Eliza would have demanded more.

"How long you planning on being in town?" Eric asked once we were outside, ambling toward my car.

"I don't really know. Why?" I didn't think he was asking to be polite, wasn't planning on inviting me over for dinner one night for old times' sake. We had always tolerated each other because we had friends in common and Ludlow was too small for avoidance, but we'd never warmed beyond basic courtesy. If not for Travis tying us together, I doubt we would have gone even that far.

"Just curious." He ran a big hand over his head, fingers scratching against his flat top. "Garrett seems pretty happy you're back."

I huffed out a laugh before I could stop myself. "He does? That's news to me." I hadn't seen Garrett since the day out back of the police station—if you didn't count him driving by my house in his police cruiser—and I was more than happy to keep it that way.

Eric stopped at the curb, squared off his stance, and stared at me. "Yeah, that's what I figured."

"What's that supposed to mean?"

He pursed his lips, gave a small shake of his head. "Garrett's always had a soft spot for you, is all. I'd hate for you to take advantage of it."

"Not planning on it," I said, my voice sharper than I'd intended. I rounded the front of my car and stopped before opening my door. "Speaking of soft spots, you had a thing for Eliza?"

Eric's face flushed, and I felt a quick jab of triumph at having caught him off guard. "I don't know if I'd go that far. But I always kind of liked her, yeah." He cleared his throat. "I never would have done anything about it, though. I wouldn't have disrespected Travis like that." Not a word about Eliza, no thought that maybe she wouldn't have been interested in return.

"Was there anyone else who liked her that way?"

"You mean besides Travis?"

I nodded and Eric blew out a long breath. "Not that I know of. But why are you bringing this up now, Greer? What does it matter? It was all such a long time ago."

He wasn't wrong; it had been a long time ago. But being back in Ludlow made the past feel immediate instead of distant, my own face in the mirror every morning surprising me because it wasn't sixteen anymore. So many conversations about things that had happened years ago making memories bubble up to the surface, where they suddenly felt close enough to reach out and touch. Like if I skidded around a corner downtown, I might catch a glimpse of Eliza disappearing into the diner. Or if I waited patiently in the park, I'd be rewarded with a flash of her hair as she rode past in Travis's truck, windows down and music blaring. If I could pull the past forward, force it into daylight, and hold it in my hands, then maybe I could see how all the pieces fit together. Figure out how the past braided into the present. See my place in it and know, finally, where it had all gone so horribly wrong.

· · · ·

For a town with fewer than two thousand residents, Ludlow had an overabundance of churches, but there was only one cemetery. People might cling to their specific faiths in life, but in death they seemed fine with mingling. The cemetery was located behind the grade school, always kind of an odd choice in my mind, but maybe it gave those who were grieving comfort to hear children playing outside, their sweet, innocent voices a constant reminder that life goes on. Or maybe the school district bought the cheapest plot of land they could find, put up a half-assed fence to block the view, and called it good.

In the years after Eliza died, my mom came to the cemetery every Saturday morning. She never invited my dad or me along, and neither of us ever asked to accompany her. I'd been to Eliza's grave only twice, the day she was buried and the day before I left for college. I didn't like to think of her there, deep underneath the ground. Sometimes I could trick my mind into believing that she was just on a trip. Or that she lived halfway around the world. But when I stood over her grave, there was no hiding from the truth. She existed only in memory now. And every year, she faded a little more.

But now that I was back in Ludlow, going to Eliza's grave felt like the least I could do for her. I'd considered tagging along with my mom, who still kept her Saturday morning vigil, but in the end, I went alone on a random late Wednesday afternoon. The day was fittingly overcast, the air sharp enough that I tucked my hands into the sleeves of my sweater, hunched my shoulders as I crossed the grass toward her tombstone.

I'd anticipated being alone in the cemetery, or at least alone at Eliza's grave, but Ryan was there when I approached, his head bowed. As I watched, he placed a tiny spray of baby's breath on the ground at his feet. I paused, unsure whether to continue forward or retreat. It had never crossed my mind that Ryan might still come here to pay his respects after all this time.

"Hey," he called when he straightened up and spotted me. He seemed completely unself-conscious to have been found here, posture relaxed, hands stuffed loosely in the pockets of his leather jacket.

"You put flowers on her grave," I said once I was within talking distance. It wasn't a question, and the words came out more accusatory than I'd intended.

He shrugged. "Yeah, Travis's, too. Once a month or thereabouts. Cassie and I take turns." He glanced down at the baby's breath. "The bank account's a little light these days. I couldn't spring for anything fancier."

"Eliza wouldn't have minded. She always liked simple things

best." The prom dress without embellishments, a bouquet of wild-flowers picked from the side of the road, tiny pearl studs instead of dangling rhinestones. My throat closed up unexpectedly, a harsh burning behind my eyes, and I turned my face away.

"We started coming after you left Ludlow," Ryan told me. If he noticed my tear-bright eyes, he was smart enough to pretend otherwise. "We figured we could be your stand-ins. Cassie's been holding down the fort the last few years while I was in Kansas City."

"But I never visited her grave," I reminded him.

"I know, but you might have eventually. And she was our friend, too."

I was ashamed to admit that until right that moment I'd never fully considered the loss Ryan and Cassie had suffered. It was true that they hadn't been close to Eliza the way they were to me, but we'd still grown up together. Ryan and Eliza spending what seemed like hours throwing a frisbee over the backyard fence. Eliza coaching Cassie on how to walk in heels without looking like she was about to topple over. Grief had made me selfish, convinced that because my loss was bigger, it was the only one that mattered.

"You're right," I said. "And thank you for doing this for her."

"Of course." Ryan laid a hand on my shoulder, gave me a gentle squeeze. "I'll leave you to it."

Eliza's tombstone was plain and to the point. A rectangle of granite in the ground. Her name, Eliza Anne Dunning, and her birth and death dates. My dad had wanted something more, an angel chiseled into the stone or maybe a dove, but my mom had put her foot down. She had known her daughter best of all.

I knelt and ran my fingers over the cold stone, picked up the spray of baby's breath and laid it across Eliza's name. I had hoped that out here, surrounded only by the dead, some words would come to me, that I might finally be able to talk to her the way I'd wanted to since the moment I found out she was gone. But when I opened my mouth, nothing came out except a sob. I bent forward, laid my cheek against the cold stone. "Eliza," I whispered. The brisk October breeze was the only thing that whispered back. I closed my eyes, felt the engraved date of her death pressing against my cheek. It was only when I opened my eyes, started to push myself upright, that I felt the prickle on the back of my neck. The fine hairs on my arms standing tall. I paused, took a deep breath, waiting to see if the sensation would fade the way it sometimes did on a dark street in Chicago, my own vivid imagination getting ahead of reality. But the feeling didn't leave; if anything, it strengthened, my shoulders tensing, my whole body poised for fight or flight.

I heaved myself upright, turned fast, one arm already coming up to ward off whatever was behind me. But there was nothing. Only a graveyard, empty except for the darkness starting to stretch out from the trees as the cloudy day gave way to moody twilight. I huffed out a breath and would have felt ridiculous, my arm still raised for battle, if that prickling awareness at the back of my neck had been gone. But it was still there, warning me.

"Ryan?" I called, and immediately wished I hadn't. It made me feel exposed, which was stupid considering I was already standing out in the open. There was no answer, and I crossed my arms, shivering suddenly in the cold. All I had to do was walk across the cemetery and to my car. It should have been easy, a few hundred yards through the grass. But the trees at the edge of the graveyard loomed, trunks dark and menacing, wide enough to hide almost anything. "You're being ridiculous," I muttered under my breath. And still my feet refused to move.

"If I didn't know better, I'd say it almost smells like snow." The voice came from behind me, and I recognized it too late to stop the jagged squawk that burst out of me before I could haul it back.

"Oh, Jesus Christ," I said, bending over to put my hands on my knees. "You scared the shit out of me."

Dean reached out, laid his hand on my back. My skin felt both icy and too hot, delayed adrenaline spiking through my blood. "Sorry," he said. "I thought you heard me."

I straightened up, pushed my hair off my face. "Have you seen anyone else out here?" The watched feeling was gone as quickly as it had appeared, my shoulders relaxing, my prickly skin returned to normal.

"Nope. But I came from that way." He pointed to the far end of the cemetery. "You're the only person I've run into. Usually I don't see anyone at all." He paused. "Which is why I come in the middle of the week." He glanced down at Eliza's tombstone and then jerked his gaze away like the sight had burned his eyes.

"Is . . ." I stopped, cleared my throat. "Is Roy buried here?" It seemed obscene, to have him in the same patch of ground as my sister.

Dean winced. "Yeah, in a manner of speaking. It's not marked. We had him in Neosho, but people kept vandalizing the grave site. Spray-painting the tombstone. Taking shits on the ground in front of it. My grandma knows the caretaker here. He agreed to allow us to move Roy's remains, but no gravestone. Since he was cremated, it made for a pretty easy transfer, all things considered."

"Can I see?" I asked, half expecting him to refuse me. But he turned and led me toward the back corner of the cemetery. A flock of crows surged out of a prematurely bare tree as we passed, momentarily blanketing the sky with black. "Wow," I said, "my kids would love that."

Dean shot me a questioning look over his shoulder.

"My kids back in Chicago," I explained. "They study Edgar Allan Poe this time of year."

"You must miss them," he said.

I hadn't been aware of missing them, but at Dean's words I felt a sharp pull in my breastbone, a sudden urge to listen to Piper

Rand talk about how much she hated algebra, or to sit on the bench outside in the courtyard and play gin rummy with Sam Logan while we worked through his anger issues. The sensation wasn't pleasant; it didn't fill me with a warm glow. It triggered only an uncomfortable confusion I didn't want to examine too closely.

"There's nothing back here," I said, ignoring Dean's comment. We'd almost reached the rusting chain-link fence that separated the far end of the cemetery from the railroad tracks that ran through town.

Dean pointed toward a leaning equipment shed, shielded from the rest of the cemetery by a meager stand of trees. "Right about here somewhere," he said, gesturing to a sliver of ground between the back of the shed and the fence. Not a single blade of grass grew here, a plastic grocery sack and a crumpled fast-food cup stuck in the fence at our feet. A horrible resting spot. Maybe it was poetic justice. But it made me sad to think of Dean and his grandma having to come here, smell gasoline from the mowers stored in the shed as they crammed into this narrow space to stare at nothing but a patch of dirt.

"Tell me something about him," I said, surprising myself. "Something good."

Again Dean acquiesced when I had expected refusal, though his expression was strained, his jaw clenched. Perhaps he thought he owed it to me, that he had no right to protect himself, his memories, his grief. All of it fair game in the wake of his brother's sins. When I'd asked the question, I'd told myself I was offering him a kindness, a chance to speak about his brother to someone willing to listen. But maybe this is what I'd been after all along— watching Dean crack his heart open in order to ease something within my own.

"He was loyal," Dean said, his gaze on the ground. "Stupidly, self-destructively loyal. He would never rat anyone out, even when he should have." He raised his eyes to mine. "Kids in the neighborhood figured it out pretty quick. They'd get up to no good, egging houses or stealing hubcaps, and Roy would take the fall. He was no angel, don't get me wrong. He was usually right in the thick of all their bullshit. But he was always the one who took the blame. He thought it was friendship, but they were using him. He just wasn't smart enough to see it." Dean tipped his head up, hiding his eyes from me. "Or maybe he knew the whole time and it was worth it to him, to feel like he had friends." He sighed. "Jesus, even when I'm trying to say something nice about him, it comes out shitty."

"He could be sweet sometimes, too, couldn't he? Like with the kittens under the porch?"

Dean's head snapped down. "How do you know about the kittens?"

"From the trial." I pushed a stray strand of hair off of my forehead, tucked it behind my ear, squinting against the breeze. My heart slammed, once, hard against my ribs. "When your grandma was on the stand during sentencing. Remember?" Dean's grandma had told a story about Roy rescuing a litter of kittens, their eyes still closed, no mama in sight. Anyone else would have let them be, she said, too much work and bother to try to keep them alive. But twelve-year-old Roy had brought them into the house, bottle-fed them every two hours for a week. Put hot-water bottles underneath them and stroked their tiny heads.

"Oh, yeah," Dean said, "I remember now. She cried telling that story. It about killed me when she cried." He kicked at the dirt. "Roy was nice to kittens and he was loyal, you could say that for the guy. What a memorial."

"Do you think that's why he never talked to you about the murders? He was keeping someone else's secrets?"

"It's possible," Dean said. "Maybe even probable." He looked at me, his face drawn, forced to a place he obviously didn't want to go. I don't think I could have been as gracious if the tables were turned. "You know, right before he was executed, when I got my ten minutes with him to say goodbye, I thought maybe he would crack. I figured if there was something he wanted to get off his chest, someone else he wanted to implicate, it was now or never. And for a split second there, right before they took him away . . ."

"What?" I asked.

"It was probably nothing. Just a look in his eyes. Like maybe he was finally going to tell me the truth. Or at least give me *something*. But then he turned away without saying a word. Let them lead him out of the room. You know, I had steeled myself beforehand for that moment. I thought he might fight them, resist. I'd prepared myself for watching him be dragged away kicking and screaming. But he went willingly. It was almost like . . ." Dean shrugged. "I don't know, he was glad they showed up so he could stop looking at me."

"And he didn't give you any clue at all about what he might have been going to say?"

Dean shook his head. "Whatever it was, in the end, he took it with him."

• • • •

Addy Johnson's family lived in a ramshackle farmhouse on the edge of town. I'd been putting off visiting because it felt barely decent, intruding on her parents' grief so soon after her death. But just the thought of a third pair of bodies made it hard for me to breathe, a jagged knife slicing through my lungs. Even if Addy's parents slammed the door in my face, I had to try.

I steeled my spine and stepped out of my car, taking in the pair of old beater trucks in the drive and the flock of chickens squawking up a storm in the side yard. Red and blue ribbons hung limply from the low branch of an oak tree next to the house, their ends tattered and unraveling. Before I'd taken a single step, a tall, skinny man holding a rake came charging from the shed I'd parked beside. He was dressed in coveralls, a battered John Deere baseball cap on his head. His grizzled cheeks were in need of a good shave, and he looked perfectly capable of taking my head off with that rake if he wanted.

"No reporters!" he yelled. "Get back in your car and get the hell outta here. Don't make me use this."

"I'm not a reporter," I said, backing up against my car, hands raised where he could see I held neither phone nor notepad. "I'm a local, that's all. Came to pay my respects."

The man stopped yelling, but he didn't lower the rake. "What's your name?"

"Greer. Greer Dunning."

The rake came down and his face crumpled. He looked a decade older than he had a moment ago. Bluster giving way to grief. "You're the sister."

"Yes," I said. "That's me."

The man nodded, took a second to collect himself before he continued. "I appreciate you coming by, but I don't got much to say right now. Not even to the well-meaning." He hooked his thumb back toward the house. "My wife's inside. You'll have better luck with her." He disappeared back the way he'd come, the rake dragging on the ground behind him leaving long furrows in the dirt.

I climbed the rickety front-porch steps, avoiding weak spots in the wood. The house needed some TLC and a fresh coat of paint, but someone was trying: baskets of mums on either side of the front door and a pretty plaid blanket draped over the rocking chair on the porch. The front door was open, and I knocked on the frame. I was opening my mouth to holler a greeting when a woman appeared in the foyer, wiping her hands on the apron tied around her waist. She was tall and thin, like her husband, with graying brown hair pulled back in a messy bun. Under her apron she wore jeans and a sensible button-down top, the sleeves rolled up on her ropy forearms. She looked about the same as the last time I remembered seeing her in the store, not long after Eliza died, like she'd worked hard every day of her life.

"Hello there," she said, pushing open the screen and motioning me inside. "What can I do for you?"

It was a wonder there weren't more murders in Ludlow, the way everyone left their doors wide open, invited strangers inside without a second thought. It had been that way when I was growing up, and although the world might have changed—gotten more cynical and wary—apparently Ludlow had not, even after the recent murders. To an outsider, this might have seemed like pure foolishness. But I recognized the touch of defiance in the gesture—Ludlow's backbone of steel sending a message, futile as it might be. *Your evil isn't going to force us to change our ways.*

"Hi, Mrs. Johnson," I said. "I'm Greer Dunning. My sister, Eliza—"

Addy's mom flapped her hand at me. "Oh, honey," she said. "I know who you are. Come in, come in. I'm finishing up some pies in the kitchen. And call me Lorraine." She turned and walked away and I followed, marveling at her equilibrium. Her daughter had been gone for less than a month. My sister had been dead for fourteen years, and my own mother was still marooned on some no-man's-land of grief. I wondered how shitty of a person it made me to wish, even for a second, that Lorraine was my mother instead.

The Johnsons' kitchen was big and airy, but probably hadn't been updated in the last forty years, other than a stainless steel refrigerator that looked out of place among the worn wood floors and original farmhouse sink. People paid big bucks nowadays for replicas of that type of sink, although the new ones came without chips in the porcelain or greenish rust around the faucet. Still, the room was homey, filled with the scent of apples and cinnamon. Again, that pang of longing.

I'd been going back and forth about what to say to Lorraine, how to launch into the topic of her dead daughter, but she beat me to it. "Addy was my youngest," she told me, picking up a knife from the cutting board that rested on what looked to be a home-made kitchen island. She used the knife to point me toward one of the stools tucked underneath, then went back to dicing apples as she spoke. "Youngest of six. It's awful quiet around here now. Some days the only sound I hear is the wind." As if to prove her point, the wind howled in off the field behind the house, wrapping around the eaves and rattling the windows. "Addy's daddy is having a hard time of it. Most days he's out in the fields before the sun rises and not back home until long after I'm asleep."

"I'm sorry," I said.

"Nothing to be sorry about. Not for him or you, neither. Everybody grieves their own way. He's got his, and I've got mine." She set down the knife and picked up handfuls of apple chunks, depositing them into a huge bowl on the island. "Personally, I'm a big fan of a bath. I get through my day, do what has to be done, and then at night I draw a hot bath. Sit in there as long as I need to, just wailing and carrying on. Some nights I worry I may never stop, turn into a human prune before I manage to wring out all my tears." She gave me a grim smile. "But I figure eventually there's gonna be a day I don't need that bath. And maybe sometime after that, a whole week will go by before I have to go up and turn on the tap. Then, later on, maybe a month. But until then, I don't worry about it. Right now, the thought of that bath is what gets me through the day."

The same way the cleaning got my mom through hers. Except she was still stuck in that proverbial bath from sunup to sundown, every damn day of her life. Maybe I should try to drag her out, but it had been so long now, I wasn't even sure how to start pulling.

"You're probably wondering why I'm here," I said, watching Lorraine dust the apples with cinnamon and brown sugar, squeeze lemon juice over the top.

"Figured you'd get around to it in your own time," she said.

"Have the police said anything to you about suspects? Do they know anything at all about who killed Addy and Dylan?"

"No suspects that I know of. Sheriff Baker doesn't tell us a whole lot more than what I read in the paper. Not criticizing the man; I know he's got to keep his cards close to his vest. But just about everybody thinks it was someone passing through. Some crazy who read about your sister and her boyfriend and decided to do the same thing all over again. Nowadays anybody can find out that stuff on the internet."

Except some random crazy would have had to look pretty hard to figure out what type of gun to use, to get all the details exactly right. "Was Addy worried about anything lately? Had she mentioned anyone following her or making her nervous?"

Lorraine shook her head, began scooping the apple mixture into homemade pie crusts already in their tins. "No, she seemed like the same old Addy to me." She paused for a moment, pinched the bridge of her nose. When she looked at me, I could see how hard she was fighting to keep the tears at bay. "Going to school. She was always a good student, no worries there. Theater practice. They were putting on *Our Town* next month. Out with Dylan or her friends on the weekends. I think she and Dylan didn't have much longer as an item. But whoever ended up pulling the plug, I don't think either one of them was gonna be too upset over it."

"Not true love?"

"Not to my eyes. More about having a steady date on a Saturday night." She laid a piece of round dough over the top of her pie, began pinching the edges together with practiced fingers.

"Does Dylan's family live around here? I was hoping to talk to them, too."

"They moved away, back to Wichita or someplace. Took his body with them and disappeared."

"That was quick," I said, watching the way Lorraine's mouth tightened, her fingers digging a little deeper into the raw dough. "What did you think of Dylan?"

"He was fine."

I waited, figured she had more to add. No mother had so little to say about her daughter's boyfriend.

"Dylan was always polite. He seemed to treat Addy right. But he wasn't from here. He never quite fit in. Always got the feeling he was looking down his nose at us a little." She huffed out a breath. "Looking down on Ludlow."

What had Ryan told me when I'd first come home? That Dylan hadn't been thrilled about moving to Ludlow. Couldn't say I blamed him. It would be a hard place to be the new kid, especially as a teenager. Ludlow stood by its own, but it took a long time to be considered a local. Buying a house and moving in wasn't enough. A few years living here wouldn't even begin to qualify. Our roots were deep and they weren't the kind that allowed for easy transplant.

Lorraine opened the oven and slid out two perfectly baked pies, the tops golden brown and so flaky I could practically taste the butter from across the room. She deposited them on the counter and then slid her unbaked pies into the waiting oven.

"That's a lot of pie."

"We're having all our kids over tomorrow for dinner. Have a few grandbabies now, too. Two of my girls are coming in from Topeka. It'll be a full house. My oldest, Bryce, loves pie. I figured he could take a whole one home with him when he goes. That boy would live on sweets if he could." She gave a fond shake of her head, began wiping down the island and stacking her dirty baking essentials in a pile.

"How do you do it?" I asked, my voice soft. "How do you go on and make it look easy?" I told myself I was asking for my mother, but really the answer was for me.

"Oh, honey. Not a single second of this is easy. But it's what we signed up for, isn't it? Life is *hard*. There's gonna be bumps and bruises and hurts big enough you wonder if you can stand to feel them. But what choice do we have? It's part of the package." She looked at me, set down her dish towel, and came around the island. She grabbed my hands in both of hers and gave a squeeze, reminding me so much of the mother I used to have that I almost burst into tears.

"Here's what I do," she said. "Every day I look around and tell myself to find three things, just three, to be thankful for. They can't be anything too far off—no being thankful for Christmas in June. They've gotta be something near, something you can practically touch. But it doesn't matter how small they are or how stupid they might sound to someone else. Even on my worst days, I can always find three." She must have sensed my skepticism because she gave our clasped hands a gentle shake. "Like this." She looked around her kitchen, closed her eyes, took a deep breath. "The sun is shining. I can smell my pies baking. My family will fill this house tomorrow."

"But what if it's not enough?" I asked, embarrassed when a few of my tears spilled over.

Lorraine opened her eyes, let go of my hands, and wiped my tears away with cinnamon-scented fingers. "It has to be, Greer," she said. "Because it's all any of us have got."

Addy

ylan was a good kisser. He never used too much tongue and he kept most of his spit to himself. Unlike fucking Todd Rowe, who'd practically drowned her every time they'd made out. Most of the time she wished they could stick with the kissing part, maybe a hand on her boobs or whatever. But Dylan, like most guys, wasn't content with that, and since they'd been dating for almost a year and she wasn't a virgin, she didn't really have a good excuse to say no. Oh, she knew she *could* say no, but it wasn't worth the grief she'd get after. "Cocktease"—that was a favorite for the guys at school to throw around. But they liked "blue baller," too. And just plain "bitch." She didn't know if Dylan was the type to say that crap, or write it in comments on her Instagram posts, but, let's face it, he probably was.

"Hey," he said, shifting her upward on his lap, his hand snaking between her legs. "Open the window a little, getting hot in here."

Addy waited for Dylan to turn the car on, then pressed the button for the window. Cool autumn air blew in, pebbling her nipples. Dylan made a guttural sound, lowered his head, and pulled down the cups of her bra.

Okay, this part she didn't mind, her back arching against the steering wheel, Dylan's fingers slipping inside her. She felt something building, everything below her waist slowly tightening. But within seconds she knew already that she was chasing it too hard, could feel the tension turning into disappointment almost as soon as it started. Maybe if he could ever actually get her there, she wouldn't mind the sex part as much. But as it was, she usually had to go home and take care of business herself.

"That's it, baby," Dylan said, oblivious. "That's it."

Addy looked at him, debating whether to fake it and get it over with or let him keep trying, when his head rocketed sideways at the same time her ears rang from a sudden burst of noise. She stared, watched Dylan's brains seep down the side of his face, the top of his skull shorn away.

"What?" Her voice was strangely calm because this could not actually be happening. Dylan was playing some kind of Halloween prank. This was not real. She saw movement out of the open window and turned her head. A dark shadow, a bright flash, and then she was slumping sideways. A hum filled her head, her vision going white and then black. A hand on her arm, pulling. Something on her skin. Tracing. Touching. She smelled blood and metal. She heard footsteps walking away. Then nothing. And nothing. And nothing.

Chapter Thirteen

Joanne Sawtell wasn't a hoarder, but she was probably only a few wrong turns from becoming one. When I was growing up, her house was always filled to the brim with knickknacks and "finds" from whatever garage sale was going on around town. Before he'd left, Ryan's dad had kept her hoarder tendencies in line. She'd go out grocery shopping and come home to find he'd dragged a trash bag full of what she deemed "treasures" and he deemed "crap" to the town dump. Nowadays it was up to Ryan to curb her enthusiasms, although I suspected he used a softer touch than his douchebag dad. I knew they drove Ryan crazy, but I'd always secretly liked Joanne's collections: the pale pink hobnail tumblers, an ancient set of Nancy Drews, the tiny ballerina figurines that took up all the surface area on her sideboard. Her house was like a scavenger hunt where you never knew what you might stumble across.

Like when I was a kid, I barely bothered knocking when I showed up on her back porch, already pulling the screen door open and yelling a greeting into her empty kitchen. She was the one person I hadn't run into since I'd been back and I wanted to make sure I said hello, especially because I still wasn't sure how much longer I'd be home. When she bustled in from the living room, she threw her hands up in the air, a huge smile flashing across her face. "Greer," she said. "Come here and give me a hug!"

She smelled the same as ever, a little musty, a little like cheap drugstore perfume. A homey scent, comforting and familiar. She looked about the same, too. Long gray hair, now streaked with some white, curled up in a thick bun on top of her head. Clothes that were always a little too bohemian for Ludlow, flowy skirts and tunic tops. Clogs in all seasons. A string of bright purple beads around her neck holding her multicolored reading glasses.

Pulling back, Joanne winked at me, her hands still gripping my upper arms. "Look at you! Where has the time gone? I swear, sometimes I glance at Ryan and think, 'Shouldn't you still be ten?'" She laughed, the sound, as always, reminding me of bells, light and musical. She ushered me into her living room, telling me over her shoulder that she was clearing out some things. She sounded proud of herself, but I could hear Ryan's voice in my mind: *She's only clearing out so she'll have room to add.* But because she wasn't my mother, I was apt to give Joanne more slack. I found her endearing rather than aggravating. I wondered if Ryan felt the same way about my parents, if he harbored the same kind of forgiving tenderness toward them that I felt for his mother.

"Where's Ryan?" I asked. "Still sleeping?" Generally, this would be my cue to run up the stairs and wake him, make fun of his bedhead and drool-encrusted pillow.

"No, actually. He had to go to work this morning. Supposed to be his day off, but Chet got a hair up his ass about something." Joanne raised her eyebrows. "You know how Chet can be."

"Poor Ryan," I said. "I don't know how he stands it. I love Chet, but he can be a lot."

"I think it's been good for Ryan, actually. Maybe not the Chet part, but being back here, spending time with you and Cassie. He was pretty raw after the split."

"I can imagine." I watched as she stacked a few books and a

couple of empty picture frames and put them in a box already labeled "Donate."

"And everyone being back has been good for Cassie, too," Joanne continued. "After you and Ryan left, I think she got lonely. She'd stop by and bring me dinner from the diner sometimes, sit with me and reminisce. But I was a poor substitute for the two of you."

I'd never really thought about Cassie being in Ludlow without us, never considered that it might have been hard for her. Mainly because she always seemed fine when we touched base, busy with work, spending time with her parents and nieces and nephews, making a life for herself. She'd never expressed any resentment at us leaving her behind, and I knew, even if given the chance, she wouldn't have followed. But that didn't mean it hadn't stung to have us so far away. At least Ryan had come back to visit regularly, which was a lot more than I could claim.

Joanne paused in her sorting, picked up a frame that still had a photo in it. One of Ryan and Bethany on their wedding day. "I had such high hopes for them," she said. "Even though I knew it wasn't going to end well." She held up the photo where I could see it. Ryan looked stiff and uncomfortable in his rented tuxedo, a fake smile plastered on his face. He'd always hated having his picture taken. Bethany looked lovely, as always. That was never a problem. It was when she opened her mouth that things usually got dicey.

"How did you know it wasn't going to work out?" I asked. The divorce still felt like such a touchy subject with Ryan. Neither Cassie nor I had been able to bring ourselves to ask the questions we were dying to have answers to.

"It was the first time he brought her here to visit. I overheard them talking after they thought I'd gone to bed. She called Ludlow a dump."

"I prefer 'shithole,' but tomato tomahto," I said with a shrug, putting the framed photo into the box. Nobody in this house needed a reminder of Bethany staring at them every day.

Joanne laughed, shaking her head. "You kids can make fun of Ludlow all you like. But it's still where you're from. Where you grew up. Ryan will run Ludlow into the ground all day, but he can't stand it when other people haven't got anything good to say about the place he was raised. Bethany's attitude about Ludlow was the tip of the iceberg. I'm surprised they made it as long as they did." She gave me a sharp look. "But you didn't hear that from me."

"Of course not," I said. I'd always been good at keeping confidences, even from my closest friends.

"And Bethany didn't need him," Joanne continued. "Didn't even bother pretending like she did. You know me, I'm all for women's lib, but Ryan likes to feel needed. Probably because he grew up taking care of me, being the man of the house. That's the last thing his worthless dad said to him, you know, on his way out the door." She lowered her voice to a gruff growl. "'You're the man around here now.'" She shook her head as her tone returned to normal. "Seven years old and the bastard lays that on him. I tried to tell Ryan I didn't need him to take care of me, that I was the adult and he was the kid. But he took those words to heart. And then he married a woman who didn't really need him for anything. They were a mismatch from the start."

"I bet she loved hearing I was back here," I said. "She always did hate Cassie and me."

Joanne's brow furrowed. "I don't think that's true. The three of you together are a hard nut to crack, is all. For someone on the outside."

For the first time I wondered what it might have been like to step into our thick-as-thieves threesome. Even with my years-long absence and Ryan's move to Kansas City, we were still tightly knit. I'd always liked to think that it was Bethany herself who was the problem, her personality the reason she never clicked with us. The first time Cassie and I met her, Bethany's face tightened up every time Cassie made a sex reference or I called Ryan a name. Rather than making her feel included, which I liked to believe had been our goal, our informality offended her. Created a barrier none of us had ever managed to breach. But maybe it was an impossible ask, for another person who hadn't grown up with us, who didn't know all our inside jokes and tangled histories, to somehow seamlessly join our group and belong. It was possible, too, that none of us had really wanted her to fit in. Not even Ryan.

It took us most of the afternoon to fill a single box with items Joanne deemed worthy of donating—old books, a few picture frames, a couple of moth-eaten sweaters. I volunteered to drop it off for her, mainly because I had a feeling she'd end up keeping it forever if I didn't take it away. As I carried the box to my car, the wind blew, a sudden sharp gust, and a clatter of browning leaves fell to the sidewalk. True autumn was fast approaching. I wondered if I'd still be in Ludlow come winter. I wondered if I wanted to be.

· · · ·

When I came around the corner on Main and saw Chet on the sidewalk talking to Merl Stafford, I didn't exactly skid to a stop, but I came pretty damn close. They hadn't noticed me yet, Merl making wide sweeping gestures with his hands and Chet nodding along sympathetically. I was debating walking backward, retracing my steps to get out of saying hello, when Merl looked over and pinned me with his dead-eyed stare. Chet followed his gaze and waved when he saw me. "Greer," he called. "Good morning, darlin'."

Merl said nothing, even as I waved and moved closer. I knew he remembered me; Merl wasn't the kind of guy to forget a face. You could tell he catalogued everyone he met, kept them filed away for possible later use. I wondered if he was going to out me, tell Chet

I'd been nosing around his place with Dean Mathews. But Merl proved to be as silent, and charming, as ever. Spitting a wad of something disgusting onto the sidewalk and walking away before I reached him.

"I'd ask if you pissed in his cornflakes," Chet said, eyes roaming from Merl's retreating back to my face, "but that's Merl. If he ever gave somebody a pleasant greeting, the whole town'd die of shock."

"How do you know him?" I asked.

Chet scratched at his stubble-marked chin. "Can't honestly say. It's like with most old-timers around here. I've known 'em so long I can't even put my finger close to where or when we first met. Merl's just always been a fixture." Chet shrugged. "He's an ornery old coot, but that's all right by me."

"I don't really remember Merl being around when I was growing up." I had memories of Stafford's, or at least of hearing about it, but Merl's wasn't a face I'd known before Dean introduced us. It was only right now that I realized how strange that was, in a town Ludlow's size.

"Well, Merl keeps himself to himself, most of the time," Chet said, his gaze shifting away from mine. And that wasn't like Chet, to try to change a subject. Generally, he settled right in and stayed a while. His evasiveness made me want to lean in, stick my nose where he obviously thought it didn't belong.

"Why's that?" I asked.

"Oh, he had some trouble with the law. It was a long time ago. No use rehashing."

"What kind of trouble?"

Chet shook his head. "You know I don't like telling tales out of school."

I managed to hold in my laugh, but barely. "I won't say a word," I said, crossing my fingers over my heart for good measure.

That was all Chet needed to get rolling. "He fiddled around

with some underage girls a time or two. Probably twenty years ago, at least."

My head jerked back, my mouth twisting. "Like rape?"

"No, no, no," Chet said. "Or at least not that I ever heard. More like lurking around. Making them uncomfortable. Maybe copping a feel here and there."

As if that was any better. Jesus Christ. "He never went to jail?"

"Nobody wanted to take it that far. The girls and their families just wanted it to stop. So Baker told him to keep his hands to himself. Knock that shit off or Baker'd knock it off for him. Far as I know, that was the end of it."

I'd felt scared when Merl's gaze had landed on me too hard, but now I felt squeamish, too. A little sick. Had he ever looked at Eliza or Addy that way? And what would it mean if he had? "Could he have been involved in the latest murders?" I asked.

"Nah," Chet said. "Merl ain't a killer. But that's part of the reason he was in such a foul mood today. Cops've been out talking to him about Dylan and Addy. He says he's kept his part of the bargain, so he doesn't appreciate Baker getting up in his business. But, like I told him, they have to ask the questions. Just doing their jobs."

The bell on the diner door jangled and Ryan came out, a couple of to-go cups in his hands. "Hey," he said when he spotted me. "I would have grabbed you a coffee if I'd known you were out here."

"That's okay," I said, leaning in to give him a quick kiss on the cheek, pushing my worries about Merl aside for the moment. "I saw your mom yesterday. I thought since you were working then, you might get today off."

"I thought so, too. But my boss here is a taskmaster extraordinaire." Ryan handed one of the cups to Chet.

"Come on now," Chet said. "You told me you didn't mind. We're already behind from . . ."

"From what?" I asked, giving Ryan a quizzical look when Chet let his comment hang in the air.

"From Dylan," Chet finished. "Dylan Short. That third pair of hands came in handy." A belated "God rest his soul" after Chet took a sip of coffee.

"Dylan was helping with your house?"

"Sure was," Chet said. He handed his cup back to Ryan. "Hold this a second. I'm gonna run into the grocery and get a few things while we're here. Won't be but a minute."

Ryan let out a long-suffering sigh, but took the cup without saying anything. At least while Chet was within earshot. The second he disappeared through the grocery doors, Ryan turned to me. "Like it's not bad enough he came around pounding on my door this morning, after having me work yesterday. And now we're wasting time running errands? Fucking Chet." But he sounded more amused than annoyed, a little grin on his face instead of a scowl.

"You told me you didn't know Dylan," I said.

"Huh?"

"That night in your gazebo, when I first got back to town. You said you didn't really know him."

"That's because I didn't." He stared at me, waited a beat. "Are you . . . are you accusing me of something?"

I wanted to deny it, but I *was* making an accusation, wasn't I? That he'd lied to me. That he was hiding something. "But Chet just said he was working on the house with you guys."

Ryan shook his head, like he was trying to shake away this conversation. Or maybe the fact that I would question him this way. "He said Dylan was helping with the house. And he was. But mainly on the weekends, when I wasn't around. Occasionally after school, but he did stuff like painting once I was done with the more difficult work. We were rarely on the same part of the project. I don't think we ever had a conversation beyond 'Hey, how you doing?' I told you as much as I knew about him that night in the gazebo, Greer. I wasn't trying to hide anything."

"Okay," I said, no longer able to meet his eyes.

"I know you're going through something," Ryan said. "But for future reference, if you want an answer, just ask me."

"I *did* ask you."

He raised his eyebrows at me. "You know exactly what I'm talking about, Greer." He looked uncharacteristically serious, seemed torn between sadness and anger. It was on the tip of my tongue to apologize, but my mouth stayed stubbornly closed.

• • • •

The morning of the Fall Festival dawned as one of those picture-perfect Midwestern autumn days. The sun clear and bright in a cut-glass blue sky. But there was an ever-so-slight edge to the air, nipping lightly at my nose and the tips of my ears. I could smell the faint scent of woodsmoke floating in from somewhere in the distance. Every time I'd sipped a pumpkin spice latte in Chicago, this is what I'd been longing for.

I'd agreed to meet Cassie and Ryan in front of the caramel apple stand, and when I found them, Cassie was already halfway through an apple, a string of caramel stuck to her chin. "Here," she said, thrusting an apple at me. "I got you one."

"Don't bother arguing with her," Ryan said. "You know how crazy she gets at this thing."

I couldn't fault Cassie for her enthusiasm. The Fall Festival was my favorite Ludlow tradition, too. The Fourth of July always made me anxious when inevitably half the town drank too much and someone ended up lighting a firecracker in their hand and blowing off a finger. And the Easter parade was a surprisingly stuffy affair, everyone decked out in scratchy dresses with lace collars or last year's suit too tight in the crotch and shoulders. We'd stand around sweating in unseasonable heat or freezing in an unexpected snow-storm. But the Fall Festival was always joyful—donut holes and face-painting, a hay bale maze set up in the park and a makeshift pumpkin patch at the end of Main. It felt like the moment when all of Ludlow came together to simply have a good time. The last one I'd attended had been the week before Eliza died. For once, it had been just Eliza and me. Travis had a family wedding to attend, and everyone else had plans. We'd gotten our faces painted and stumbled, laughing, through the maze while the sun went down. It had been a brief, magical glimpse into the sisterhood I'd always assumed we'd have one day. But instead of being the start of something for Eliza and me, it turned out to be only a prelude to the end.

I followed dutifully behind Ryan and Cassie as we traipsed along Main Street, the three of us trying our hand at the ring toss, sharing a powdered-sugar-encrusted funnel cake, and getting temporary tattoos applied to our cheeks. I kept waiting for the right moment to bring up Dean, now that we were all together. It was only a matter of time before word got out, and I wanted them to hear it from me first. Part of me wondered if they already knew. But they seemed oblivious. Or maybe they didn't want to ruin the day. Either way, in the absence of confrontation, I was left with an odd, barbed tension that made everything, even simple conversation, feel harder than it should have.

"Wanna do the dunk tank?" Cassie asked, peeling off a strip of Ryan's cotton candy and stuffing it in her mouth.

"No way," Ryan said, swatting her away. "But I'll happily watch you get soaked."

"I'll meet you guys over there," I told them. "I'm going to hit the bathroom."

"Porta-potties are thataway," Cassie said, making a vague gesture with her hand.

I headed in the direction she'd instructed, although I didn't really need to use the bathroom. What I was looking for was a few minutes of quiet, not a toilet. I spied a picnic table in the shade of an oak tree, only one spot on the bench occupied. As I got closer, I realized it was Sheriff Baker camped out there. He was in civilian clothes and clutching a huge teddy bear.

"Looks like you made a new friend," I told him.

"Grandkids," he said with a shake of his head. He scooted down the bench. "Here, make yourself comfortable. You enjoying the day?"

"Yeah, I guess so," I said. "It seems smaller than I remembered."

"Well, you're a big-city girl now. I'm guessing everything in Ludlow feels small."

"Maybe that's it." Or maybe I would never again be able to see my hometown the way I had before Eliza died, back when it had been safe and magical and my life made sense.

"It's good to see you out here," Baker said. "Saw you three earlier getting your face tattoos." He pointed at my cheek. "Always thought butterflies were Eliza's favorite, though. Seem to recall you preferring bees."

My hand fluttered upward, cupping my cheek. "Oh, yeah, well. Guess I was in a butterfly mood today."

"Anyway," Baker said, "I'm glad you're spending time with your friends."

"As opposed to what? Lurking in bushes and spying on people?"

"Hey now, I didn't say that."

I raised my eyebrows. "But it's what you meant."

Baker sighed. "It's like I told you the other day at the station. Nothing good can come of going backward, is all. It's time to move on."

"Easier said than done."

"Well, I can't argue with that," he said. "Most things are. But doesn't mean it's not worth trying." He stifled a yawn behind his closed fist. "Sorry about that. Not sleeping like I should."

"Work?" I asked. If the past was anything to go by, he was burning the midnight oil over the latest murders.

"Yup."

"Are you looking at Merl Stafford?"

Baker stared at me. "Why would we be looking at Merl?"

I sighed, wishing we could skip the part where he pretended not to know anything just so he wouldn't accidentally give something away. "Because he has a thing for teenage girls. Maybe stalking and molesting them wasn't enough for him anymore."

"We're looking at every lead, Greer," Baker said finally. "Every single one."

"Does that mean you don't think Merl was involved? Or that you do?"

He gave me a warning look. "You know I'm not going to talk about this with you."

"Was there anything different this time around? With Dylan and Addy? Anything that stood out?"

"I'm free next Saturday," he said. "Can take you out to Murdock's pond. We can work on your fishing skills."

That surprised a laugh out of me. "Hey, it was worth a try."

"Maybe. But only on a fish a lot dumber than me."

I ignored that. "Do you think it was someone local?"

Baker huffed. "You are relentless. And I don't think much of anything yet. I will say, it's a lot easier to solve a double murder when the killer's brother marches right into the police station and turns him in. Unfortunately, that hasn't happened this time."

It took a few seconds for what he'd said to sort itself out inside my head. "Wait . . . what? Dean Mathews turned Roy in?"

Baker looked at me, surprise running across his face. "How can you not know that? It was in the paper. And they talked about it at the trial."

"I don't . . ." I shook my head. "I don't have a lot of clear memories from back then." Certain things I could recall with the kind of crisp, clean clarity of a photograph: Baker knocking on the front door and the sound of my mother's scream; the stiff black dress I wore to the funerals; Roy Mathews's face in the morning paper; the blood red heart on our hallway floor. But I couldn't remember my own reaction to the news of Eliza's death, couldn't recall a single word of the article that had accompanied Roy's photograph in the paper; could conjure up only small flashes of the trial—the back of Dean's head, his grandma crying on the witness stand, Roy shuffling out after the guilty verdict. I didn't recall ever hearing that Dean had been the one to hand Roy over to the police. I wondered how much that had cost him.

I watched a father across from us hoist his daughter up onto his shoulders, her spindly legs dangling around his neck while she clutched a spool of pink cotton candy. A cheer went up as a teenage boy emerged victorious from the apple-bobbing bucket next to them, water plastering his shirt to his narrow chest. The sun filtered down, warm and bright, turning the whole street to gold. If I'd been back in Ludlow for any other reason, it would have been a glorious day.

"I swear, one of these years somebody is going to drown trying to get those damn apples. They're slippery suckers," Baker said. He slapped his knee with his teddy-bear-free hand. "Guess I'd better go rejoin the fray."

"Wait," I said. "Can I ask you something before you go? It's not about the murders."

He glanced at me. "Okay," he said, but the word came out reluctant, like he was already anticipating the turn this conversation was taking.

"Did my dad have life insurance on Eliza?"

Baker rested one elbow on the back of the bench, angling his body toward mine. "Have to admit, that was not the question I was expecting. Have you asked your dad about this?"

"No." I scoffed. "The other night he thought Eliza was still alive. He's not exactly the most reliable source for information."

Baker paused, seemed to be weighing what he said before he opened his mouth. "He did have life insurance on Eliza."

I wasn't surprised—Chet was a talker, but he wasn't a liar—but my stomach sank all the same. "Just on her? Not on me, too?"

"He'd planned on getting it for both of you. That was the year before Chet retired and he was giving everyone in town the hard sell on life insurance. We'd all regret it if our whole family wasn't covered, blah blah blah. He managed to wear your dad down at some point, and he bought the policy on Eliza. But he couldn't really afford it, so he never followed through on yours. I don't think he ever anticipated using it. He did it more as a favor and probably figured it was the quickest way to get Chet to shut his yapper about it. He bought Eliza's first because she was older." Baker shook his head. "Turned out to be the unluckiest of lucky guesses."

"Why wouldn't he have mentioned it to me?"

"The better question is why would he have? You were sixteen years old, Greer. What business was it of yours? Besides, it wasn't a windfall, for god's sake. It was enough to cover the cost of Eliza's funeral and to keep the store afloat a little longer." He squinted at me, realization swimming into his eyes. "Oh, good lord, don't tell me you're suspicious of your father now."

"I didn't say that," I said, glancing away. I knew my father would've died before he'd ever hurt Eliza. But I'd also thought I'd known him, inside and out. I'd never imagined that Chet and Ryan would be privy to facts about him that were news to me. It made him feel even further away than he had before.

Baker reached over and gave my shoulder a gentle shake. "Greer, sweetheart, come on now. You don't really think your dad had something to do with Eliza's murder, do you? Because that would be . . ."

"What?" I demanded. "Crazy? Nuts? I'm off my rocker? I know that's what you want to say. Just like you wanted to say it after Eliza died."

"Never thought you were crazy," he said, calm, looking at me with those eyes that always made you feel stripped naked, every secret or bad thought you'd ever had right there on display. It reminded me of a conversation I'd overheard years ago between my dad and Chet when I was stocking cans at the store. How my dad said Baker was the perfect sheriff because he knew people's bad deeds before they did. "One glance from Baker," Chet chimed in, "and people start confessing things they haven't even done yet. Running their mouths so fast, they about beat their own gums to death."

Well, that might have been most people, but it sure as hell wasn't going to be me. Not yet and maybe not ever. I was starting to wonder if I'd ever have the strength to shine a light into all the hidden corners of my mind and lay bare what lurked in the shadows. I stood up with a jerk, sending the teddy bear spilling onto the grass.

"Never thought you were crazy, sweetheart," Baker repeated to my back as I walked away. "Thought you were grieving, is all, and having trouble finding your way out."

At his words I was sixteen again, sobbing into my pillow at night and leaning hard on dark humor during the day. Keeping my face a careful blank when I heard someone call Eliza a dirty whore, while inside bile rose fast in my throat. Missing my parents with a fierceness that stole my breath, even as we sat right next to one another. Fourteen years later, and I guess some things never changed.

Dylan

*ound in the back of Dylan's world history notebook after his
death:*

Goals

- Get out of Ludlow

- Throw a no-hitter

- Raise my GPA to a 3.5

- Get out of Ludlow

- Make some money

- Find a way to break up with Addy without hurting
  her feelings

- Win a baseball scholarship

- Stop fighting with my dad about everything

- Get out of this fucking town!

Chapter Fourteen

nstead of having another painful dinner at home, I'd told Cassie I'd meet her at the diner at the end of her late-afternoon shift and we could grab a bite. The day was overcast, like all of them since the Fall Festival, but the air was mild, and I decided to take advantage of the weather and walk uptown instead of driving. I was just turning the corner toward the park when I spotted Garrett pulling his squad car into a parking spot closest to the clumps of trees that were the preferred destination for teenage lovers or kids smoking pot. One of the few places in Ludlow where you could at least make an attempt at privacy. I raised my hand in a reluctant wave, but Garrett didn't see me. He got out of the car, head down, and moved into the trees, walking fast.

Without making a conscious decision to do it, I stepped off the sidewalk and onto the grass, heading across the park in the direction Garrett had disappeared. Furtive wasn't generally Garrett's style, and my curiosity was getting the best of me. What was he doing? I had no business following him, but my feet kept moving forward regardless. Once I was among the trees, ground littered with sticks and seed pods, I stopped and listened for the sound of footsteps over fallen leaves, the murmur of voices, but there was nothing. I continued walking, telling myself I'd turn around in two minutes, when a moan floated toward me on the breeze. I stopped, cocked my head. Maybe it had been a dog. But it came again, low and guttural. Definitely human. Pleasure or pain, it was hard to tell. I stepped cautiously in the direction of the sound, making sure not to tread on anything that would give my presence away. Ahead of me was a huge oak, its trunk riddled with scars from overzealous teenagers anxious to leave evidence of their passing, and I ducked behind it. The moan came again, and I peered around the tree, feeling faintly ridiculous.

It was two people against a tree, and at first all I could register was Garrett's bare ass pumping away and her fingernails digging in, long and ragged and painted with chipped red polish. Then I noticed his duty belt tossed carelessly on the ground. Sheriff Baker would have his badge for that if he knew, never mind the screwing on duty. Garrett turned his face, and I could see his mouth hanging open like an overheated dog's. I would have bet good money the woman pinned to the tree was not his girlfriend, her bleach-blond hair dark at the roots, her limbs skinny and pale. Her face pinged something inside me, but I couldn't place her. She moaned again, her eyes screwed tightly shut. I still, for the life of me, couldn't have said whether the sound was pleasure or pain. Maybe a combination of both, considering her ass was getting slammed into tree bark. And I knew from experience that Garrett was probably going to have a much better time than she was.

As if to prove my point, Garrett shoved into her, making me wince in sympathy. The woman cried out, but Garrett didn't slow his pace. Suddenly what had been a little amusing felt anything but, the sandwich I'd had for lunch sitting leaden in my stomach. I pushed away from the tree, fingers slipping over rough bark where something had been hacked into the trunk. I glanced down, snatched my hand back from where it was resting on a gouged-out heart, a pair of initials carved inside. I stumbled sideways and stepped down hard on a fallen branch, the crack sending a clatter of birds wheeling skyward.

"What the fuck?" I heard Garrett say, but I was already running, darting between trees, breath whistling out of me. I didn't look back, but I heard the thud of footsteps, each one gaining on me. My shoulder blades tensed, my body ready to be yanked backward. I leapt over a divot in the ground, adrenaline shooting through me like lightning, and my foot came down wrong on a rotting mass of slippery leaves. I hit the ground, arms outstretched, the breath whooshing out of me. I rolled over, mouth sucking air, waiting for Garrett's angry face above me. But everything was silent and still, only gray sky bearing down on me between branches. I could have sworn I'd felt Garrett's fingertips brushing the back of my neck, had prepared myself for what he might do when he caught me. I'd felt a lot of things toward Garrett Bloom in my life—lust, annoyance, irritation—but until now fear had never been one of them. But something about his face when the woman moaned, his disregard for anything but his own pleasure, had sent unease rippling along my spine. I don't know why I was surprised that Garrett had a dark side. Didn't most people? Maybe none of us were the same when we thought no one was watching.

• • • •

If the Fall Festival was the family-friendly tradition in Ludlow, the annual bonfire out at Frank LeBeau's farmstead was the semi-adult one. Pretty much everyone between the ages of fifteen and sixty showed up, provided they could get a ride or pawn their kids off on a relative. My parents never attended, even when Eliza was alive, but I'd seen Ryan's mom a time or two, and Cassie's parents were fixtures. I hadn't planned on attending tonight, but Cassie and Ryan hadn't given me a choice, captive as I was in the backseat of Cassie's truck.

"We won't stay long," Cassie said over my protests. "I promise."

"If you're not having fun, I'll run you home," Ryan said. Which was a vow easier made than executed. The bonfire usually drew hundreds of people, from not only Ludlow, but also Neosho, Boone, and every tiny burg in between. Finding Ryan if I lost track of him could take all night.

By the time we arrived, after a quick stop at Sonic for cheeseburgers and shakes, the bonfire was already hopping, cars parked haphazardly along the road and ringing the edge of the field where two giant fires were burning, sending furls of black smoke into the darkening sky. Music blared from speakers set up next to dozens of large coolers stuffed full of beers and hard seltzers, and clusters of people dotted the field, some dancing, some chatting, some playing cornhole by the light of the fires. The same as it had always been, but there was a new edge to the proceedings tonight: the faint feeling that things could go off the rails at any second, the need to blow off steam and have some fun after the recent murders easily crossing the line into chaos.

"I can't even hear myself think," I yelled, taking the drink Cassie passed me.

"I'm pretty sure thinking isn't required," Ryan said. "That's kind of the point."

"Touché," I said, knocking my can against his as I scanned the crowd. Most people looked to be in the early stages of getting sloshed, but a woman about our age, looking none too steady on her feet, performed a sad, solo bump-and-grind, arms aloft, cigarette in one hand and beer in the other. Her bleach-blond hair was tangled and greasy, and her skinny legs were mottled with bruises. Chipped red polish on her fingernails. "Holy shit," I breathed. No wonder she'd looked familiar yesterday in the park. I pointed with my chin. "Is that Amber Stevens?"

"Uh-huh," Cassie said. "She's come down a few pegs."

Amber had been the most popular girl in our high school class. She'd claimed the crown at the end of sixth grade and hung on for the next six years with teeth and nails, equal parts malice and manipulation. The kind of poison package most high school boys are too dumb to resist. "I thought she married Chad right after we graduated? Had her perfect life all worked out."

"She thought she did, too," Cassie said. "Until Chad divorced her, moved away with some new chick, and left Amber with three babies, no job, and a ton of debt. Last I heard, she was courting a pretty serious Oxy habit and her kids were in foster care."

"I'm surprised she's not in jail," Ryan said. "She tried to steal a bunch of shit from the hardware store recently, but was too fucked up to even make it out the door."

Amber and I had never been friendly, but I felt a sharp pang of sympathy when I thought of her pinned to a tree. I had a pretty good idea how she'd gotten away with her attempted hardware heist.

"Remember how pissed she was when Travis picked Eliza over her? 'Oh, my god, like what does he see in her?'" Ryan said, voice high in imitation.

I remembered. And I remembered how after the murders she'd told everyone who would listen how lucky she was that she hadn't been interested in Travis way back when; otherwise she could have been the one dead in his front seat. Revisionist history rendered with a spiteful kind of glee.

We watched as Amber tripped over the couple next to her, landing hard on her ass. She tossed her beer can at the woman, who dodged out of her way. "Stupid cunt!" Amber screamed.

"Jesus," I said. "What a mess."

"I try to feel bad for her," Ryan said. "But she makes it hard."

"Come on," Cassie said. "Let's mingle."

Mingling with this crowd was the last thing I wanted to do, but

I let myself be led into the fray, finger hooked loosely through the back belt loop of Ryan's jeans. I threw vague smiles out when I heard people call my name, but let my gaze skate over most of the faces, getting just a glimpse before we moved past. I saw Eric and Faith in the near distance, his arm slung across her shoulders while she chatted with the woman next to her. When Eric spotted me, I raised my hand in greeting, but he only stared back, his mouth a grim line. I looked away, and my eyes snagged on a newly familiar face. Loosening my grip on Ryan's jeans, I spun back into the crowd.

"Hey, Libby," I said, sidling up to where she stood near the largest bonfire. The smoke burned my eyes and coiled its claws into my chest.

She squinted at me, recognition dawning. "Oh, hey, Dean's girl, right?"

"Close enough."

"He here?" Libby asked, downing the last of her beer and tossing the can to the ground.

"I have no idea."

She hooted at that. "See? Already moved on, huh? Told ya. He's a real son of a bitch. He pretends to be nice, pretends to care about you. But his brother wasn't the only one with a mean streak. Only difference is, with Dean you don't expect it."

A gust of cold air blew hard across the field, and I was suddenly glad for the bonfire, smoke and all. Libby took a step away from me. "I need another beer."

"Here," I said, passing her mine. "It's practically full."

"Thanks." She took the can and tipped it to her mouth, swallowing what had to be half the contents in one long gulp.

Someone pushed into me from behind, sending me stumbling forward toward the bonfire. "Oops, sorry," a voice said close to my ear. I glanced over my shoulder, found Amber's smirking face.

"Libby, girl," she screeched, her eyes falling away from mine. "How you been?"

"You two know each other?" I asked.

"Not really," Libby said. "We worked together for a while. Couple years ago."

"Where your friends at?" Amber asked me. "You always did travel in a pack." She hooked her thumb at me, but turned her face back to Libby. "Her best friend's a carpet muncher."

"Nice," I said.

She cackled. "God, you've always been so easy to fuck with. But tell me the truth, you into that girl-on-girl stuff now, too?"

"Not yet. But the night's still young."

Libby snorted into her beer can and Amber's mouth twisted. "You better stay away from her, Libby," she warned. "That shit rubs off."

"Well, considering the men around here, might not be a bad choice," Libby said. She held out her fist to me, and after a second's awkward hesitation, I bumped mine off it.

"You know who she is, right?" Amber said, giving me a vicious side-eye. I should have known that even drunk and drugged up, she always held this trump card in reserve. She never did like anyone stealing her thunder.

"Who who is?" Libby asked, eyes scanning the crowd instead of focusing on Amber.

"This one." Amber stumbled into me again, harder this time. "Her sister's the girl that Roy murdered." She made her fingers into a gun and pointed it at her own head, lips blowing a raspberry as she pulled the trigger.

Libby's gaze flew to mine, her mouth forming a round O of surprise. "Wait . . ." she said. "But you were with Dean the other day. Why—"

"She was with Dean?" Amber screeched. "Like *with* him? Holy fuck!" A laugh brayed out of her, scraping along my nerve endings.

I pivoted away from both of them, Libby with her confused eyes and Amber with her cruel mouth, and pushed my way into the crowd, let it swallow me up. I'd only made it about five steps before someone collided with me, grabbed my arm as I staggered sideways.

"Hey now," a familiar voice drawled. "How drunk are you?"

Judging from the look of him, and the smell, too, Garrett was the drunk one. I was about one second away from telling him that, shaking off his arm and demanding that Ryan and Cassie get me out of here, when my conversation with Baker at the Fall Festival suddenly came back to me. Here, right in front of me and a few too many beers in, was definitely a dumber fish.

"Not drunk at all," I said with a smile, adding a little slur to my words for good measure. "You're the one who bumped into me."

Garrett laughed, slid his hand down my arm, and laced our fingers together, like prom night was only yesterday and we were still on a date. "I don't know about that. You're looking a little unsteady on your feet." He tipped his head down to me, and I fought not to recoil from the stale beer fumes on his breath. "Wanna go someplace less crowded? You can sit down. Rest that pretty ass of yours."

What a charmer. That third-grade teacher Garrett was attempting to two-time sure was a lucky gal. But I nodded, let him lead me through the crowd and into the dark edges of the party. The kind of shadowy no-man's-land where nothing good ever happened.

"Here," Garrett said, pointing to a log on the ground. He sat with a grunt, pulling me down beside him. Any hope I'd had of some space between us disappeared as he used our still-joined hands to yank me closer, mashed his thigh up against mine. "Don't want you getting cold."

"Thanks," I said. He was right about one thing; it was definitely brisk out here, beyond the reach of the bonfire and the press of too many bodies. Overhead, black clouds scudded across the navy blue sky. A storm was rolling in. I could smell damp and ozone on the breeze.

"Why've you been driving by my house at night?" I blurted out. Not exactly the conversational opening I'd planned, but Garrett seemed completely unfazed by the question, took a long swallow from his beer before he answered. "Keeping an eye on you, is all," he said. "And rumor has it you've been hanging around some unsavory company."

I sighed, tried unsuccessfully to wiggle my hand out of his. Between Garrett and Libby, the whole town was going to know my business by morning. I thought briefly about arguing, but didn't see the point. Someone had seen me and Dean together, either Garrett himself or someone he trusted. Denial seemed like a waste of my time. "You're talking about Dean Mathews, right?"

Garrett turned to face me. "Yeah, I am. What in the hell are you thinking, Greer, hanging around with that loser? What bullshit is he feeding you?"

"He's not feeding me anything."

"Right," Garrett scoffed, tossed his beer can into the shadows behind us. "He's got an interest in having you believe certain things. Let me guess, he's trying to tell you Roy was innocent or that he was framed." He kicked out at the grass. "What bullshit."

"He's not trying to get me to believe anything," I said. "I barely know the guy. I've talked to him once or twice."

"Not what I heard," Garrett muttered.

"Well, then you heard wrong. I'm not hanging around with him."

Garrett glanced at me. "Yeah?"

I scooted closer, pushed my shoulder against his, trying hard to conjure up the flirty tone of voice I'd used on him back when we were teenagers. "Yeah."

"Why'd you want to talk to him in the first place?"

I shrugged. "I don't know. I wanted to see if he knew more

about the new murders than what I'd heard around town. Nobody will tell me anything. I guess I got desperate. It was dumb of me." Baiting my hook and holding my breath.

"You could have asked me." He stroked the back of my hand with his thumb.

"I tried that before. You said you couldn't tell me." Infusing my voice with the right amount of pout was harder than I remembered. Did I really used to put this much energy into pleasing boys?

"That's because there's nothing to tell." But his eyes slid away from mine as he spoke. The oldest tell in the book. Garrett wasn't only the dumber fish; he also wasn't a very good cop.

"Oh, come on," I said. "I know you're hiding something." I pulled my hand out of his and laid it on his thigh instead. "I won't tell anyone, I swear."

He looked down at my fingers splayed across his jeans and reached for my arm. For a second I thought he was going to drag my hand higher, onto his dick, and I wondered how far I was willing to go with this charade. But he only turned my hand over, exposing my wrist. "The killer drew something with Addy's blood," he said, voice low enough that I had to lean closer to hear him. "On her arm, right here." He tapped his index finger against the pale, delicate skin of my inner wrist. My pulse thrummed, blue veins jumping, but not from his touch.

"What was it?" I asked. My breath was coming too fast, shimmering black stars exploding in my peripheral vision.

But I already knew. Knew before he traced the familiar shape with his finger, goose bumps racing up my arm. Knew before the words ever left his mouth.

"It was a red heart," he said. "A valentine."

Chapter Fifteen

caught a ride back into town with a carload of teenagers I didn't know. They were amused to have someone my age begging for a lift, and I could imagine the embellishments they'd add to the story at school on Monday. But I didn't care, ignored their jokes about drunk old ladies as I hunched over my phone in the backseat, frantically texting Dean. I'd left Garrett sitting on the log, yelling after me as I careened back through the crowd, not caring who I slammed into or how many people called my name.

I told Dean I'd found out something, and we agreed to meet at the refinery, a private spot I was pretty sure would be empty because the teenagers who usually hung out there on Saturday nights were at the bonfire instead. The kids dropped me off a block from my house, and I ran the rest of the way, scrambling up the front-porch steps and to my room to grab what I needed.

"Greer?" my mom called from her bedroom. "Honey, is that you?"

"Yeah," I said, popping my head into her doorway. She was already in bed, alone, a book propped in her lap. "I'm heading out again."

"Okay," she said with a faint smile.

I started to turn away and paused. "Can I ask you something?"

She nodded, but I didn't miss the way her hand tightened on her book.

"Did you come across any photos in Eliza's room when you cleaned it out? Ones that might have been taken with a phone and then printed out?"

"Photos?" Her voice was faint. "She had lots of photos, Greer."

I shook my head. "Not like her albums." Eliza had gone through a scrapbooking phase her first two years of high school. She'd spent countless hours hunched over at the kitchen table with a pile of stickers and craft scissors at the ready. I'd called her Grandma every time I caught her working on her new hobby. I wished I'd paid more attention to what she'd created. How could I have lived sixteen years with her and not known her better? I cleared my throat against the lump forming there. "These would have been loose photos."

"No," my mom said, eyes dropping back to her book. "There was nothing like that."

I wanted to push—*What if it happens again?*—but I could see her retreating from me. The same way she had years ago when I'd asked too many questions. As if she feared any mention of Eliza might send me off the deep end again and drag her down with me.

"Okay," I said, still lingering in the doorway.

She didn't look up. "Be careful tonight, Greer. There's rain on the way."

. . . .

The drive to the refinery was dark, along a highway that people I knew in Chicago would call a lonely country road, devoid of any streetlights and surrounded by empty fields. The only illumination was an occasional flash of lightning in the distance, each one leaving behind jagged white streaks in my vision. It was almost a relief to see headlights coming toward me, to know that I wasn't alone out here in the relentless night. I slowed, turning into the refinery, and Dean's SUV eased in behind me, his headlights bouncing off my rearview mirror.

We parked and got out of our cars, Dean's eyebrows knotting up as soon as he saw me. "Hey, are you okay?"

I thought of the heart on Addy's arm and just managed a nod. "I'm fine."

"Okay," he said, brows still drawn together. "What did you need to tell me?"

"Not here," I said, suddenly feeling exposed, even though we were shrouded in darkness. "Let's go in."

Dean turned to look at the building looming behind us. "Really? Inside the refinery?"

"Really," I said. "Come on."

"Isn't this illegal? I've heard they have to rescue people from inside every once in a while." He paused. "I sound like a chicken-shit, don't I?"

"Little bit," I said, grateful for the moment of levity. "Besides, those are probably idiot kids who don't know their way around. I could navigate this place with my eyes closed." I pulled a flashlight from my bag and turned it on, held it under my chin to illuminate my face, cheeks glowing ghostly orange in the darkness. "But lucky for you, I brought this." I wiggled my eyebrows at him until he huffed out a reluctant laugh.

"We could have just used our phones," he pointed out.

"Yeah, but the old-school flashlight really adds to the vibe. Trust me."

We skirted the perimeter of the fence until I spotted a piece of loose chain link rolled up slightly from the ground and detached from its metal post. Dean held it aside while I wiggled through the gap, and then he followed, shoving my bag ahead of him. Thunder cracked, loud and strong enough to make the ground thrum under my feet.

"This way," I said, gesturing with the flashlight as we picked our way across the expanse of cracked concrete, skirting around shards of broken glass and tufts of dying weeds. "You really never came here when you were younger?"

"Once. Maybe twice. It was more Roy's speed. He liked to come out here and smash bottles. Rage against the world. Personally, it always creeped me out."

"Yeah, Eliza never liked it, either. She came once, that I know of, and never again."

Our entry into the refinery was through a busted-out window with a piece of plywood leaning drunkenly over the opening. Inside, dim silvery moonlight rained down from a hole in the roof, a few birds or bats wheeling in the cavernous space overhead. The concrete floor was littered with the waste of a hundred other trespassers: fast-food wrappers, empty beer cans, shriveled condoms, a random flip-flop. In one corner was a pile of broken glass, Roy obviously not the only one who got out his anger with a crate of beer bottles and a concrete wall. Dean turned in a slow circle, following the beam of the flashlight in my hand. "Jesus," he said finally. "What a hellhole."

"It's not that bad," I said. "Especially when you're rebellious teenagers desperate for some privacy." I stepped past him, farther into the shadows. "This is where we spent most of our time."

He followed me across the vast space, around the far corner into a tucked-away spot near an open stairwell. The walls were covered in graffiti, bright tags of paint professing love or hate, pictures of flowers and odes to the Class of 1989, a swastika that someone had tried to paint over with a peace sign, a giant Kansas Jayhawk. I used the flashlight to point out a scrawl of hot pink paint—a daisy, one side of the petals too long and pointy. "My friend Cassie did that one. The hot pink was her signature."

We lowered ourselves to the floor, kicking trash and pieces of rock out of the way. From outside I could hear the sound of rain falling, great sweeps of thunder rumbling across the sky. We'd made it just in time. "You realize this whole place is probably contaminated, right?" Dean said as we sat. "An EPA nightmare."

"I think we're fine for a few minutes. But I definitely wouldn't want to build a house downstream from here."

In the glow of the flashlight, I watched Dean's gaze rove over the graffitied walls. "I stand by my earlier statement. This place is creepy. And dangerous. But I can kind of see the appeal. Especially to teenagers."

"Yeah," I said. This had been a place hidden from adults, a spot meant for the young and brave, where you could do what you wanted with no one around to watch. A place where good, responsible Greer Dunning could paint graffiti and drink beer and transform into someone else for a little while.

"Are we done stalling now?" Dean asked. "Do you want to tell me what's going on?"

"I went to the bonfire tonight. Saw Libby, by the way. She still wouldn't cross the street to piss on you if you were on fire."

"Greer . . ." He laid his hand over mine, stilling my fingers from picking at a loose thread in the hem of my jeans.

"Okay, yeah, sorry, getting to the point." I took a deep breath, tipped my head back. Above me, the painted, pockmarked walls stretched up and up, something fluttering in the echoing darkness. "I ran into Garrett Bloom while I was there. He was drunk, and I figured I'd use that to my advantage."

Dean stiffened next to me, and I glanced at him. "Don't worry. I didn't have to go too far. Just played nice to get what I needed, same as you."

"What could you possibly need from Garrett Bloom?"

"He told me something about the latest murders." I reached over and grabbed Dean's arm, the same way Garrett had done to me earlier. "He said there was a heart drawn in blood on the inside of Addy's wrist, right here." I watched his face closely as I spoke, searching for a glimpse of shock, recognition, anything that would tell me the heart had meaning for him, too. But all I saw was confusion chasing its way across his features.

"A heart?" He looked from his wrist back to me. "I don't get it. Roy didn't do anything like that with your sister or Travis."

"No," I said, reaching into my bag. "Roy didn't." I pulled out the paper heart, set it carefully on the ground between us. "But someone put this through my mailbox after Roy was arrested."

Dean picked up the heart, turned it over once, twice. He held it the same way I always did, like it might come to life at any second, dark blood dripping into his hands. "'I did it. For you.'" His jaw tightened. "What the fuck, Greer? And you're just now telling me this?" He waved the heart in my direction.

"I wasn't sure if it meant anything," I said, stomach knotting at the lie. "But now we know it does."

Dean dropped the heart onto the concrete, pinched the bridge of his nose with his fingers. "A heart," he said finally. "Is this why you freaked out about my tattoo?"

"Yeah. Sorry. It just caught me off guard."

He stared down at the heart. "Did you have a thing for Travis? Unrequited love. Is that what this whole mess was about? Somebody thinking if you couldn't have Travis, you wouldn't want anyone else to have him, either?"

"What?" I breathed out. "No. I didn't even like Travis that much. I mean, he was fine. Nice enough. Good to Eliza. But talking to him was like watching paint dry."

Dean let out a reluctant laugh. "Okay, got it. But I had to ask." He pointed toward the heart. "It seems like the most obvious reason. A woman scorned and all that." He winced. "That sounds really shitty now that I'm saying it out loud. Sorry."

"It's all right," I said, waving off his apology. "And it may be the most obvious reason. But it's not why."

Dean's head swiveled toward me. "Do you know why?" His voice wasn't sharp exactly, but his eyes were, searching my face and leaving no room to look away.

"No," I said. "I've thought about it a thousand times. What those words mean, why someone would write them, why anyone would think killing Eliza and Travis would help me. What connection it could all have to Addy and Dylan. I don't know. No matter how many ways I come at it, I still don't know."

Dean didn't answer right away, and I could practically hear the cogs in his brain turning. "Maybe it wasn't killing Eliza and Travis that was supposed to help you. Maybe it was what killing them caused."

"My whole life to fall apart?" I asked, voice dubious. "How exactly did that help me?"

"I have no idea. I was just thinking about what you said that day we went to see Libby . . . that maybe Eliza and Travis were collateral damage. But I don't know how it all comes together in a way that makes sense." He sighed. "I've been driving myself crazy, too. Trying to piece together some kind of connection between the first set of murders and the second." He gestured toward the heart. "So far, that's the only thing that links them, really. And we don't even know what it means."

"It could be a coincidence, I guess. Maybe the murders didn't have anything to do with me and someone just wants to mess with my head." *God, you've always been so easy to fuck with.* I could almost picture Amber Stevens, or someone like her, making the heart, cackling to herself as she slipped it through my front-door mail slot. Mean Girls 101. But that didn't explain the heart on Addy. No high school rival with a bitchy streak was going to go that far.

"What if the heart wasn't for you at all?" Dean said. "What if it was meant for your mom? Or your dad?"

That stopped me. I'd never really considered the possibility that the heart had been aimed at anyone else. From the first second I'd held it in my hand, it had belonged to me. "I don't see how Eliza's death benefited either of them." The life insurance policy notwithstanding, Eliza's death had crushed them both in one fell swoop.

"Yeah." Dean sighed. "It's probably a stretch."

We sat in silence for a minute, all the things we still didn't have the answers to hanging heavy over us. Something pulsed hard in the dark shadows of my mind, and I could feel myself giving under the pressure. I wouldn't be able to keep looking away much longer. I lowered my forehead to my bent knees and closed my eyes.

"Roy died five months ago tonight," Dean said finally. "That's why I was home with my grandma instead of at the bonfire. She was having a hard time. I'd been hoping she wouldn't remember, would have one of her bad days that sometimes come as a blessing instead of being lucid and dredging it all up again."

I raised my head and looked at him. "Was your grandma at the execution?"

He sighed. "Yeah, of course she was there. How could she not have been? Wouldn't your mom have been there when Eliza died, if she could have? Even if her being there wouldn't have changed the outcome?"

"Yes," I whispered, picturing my mom cradling Eliza, wiping blood off her face and crooning the old lullabies she used to sing when we were babies. My mom would probably give every day she had left in exchange for those final seconds with Eliza, for the chance to let her know she wasn't alone. "What was it like? The execution?" I hadn't realized the question was waiting there, perched on the tip of my tongue all this time.

Dean shifted his body away from mine. "I'm not the person you should ask."

"Why not?"

"Because whatever I say is going to sound self-serving. Like I'm comparing pain, asking you to feel sympathy for me or for Roy."

"I'm never going to feel sympathy for Roy."

"That's my point. I'm not asking you to." He looked at me, blew out a long, stuttering breath. "It was awful, Greer. Is that what you want to hear? It was the most awful thing that's ever happened to me, and my life wasn't all that great to begin with." I watched his knuckles turn white where they were clenched in his lap. "It took him over ten minutes to die, did you know that?"

"Yes," I said.

"Yeah, I figured that got out. What probably didn't is that it took them twice that long to get the IV into his vein. Kept poking and poking at him. They say that fear can make your veins contract. Or maybe he was dehydrated. But for a few minutes there I thought it was going to be one of those horror shows where they put him back in his cell to try again another day. There was no way I was going to be able to come back and go through it again. I was praying under my breath, begging the universe to let them get the IV going. Hoping they'd be able to kill him and get it over with. Wishing for my brother to hurry up and die. He cried the entire time, silent, not making any noise, but his body wouldn't stop shaking. At the end, he called out for my grandma. Are those the kinds of details you're looking for?" The muscle in his jaw looked tight enough to snap.

I shook my head, unable to speak. I'd pushed him too far, I realized. The grace he'd shown me that day at the cemetery his line in the sand, and I'd just overstepped.

"Yes, my brother was a killer," Dean went on. "And maybe he deserved what he got. But we paid for it, too, my grandma and me. Even though we hadn't done anything wrong, we paid by having to watch him die that way. With waking up every morning for months knowing the exact day, the exact hour, the exact *minute* that Roy was going to stop breathing. None of us deserved that." He ran a weary hand over his face. "I'm not here to be your entertainment, Greer. I know my brother hurt your family in a way that can't ever be repaired. Believe me, I never forget that fact. But we're hurting, too. And I'm not going to lay it all out for you to salivate over."

"That's not what I'm doing," I managed.

"Then what?" Dean demanded, his voice harsh, but his eyes a raw bruise.

I wasn't sorry Roy was dead. But I was sorry his death had hurt the people who loved him. I was sorry that it had hurt Dean. I couldn't offer him the kind of words he probably deserved, the ones he might have gotten from someone with no connection to what had happened. Because as much as I ached for him, there was always going to be a piece of me that compared his loss, his pain, to ours and found his came up short. That would never understand how he could love his brother even now. Since I couldn't give him words of comfort, I did the next best thing. Pushed myself forward and put my arms around his neck, pulled him into a hug. He made a startled sound in his throat, and it took him a second to touch me back, but then his arms banded around me, squeezing tight. He smelled like the outdoors, wheat and sun and sweat. The skin of his neck was warm against my face, and I closed my eyes. It had been a long time since someone had held me, even longer since I'd wanted someone to. He stroked the back of my head, fingers sifting deeper into my hair with each pass. When I finally pulled back, his hand knotted in my hair kept me from going too far, our breath mingling as we stared at each other.

"This is all kinds of fucked up," Dean whispered. "You know that, right?"

"Fucked up is my current specialty," I whispered back, and then pressed forward to kiss him while a laugh still lingered on his mouth.

I wondered briefly if this had been inevitable. All the things we shared—our fear, our resentment, our distrust, our guilt—finally finding the most obvious, and easiest, outlet. The one that meant we wouldn't be forced to have another painful conversation. But if our coming together was partly avoidance, there was also a rightness to it that I couldn't deny. His wounds were different from mine, but they'd been made by the same weapon. All our raw, jagged edges scraping against each other and smoothing out the roughness.

He tasted like toothpaste and beer, and his lips were sure and steady under mine. He'd thought about this before, how we'd move together, and the knowledge sent a bolt of pure pleasure rocketing through me. I tilted backward and he went with me, hand behind my head to ease my impact with the floor. Goose bumps from the cold concrete chased away by the warmth of his hand, calluses scraping my delicate flesh as I arched my back to help him shove my shirt up and my bra aside. A low moan wrenched out of me when he pinched my nipple between thumb and forefinger while heat gathered between my legs. He lowered his head and I looked at him, mouth poised right above my breast, and then I stilled, gaze drawn to the stairs above us—the dark outline of a body in the gloom. I jerked, fumbling out from under his hands.

"What's wrong?" His eyes were heavy-lidded in the dim light, gaze unfocused, and for a split second all I could see above me was Roy. I pushed him off and rolled to the side, breath heaving out of me as I straightened my clothes.

"What—?" he asked again.

"I saw something," I said softly, not looking at him. "On the stairs. Someone's in here."

He rolled up to standing in one fluid movement, all slowness gone. "Where?" His voice was low and intense, one hand held out for mine. I took it and let him pull me upright. His face was his own again and, god help me, I still wanted him. The fucked-up part hadn't been a lie.

"Maybe it was a teenager. You said they like to hang out here." He was talking in a whisper, eyes raking the space above us.

"Could be. But whoever it was, I think they were watching us."

"Man or woman?"

"Couldn't tell. It was a dark shadow, that's all."

He took a step forward, started to let go of my hand, but I hung on. "I'm going up there," he told me. "You stay here."

"Hell no," I said, falling into step behind him. "We're going together or we're not going at all."

To his credit, he didn't waste time arguing with me. He hugged the wall as we made our slow way up the stairs, and I did the same. The steps felt secure enough, but the metal occasionally groaned under our weight in a way I didn't find particularly reassuring. There was no one on the second-floor landing, and I pointed upward. The next set of steps dumped us out into an empty loftlike area. Standing at the railing, we had a clear view down to where we'd entered the refinery, where we'd been sitting on the floor, the corner broken-glass pile. Or we would have if there had been lights. As it was, the glow from my flashlight was enough.

"No one's here," Dean said just as metal creaked above us, followed by the sound of footsteps fading away.

"There's one more flight," I said. "Someone's up there. Keep going."

When we got to the top, the landing was empty, and Dean raised his eyebrows at me. "There's another way down," I said, gesturing behind him with my head. "If we follow that catwalk."

I went first this time and Dean took control of the flashlight, lighting my way but holding it more like a weapon than a source of illumination. We inched along the catwalk, acutely aware of the spots where the railing was rusted away on one side.

"This is beyond stupid," Dean muttered, echoing my own thoughts, as we cleared a stretch with nothing between us and a long drop to the concrete below.

"Almost there," I said. From up ahead I could feel cold air, hear the distant whoosh of a car passing by on the highway, a gentle drumbeat of rain. The storm was winding down. We were almost to the end of the catwalk when a loud snapping sound stilled me, my heart tripping double time. "What the fuck was that?" I whispered.

Dean cocked his head, listened as the sound came again. Less alarming this time, but still not immediately identifiable. "Sounds like plastic?" he said.

The catwalk ended in a small room, the single broken-paned window I remembered completely missing now, a tacked-up piece of plastic in its place, whipping in the breeze. The space was empty save for a couple of sleeping bags twisted in a corner and the same trash and dirt as downstairs. "How the hell would someone get out of here without us seeing them?" Dean asked.

"There's a fire escape ladder out this window," I told him. "Or at least there used to be. You can climb down it in a pinch. Did it a time or two myself when the cops showed up."

He glanced my way. "And here I always had the Dunnings pegged as good girls."

"Eliza was, all the shitty things people said about her after she died notwithstanding. But for me, it ebbed and flowed." I pulled back the plastic sheeting and pointed. "See?" The rusting metal ladder was still there, if you were brave enough to risk the four-story fall.

"So what are we thinking? Whoever was watching us came back this way and then climbed down?" Dean leaned partway out the window. "Had their car waiting or took off on foot. Either way, they'd have to know this place pretty well to know an escape route." He clapped his hands together where dust and dirt had gathered from the windowsill. "And why would someone be watching us in the first place?" He reached for me, his warm hand sliding down my arm reminding me that I was cold, the air through the broken window icy against my skin. I leaned into his touch without thinking about it, threaded our fingers together and hung on.

"It could mean we're getting close somehow, right? Somebody is nervous." As we talked, I swung the flashlight in a lazy arc across the ceiling, back and forth, illuminating the graffiti that had found its way even back here.

"Okay, but—"

I didn't hear the rest of what he said, my attention caught on a hot pink splash of paint in the corner. "CJL + EAD = LOVE 4EVER."

No, my mind kept saying, long after my eyes had accepted what they'd seen. Long after I'd run back down the catwalk and out to my car, yelling excuses to Dean over my shoulder. Long after I'd peeled out onto the highway, racing back to Ludlow.

I'd known people were keeping secrets about that endless hot summer before Eliza died. But I'd never considered, not even for a single second, that Cassie was one of them. Or that the secret she'd been keeping was my sister.

Chapter Sixteen

I t was maybe lucky for both of us that Cassie hadn't been home when I'd run up the steps to her apartment and smashed my fist against the door over and over the night before. Things might have been said, or done, that could never be unsaid. When she hadn't answered the door, I'd texted her with shaky fingers, demanding to know where she was. But she'd never responded. I'd eventually gone home, ignoring Dean's texts the way Cassie was ignoring mine, and fallen into an uneasy sleep. I dreamt of red valentines and pink spray paint. Wind blowing through tattered sheets of plastic. Taste of gunpowder on my tongue. Woke in my childhood bed with a scream snagged deep and heavy in my chest. I got up and splashed cold water on my face, hands clenched on the sides of the pedestal sink. "You said you wanted answers," I reminded my pale reflection. I should have known to be careful what I wished for.

When I got to the diner, it was a full house, Cassie running interference behind the counter and Mabel taking care of the tables and booths. "Hey," Cassie said, sending a distracted smile my direction. "Sorry I didn't—"

"I need to talk to you," I said. "Out back." I didn't wait for her to answer, kept right on walking down the length of the diner and through the screened door to the alley beyond. It took her a minute to join me, her face torn between concern and annoyance.

"I only have a second," she said. "We're slammed in there. Is everything okay?"

"I was at the refinery last night. I saw your graffiti."

Cassie's head jerked back. "My graffiti? You mean from years ago?"

"Yeah. CJL plus EAD equals love forever. Cassandra Jane Lloyd. Eliza Anne Dunning. Ring a bell?"

Cassie's eyes closed, opened again slowly. She looked far away, like she was back in the refinery, a can of spray paint clutched in her hand. "God, I'd forgotten I even painted that. In the back room at the end of the catwalk, right?"

"Right," I said. My voice was like a whip, and it snapped Cassie back to the present.

"It didn't mean anything," she said, too fast.

"How could it not mean anything? What the fuck, Cassie? How could you not tell me this?" My voice was spiraling higher and higher with each word, and Cassie pushed down with one hand, trying to shush me as her eyes cut back toward the diner. A shadow appeared on the diner side of the screened door and then Ryan shouldered his way outside. "Hey," he said. "What am I missing out here? Mabel's about to have a panic attack."

"Oh, shit," Cassie said. "I have to go help her."

"No way," I said, shooting my hand out and holding the door closed. "She can manage for a couple more minutes."

Ryan's gaze shifted from me to Cassie and back again. "This looks intense. Do I need popcorn?" He pointed at Cassie. "Hey, is it your turn in Greer's hot seat? Believe me, it's a good time."

"Shut up, Ryan," Cassie said, not even glancing at him. "No, Eliza and I weren't together. We weren't in love. She had no idea that I had a crush on her, Greer. It was dumb, but for that one summer I was obsessed." She threw up her hands. "I have no idea why. Nothing that happened when I was sixteen made any sense. I woke up one morning and Eliza was who I couldn't stop thinking about. So I painted that stupid graffiti. And by the end of the summer my crush was over."

"You were never over anybody that fast," I reminded her. "There was always drama and fireworks. Or months of pining. You want me to believe it was magically different when you had a crush on Eliza?"

She shrugged. "I can't make you believe anything. But that's what happened."

"Wait," Ryan said. "You had the hots for Eliza? Did Travis know?"

"Oh, my god," Cassie said. "Nobody knew! That was the whole point. It was a secret and I couldn't tell anyone. I painted it on a wall instead."

My anger from the night before was fading a little with every passing second; Cassie's explanation made sense if you looked at it through a sixteen-year-old's eyes. And yet I'd always thought of Cassie as someone who shot straight from the hip, who never bothered keeping secrets. But that had been stupid of me because everyone had something to hide.

"I was embarrassed," Cassie went on. "I'd just come out the year before, and now I had a crush on your sister, the straightest of straight girls? Besides, I worried you'd slip up and tell her and then things would be weird when I was over at your house. I knew it would pass, and it did. Because it wasn't real. No harm done."

Except there was harm done. Like finding out my father had an insurance policy on Eliza, but not on me. Like discovering Ryan knew Dylan better than he'd let on. Doubt crept in. Only a little, but enough to shift perspective ever so slightly. To leave me questioning the people I'd always thought I could trust the most. I didn't understand how I'd gotten to this point, where I looked at the people I loved and saw only secrets.

"You could have told me," I said. "You should have told me."

Cassie's eyes cut away from mine, finding Ryan's, exchanging a look I couldn't read. "Same goes for you," she said after a few seconds of silence.

"What's that supposed to mean?" I asked, but I was pretty sure I knew.

Ryan edged closer, the three of us forming a tense little triangle. "We ever going to talk about how you're hanging around with Roy Mathews's brother?"

I closed my eyes for a second. "Jesus. That didn't take long to get around."

"Did you think it would?" Ryan sounded genuinely curious. "Cassie saw you two chatting it up at the drive-in. She wanted to say something right then, but I told her to give you some time."

"I guess time's up, then?" I raised my eyebrows at Cassie.

"What are you doing, Greer?" she asked. "Palling around with that guy? What's the point of it?"

"Maybe I like him," I said, trying out the words to see how they sounded. To gauge whether they were true.

Ryan laughed. "Are you serious? Maybe you *like him*? His brother fucking murdered your sister. Or has that fact slipped your mind?"

"Fuck off," I snapped. "Of course it didn't slip my mind. But he didn't kill them, you asshole. He's not his brother. How would you like it if every girl you met assumed you were like your cheating, disappearing-act dad?"

"That's not the same thing, and you damn well know it." Ryan took a deep breath. "Look, Cassie and I are worried, that's all. You show up here out of the blue. Start hanging around with Dean Mathews."

"I thought you guys were glad I was back."

"Not the point," Cassie said. "And you know we're happy you're here. Don't pretend that you don't."

"Then what *is* the point?" I demanded. I didn't know why I was angry. I'd known Ryan and Cassie would find out about Dean eventually. But I thought I'd have more time, a few more weeks, or at least days, to figure out what I wanted to say, to come up with the right combination of words that might make them understand. More time to find the answers I needed. Now I felt ambushed, and that only made me want to fight back.

"The point is, we just want to know what the hell is going on." Cassie laid her hand on my shoulder, and I jerked away. "How worried do we need to be?"

"I never asked you to worry about me. I'm fine."

"Yeah, fine like after Eliza died and you wouldn't stop talking about how the cops were missing something?" Ryan asked. "Or fine like all these years in Chicago when it was obvious to anyone with a pulse how miserable you were? Fine like that?"

"I don't need you or Cassie to babysit me. I'm looking for answers, that's all. And Dean feels the same way. That's it."

Cassie and Ryan shared another glance that made me feel childish and stupid, wondering how often they talked about me behind my back, lamenting all the dumb decisions I was making. "I have to go back in," Cassie said. "But remember, just because you and Dean are both looking for answers doesn't mean you're on the same side."

• • • •

This time when I walked into the police station, Sheriff Baker wasn't eating scrambled eggs. He was engaged in the slightly more cop-like behavior of explaining to a disgruntled middle-aged man why he couldn't park in the no-parking zone in front of the fire station. I clocked Garrett sitting at his desk, hunched over paperwork, and another deputy in the back pouring himself a cup of coffee. The receptionist up front started to ask me what I needed, but I pointed at Baker and moved past her.

"You lied to me," I said when Baker looked over and caught my eye. The whole station didn't exactly fall silent, but there was a definite hush, heads turning to watch what might unfold.

"Well, good morning to you, Greer Dunning," Baker said, voice easy but eyes a warning. He said something I didn't catch to Mr. Parking Ticket and then ushered me toward the empty interrogation room. Once the door was shut behind us, Baker sighed, leaned back against it, and crossed his arms over his chest. "What the hell are you talking about?" he asked, sounding more worn out than angry.

"You told me there was nothing different about the new murders."

"No," he said slowly. "I didn't tell you anything at all. That's not the same thing."

"I know about the heart on Addy's wrist."

Baker's arms dropped fast. He pushed himself away from the door, and the alarm on his face gave me a hot rush of satisfaction. Not so tired of me now, was he? "Where'd you hear that?" he asked. "About Addy?"

I didn't hesitate. "Garrett. You need to do a better job picking your underlings. That dumbass can't keep a secret to save his life."

Baker shook his head, muttered something under his breath.

"Why didn't you tell me?" I asked. "You've had plenty of chances."

"Because it's not for you to know, Greer," he said, frustration roughening his words. "You're not a cop. And the last thing we need are civilians out there sticking their noses into things, messing up the investigation."

"What investigation?" I countered. "No offense, but it sort of seems like this one is going nowhere fast."

"You have no idea what you're talking about."

"The copycat stuff, that's all bullshit, right? To throw everyone off the scent?"

"Why would you assume that?" he asked, brow furrowed.

I opened my bag and pulled out the paper heart, laid it carefully on the table.

"What in the hell?" Baker breathed, looking down and then back up at me.

"I got this a month after Eliza died." My finger skated lightly over the red paper, flipped it over so he could read the back. "Someone put it through our mail slot."

"And you're just bringing it to me now?" His voice was level, but every word dripped with accusation.

I shrugged, even though my own heart was clawing its way through my rib cage. "Last time I tried to talk to you about Eliza's murder, you had me sent to a therapist. I don't owe you anything. But when I heard about the heart on Addy, I figured it was worth letting you know."

"Goddamn it, Greer," Baker said between clenched teeth. "Do you know who sent it?"

"No." I drummed my fingers on the tabletop. "But I'm guessing this definitely throws a wrench in your copycat theory. Because from where I'm sitting, the heart on Addy's arm, combined with this, pretty much shoots the whole random-killer idea right out the window." I paused. "No pun intended."

Baker shook his head. The man was known for having a very long fuse, but I had a feeling I was causing him to reach the end of it. "I don't think it's a coincidence. But I do think people talk. People you told about the heart. People who saw it. People who love to gossip. This town is filled with them. It wouldn't be hard for the wrong person to get that information, use it to try and throw us off track."

"I didn't tell anyone," I said. "Not even my parents." I hadn't wanted to watch them read the words on it. It was bad enough for me to be haunted by them; I didn't want them haunted, too.

"Even if you didn't tell anyone, there's always the possibility that someone saw it. Put together the heart with something you might have said. People's memories fade over time, Greer. Even yours. You may have given away more than you think."

"That's bullshit," I told him. "The only people who know about the heart are you, me, and whoever put it through my mail slot." I left Dean off of the list. The last thing I needed right now was another lecture.

Baker sighed. "Nothing stays a secret for long, Greer. The hearts aren't necessarily as important as you think they are, is all I'm saying. The one you got could have been a mean-spirited prank. And then the wrong person learned about it, like I said, left the one on Addy's arm as a way to lead us down a false path, make us assume the two sets of murders are connected."

"You don't really believe that," I said. Mainly because I couldn't. The heart had been what I'd clung to all these years, the horrible, hateful clue that would solve it all. I couldn't accept that it might mean nothing in the end.

Baker shook his head, his eyes never leaving mine. "I'm going to ask you this one more time, Greer. Do you know who gave you the heart?"

"No," I said. "But whoever it was, they know something about Eliza's and Travis's deaths. And they killed Dylan and Addy. If you want to think otherwise, go right ahead. But you'll be wrong."

I pushed past him and opened the door, strode strong and angry back toward the front of the station, his footsteps right behind me.

Garrett looked up and caught my eye as I passed his desk, shot me a grin and a wink. I hooked my thumb at him as I kept walking. "And he's fucking Amber Stevens in exchange for not arresting her. Just another detail you missed." Baker's footsteps stopped dead.

I glanced back at Garrett and gave him a wink of my own. The look on his face—dumbfounded, pissed, mortified—almost made the memory of my hand on his thigh worth it.

• • • •

Turns out the Do wasn't that bad once you had a few drinks in you. Maybe my dad had been on to something when he'd started coming here. Maybe the world *was* easier to take when you used bourbon as a shield. When I'd first moseyed up to the bar and pulled out a stool, Jim had seemed glad to see me, not all that concerned about me rolling in alone at six p.m. But the worried looks he kept shooting me were increasing in direct proportion to the number of empty glasses lined up in front of me.

"What?" I said, downing another gulp. "Like father, like daughter, right?" Bravado and belligerence barely hiding the fact that my stomach was in full rebellion, every sip I'd taken about ready to head in the opposite direction.

"How about a water?" Jim didn't wait for my nod, already sliding a large glass of ice water toward me.

"I can take the rest of that bourbon off your hands."

It took me a second to connect the voice to the person suddenly standing next to me. "Dean!" I said, looking up. "You're here!" I lowered my voice. "Why are you here? You looking to get your ass kicked?"

Dean slid onto the stool next to me and grabbed my bourbon. "You texted and told me to meet you here. And this place is practically empty. I'm not too worried about my ass." He nodded toward the water. "Drink that."

208 • Amy Engel

"God," I mumbled. "Everyone's so bossy." But I dutifully sipped at the water, not wanting to admit how good it tasted.

"What kind of drunk are you anyway? Mean? Funny? Head in a toilet?"

"I'm not drunk. I'm never drunk." I paused. "But if I were, I think I'd be the toilet kind."

"Good to know," Dean said. "We're definitely cutting off that bourbon then."

"How about something to eat?" Jim asked. "I got chicken tenders or nachos." He didn't seem to mind Dean being in his bar, but I noticed he wasn't making eye contact with him, either.

"Yes," I said, nodding too hard. My vision blurred, and I covered my face with my hands and moaned.

"We'll take both," Dean said. "You really are never drunk. You suck at this."

"Thanks," I said from behind my palms.

He laid his hand on the back of my neck, underneath my ponytail. His fingers were a cool relief against my burning skin. We hadn't talked about what happened between us at the refinery. I could feel it sitting there, fighting for our attention. We stayed like that until Jim returned with our food, me breathing into my palms and Dean rubbing light circles against my neck.

I lowered my hands and stared down at the nachos in front of me, swimming in canned cheese and sour cream, the top dotted with blood red salsa and jarred jalapeños. "I can't tell if this looks amazing or disgusting."

"Go slow," Jim said, pointing at me. "If you puke on my bar top, Greer Dunning, I'm putting your ass out."

As I took a tentative bite of chip, the jukebox started up behind me. Garth Brooks singing about low places. Maybe he'd had the Do in mind when he wrote those lyrics.

"Does it always have to be this song?" Dean asked. "Every damn time I'm here?"

"And does it have to be this loud?" I chimed in, wincing.

"Oh, quit your bellyaching," Jim said. "You're not even hung over yet. Besides, you should count yourself lucky you didn't wander in here tomorrow."

"What's tomorrow?" I asked.

"Eighties night," Dean said. "And the volume is turned up to eleven."

"Wait." I held up a hand. "Tomorrow is eighties night? That makes today . . . Thursday?"

"Yep," Jim said, looking amused. "He's right. You do suck at this."

"Oh, shit," I muttered at the exact moment the door of the Do opened and Ryan and Cassie walked in like they'd choreographed it. I watched them notice my appearance at the bar and then register Dean sitting next to me, one of his arms slung across the back of my stool. Ryan's whole face tightened up and Cassie looked away, disapproval etched across her features. A flare of anger shot through me, zipping hot and electric under my skin.

"I should go," Dean said, his gaze following mine.

"No. Stay. It's fine." I pushed our untouched plate of chicken tenders toward him. "We haven't even finished eating." But I knew I was full of shit. I wasn't going to be able to choke down another bite. I could feel eyes on the back of my neck, knew Ryan and Cassie were probably huddled behind us at their regular Thursday night table whispering about what an idiot I was. "Fuck this." I slid off my stool and grabbed Dean's hand. "Come on," I told him when he didn't immediately move to follow me.

"What about our food?"

"Oh, good thinking." I grabbed the plate of nachos with my

free hand. "Mind if we join you?" I asked when we reached Ryan and Cassie's table. I didn't wait for them to answer, just set down the nachos with a clatter and pulled out a chair. "Take a seat," I said to Dean, gesturing at the empty fourth chair when he hesitated.

I looked across the table at Ryan and Cassie. I could feel a flush working its way up my face, a combination of anger and booze. I wished I had a cold beer bottle to lay against my cheek. "This is Dean," I said, eyebrows raised, daring them to say something. "Dean Mathews."

"We know who he is," Cassie said, eyes only on me. There was a pause where no one spoke before Cassie's Kansas manners got the better of her. She glanced at Dean. "It's nice to meet you. I'm Cassie."

"Nice to meet you, too," Dean said. He had to be wondering what the hell was going on here, but he seemed okay with sitting back and letting me lead.

Ryan set his beer down on the table a little too hard. "What the fuck are you doing, Greer?"

"I'm having a few drinks, eating some nachos, hanging out with my friends. What does it look like I'm doing?"

"I couldn't tell ya," Ryan said. "But what I do know is that you normally barely drink, these nachos look like shit"—he put one finger under the edge of the plate to lift it up and then pulled his hand away to point at Dean—"and he is not your friend."

I opened my mouth to protest, but Dean got there first. "I am, actually," he said, voice easy. "Her friend. Or at least I'm trying to be."

"How can you even say that with a straight face?" Cassie shot back. "Because I distinctly remember sitting in a courtroom listening to you spew some bullshit about how hard your brother's life had been and how he should be spared the death penalty, be allowed to live out his years all nice and cozy in prison while Eliza and Travis are rotting in the town cemetery." Cassie's breath huffed out of her, and she shrugged off the hand Ryan tried to lay on her shoulder. "I need another beer," she muttered, flagging the waitress as she walked by and pointing to her half-empty bottle.

I looked at Dean, trying to telegraph an apology with my eyes. I regretted bringing him over here, regretted whatever kind of fucked-up message I was trying to send to Ryan and Cassie by doing it. Because I should have known Dean was the one they were going to take it out on. But he wasn't looking at me. He was staring straight at Cassie, and that muscle in his jaw was tick-tick-ticking away.

"He was my little brother," he said finally. "I was always going to try and save him."

"Whatever, man," Ryan said after a moment of silence. "You need to leave Greer alone. You're not good for her."

"Hey—" I said.

"And if I don't?" Dean asked, cutting me off.

"Then we have a problem," Ryan said, leaning forward in his chair. I looked at Cassie, expecting her to have the same disbelieving look on her face that I probably had on mine, but she was looking straight at Dean, her expression hard.

Dean smiled, but it wasn't a version I'd ever seen before, his lips pulled back, stark and predatory, his eyes flat. "Go fuck yourself," he said, low and even and a hundred times more threatening than if he'd raised his voice. Goose bumps erupted along my limbs. Nobody moved, it felt like nobody breathed, and then Dean stood, his chair legs scraping back breaking the spell. He looked down at me. "Stay or go?" he asked.

"Go," I said, taking his hand. I didn't give myself a second to think about it, and I didn't look back as we walked away, out the front door of the Do and into the dark parking lot. "I'm sorry," I said to his back, trying to match my strides to his. "About them.

They're being overprotective and taking it out on you. They loved Eliza, too, and they mean well. But they're acting like assholes."

Dean stopped next to his SUV and dropped my hand. He didn't seem angry, exactly. Just bone tired, all his earlier menace drained away. "I can't really blame them. I know this is a screwed-up situation. I shouldn't have let them get to me." He scrubbed one hand down his face, the drag on his features adding years to his age. "Listen, I'm going to take off. It's been a long day."

He turned to unlock his door, and I stepped forward, wrapped my arms around him from behind, laid my cheek against his back and held on.

"Greer," he said, voice low.

I squeezed tighter, breathing him in. "I like you. I wish I didn't like you so much." His steadiness, his voice, the way being next to him made me feel not so alone. It was the truth, despite everything. I didn't know him, not really, and I couldn't trust him, not fully, but I liked him anyway. More than I should. More than was good for either of us.

He folded his hands over mine, his heart beating against my palms. "I like you, too." He took a deep breath, let it out slowly, and when he spoke, I could hear the smile in his voice. "Remember that first day on the bench, when you said we'd give Ludlow a collective heart attack if they saw us sitting together?" I nodded against his back, and he squeezed my fingers. "What about now?"

"Aneurysm," I said, not missing a beat.

"Stroke," he countered.

I smiled. "Total organ failure, for sure."

Dean laughed and turned in my arms, bracketing my face with his calloused hands. When he kissed me, it was different from the kiss at the refinery. This time we knew exactly what we were doing. But like before, the heat spiraled up fast. It felt like someone had lit a burner under my feet, the instantaneous whoosh of ignition racing up my body. But as I surrendered myself to it, pushed my body into Dean's, Roy's face swam up again, a nasty mirage against my closed eyelids. Like it was his lips on mine, his hands on my body, his voice in my ear. I pulled back fast, breath panting out of me, heart slamming against my ribs.

"What?" Dean asked.

I shook my head, took a step backward. "It's just . . . I keep thinking . . ." I couldn't bring myself to finish my sentence.

"It's Roy, isn't it?" Dean said, voice flat.

I gestured between us. "He's here, even when he isn't. I see his face . . ." It pained me to know that I was the same as everyone else—looking at Dean and seeing only Roy.

"I could put a bag over my head, if it would help."

Laughter burbled out of me, and I leaned forward, rested my forehead against his chest. "This is all the bourbon's fault," I said, my words muffled against his flannel shirt.

"I don't think it's the bourbon," he said, his hands running gently up and down my spine.

I tilted my head back to look at him. "Are we good?"

Dean nodded, his eyes serious. I wondered what level of fucked up it made me that a big part of me still wanted to kiss him, mold my body to his until we burned away Roy's memory. "We're good."

"Do you want to meet up tomorrow sometime, after my hangover wears off, and decide where we go from here? About the murders, I mean?" I hated how awkward I sounded, how awkward this felt. That had always been the one magical thing about Dean and me—the unearned, unexpected ease between us. I should have recognized how fragile it was, protected it better. And maybe now it was gone for good.

He looked away. "I don't know. Tomorrow is kind of busy. And it seems like you have some things you need to sort out with your friends."

I waved a dismissive hand toward the bar. "It's fine, really."

"Let's just play it by ear, huh?" he said, still not looking at me. "I have a couple things I need to get done tomorrow anyway."

"Dean—"

"We'll talk soon, okay?" He hopped in his SUV before I could say anything more, and I stood in the parking lot and watched him drive away, his taillights growing smaller and smaller until I could no longer see them at all.

Roy

The noise bothered him the most. You'd think it would be the smells, or the tiny cell, or the knowing he was going to die soon, whenever they finally got around to killing him. But he could handle those things. It was the fact that this place was never quiet that really got to him. Didn't matter if it was day or night, there were always sounds. Clanking, screaming, crying, yelling, rattling, howling, banging. He'd tried stuffing his sheet in his ears, covering them with his hands, humming under his breath, but nothing drowned any of it out. He'd never really paid attention to noise before prison, only knew that he liked the quiet, but now sound was everywhere.

When he was a kid, classmates had made fun of him for all kinds of things—his ratty clothes, his missing mom, how hard he breathed right before he lost his temper. But a favorite had been standing next to him and pretending they could feel a breeze blow clean through his ears, one side to the other. He wasn't so dumb that he didn't get what they were saying—his head was empty—but he hadn't really understood the joke. But now he thought maybe he did. Because all this constant noise made him realize that before prison most days his head was quiet. He could work a ten-hour shift in Merl's garage, look up and see it was quitting time, and nothing would have gone through his mind except a few thoughts about which wrench to use. As a teenager, Dean sometimes couldn't sleep at night, tossing and turning in his narrow bed across from Roy's, keeping them both awake. In the morning, when Roy asked him why he hadn't slept, Dean would say, "Couldn't turn my brain off," or "Couldn't get out of my own head," and Roy would have no earthly idea what that meant. But maybe it was like the noise in prison. A constant rumble you couldn't escape. He wouldn't have liked that, wondered how Dean ended up with a brain so different from his.

But he wouldn't have to listen much longer. They'd set the date for his execution finally. His lawyer had come to give him the news, not realizing one of the guards had already spilled the beans. Some guards were like that. They loved passing out bad news. But Roy hadn't reacted when he'd been told, and he could tell that pissed the guard off. Especially because Roy could usually be counted on to lash out, give the guards an excuse to take out their frustration. Even when Roy's brain knew better, his fists never quite got the message. But learning his execution date hadn't bothered him much, definitely not enough to throw a punch. It was hard for Roy to get worked up about dying. Not when he'd never cared that much about living in the first place.

He worried about his grandma, but only a little. Dean would take care of her. Dean was good at that kind of stuff. And it didn't occur to him to worry about Dean—his strong, smart older brother. Dean would be fine. And he didn't worry about himself, either. Whatever was going to happen to him was going to happen. He couldn't change any of it now. And really, he wasn't sure he would if he could. Maybe not killing those kids. Even though he'd thought it was the right thing to do at the time, maybe it hadn't been. He got upset when he thought about it too much, confused and anxious, angry about how wrong things had turned out in the end. So most of the time he chose to pretend it hadn't happened. But the rest of that summer? He wasn't sorry for any of it. It was the happiest he'd ever been.

He'd asked for chicken-fried steak and twice-baked potatoes for his last meal. Figured he didn't have to eat a vegetable like his grandma always said, not this time. And strawberry shortcake. He knew it wouldn't be as good as his grandma's, with the homemade biscuits and fresh whipped cream, but that was okay. It would still remind him of the best meals he used to eat around the table with his family.

Yesterday there'd been a visit from the prison chaplain, which was like a minister, he'd found out. He'd only agreed to meet with the guy because his grandma had begged, wanted him to get right with the Lord before he died. Roy thought that was stupid and a waste of everybody's time, but he did it because Dean said he should. "Don't make this any harder on Gram than it already is, you selfish asshole" had been Dean's exact words. In the past that would have led to them rolling around on the ground, beating the shit out of each other. But what was Roy going to do now? He couldn't exactly reach through the glass and punch Dean in the face. Besides, could be Dean had a point.

The chaplain had asked him if he was going to say anything before the execution, any final thoughts. "About what?" Roy'd asked, and the chaplain had sighed. "About what you did, Roy. Anything that might help the families find some closure." But those kids were already dead; Roy didn't see how anything he said or did now could make a difference. "The families are going to be there?" he'd asked instead. "The dead kids' families?" He pictured them watching him through the glass. Watching him maybe crap his pants or drool and jerk around on the table. It was the closest he'd felt to panic since he'd learned his execution date. According to the chaplain, the boy's mom was coming. But Eliza's family probably wouldn't be there. "Word would still get back to them about anything you said," the chaplain told him, like that was a good thing. Roy shrugged, promised to think about it. But he'd never been good at talking. He wished there was a way to explain what he'd been

218 • Amy Engel

trying to do that night. But he barely understood what had happened himself, didn't think there was any way he could make someone else understand. And even if he could, he'd still pulled the trigger. He'd been the one to fire that gun.

Dean had asked him a hundred times, especially at the beginning, why he'd done it. Or if someone else had been part of it. Dean kept saying that maybe Roy knew something that would help him get a lighter sentence, like life in prison. Something besides the death penalty. But Roy had kept his mouth shut. Hadn't said a word. Because it wasn't only his secret to tell. He was proud of that one thing, if nothing else. He knew how to keep secrets. How to protect people. Just like he'd never told anyone that he'd liked pulling the trigger, all the anger and resentment and uncertainty he lived with every day bursting out along with the bullets. It had been a release to watch the blood flow, to know that he was the one in control. For those few minutes, his entire life made sense. He knew exactly what he was doing and exactly why he was doing it. But he hadn't thought much about what would come after. The handcuffs on his wrists, the trial he barely understood, the tears on his grandma's face, the disappointment in Dean's eyes. He knew now that he'd done a bad thing. He wasn't so dumb that he didn't realize that. But a bad thing for what he'd thought was a good reason? He had to believe that was something different.

He wasn't scared yet, but he knew he would be as the day got closer. Could feel the fear churning just behind his ribs, dark and snapping, gathering strength. He hoped he'd be able to look through the glass and see Dean in the final seconds, focus on at least one face that didn't hate him. Before he'd left, the chaplain had talked about forgiveness in heaven, but Roy wasn't looking for that. He didn't care about angels and pearly gates. He didn't need mercy or a warm white light. Quiet, silence, an endless nothing. That's all he wanted from what came after.

Chapter Seventeen

We rarely used our living room. It was a formal space my grandparents had carved out, and all these years later it still held the original furnishings. A stiff horsehair sofa that poked the back of your legs when you shifted against its cushions. Heavy dark wood tables and floral draperies that smelled faintly of the mothballs my grandmother had sewn into the linings. My grandparents were long dead now, but the living room had remained untouched. Probably because we never really needed the space. There was a family room addition off of the kitchen, with a comfy sectional sofa and a television big enough for a crowd. And my dad had his study on the second floor—a cigar retreat before Eliza died, his own personal speakeasy now that she was gone. Over time, the living room became the place where we had serious family discussions, the formality of the room lending itself to weightier topics: a bad grade in school, a necessary cutting back on spending money, a grounding after missing curfew or talking back to our mother. Or, like tonight, a daughter's betrayal.

I'd come through the front door exhausted, wanting nothing more than to take a hot bath and then fall into bed. For once thankful that my parents weren't interested in interacting, that we could all go about our separate lives and barely cross paths. But I'd been greeted by my mother standing in the doorway of the living room. "Greer," she'd said. "Please come in here. We need to talk."

She'd sounded exactly like the mother of my teenage years, and I'd been hit by a powerful sense of déjà vu. Was I fourteen again? But a quick glance in the hallway mirror confirmed I was an adult now, one with dark smudges under her eyes and panic in her gaze. I knew what this sudden meeting was about. I'd known it would come, but still felt unprepared. My second shock of the evening came when I walked into the living room and found my father sitting in one of the armchairs next to the fireplace, no bourbon in hand and his eyes only half glassy.

My mother took a seat on the prickly sofa, gestured for me to sit beside her. But I remained standing, leaning in the doorway with my arms crossed. Trying to project nonchalance, a touch of defiance, already. But my heart hammered in painful beats. I didn't want to do this. I wished there was some way to make it stop.

"We heard about you and Dean Mathews," my mother said.

I had a sudden vision of Dean and me tangled together on the floor of the refinery, his hand on my breast and my tongue in his mouth. I knew that wasn't what she'd meant, or at least I hoped it wasn't. The PG-rated version was already bad enough. I wanted to deny, but that would only be prolonging the inevitable. I owed them the truth of it, at the very least.

"We're friends," I said softly. "He's not a bad person."

My dad made a strangled sound, like he was choking on a mouthful of booze. "How could you?" he rasped.

"What would Eliza say?" my mom asked.

"He didn't kill Eliza!" I said, voice rising. "And she was always the very first person to forgive." Actually, I had no idea what Eliza would think about me befriending the closest blood relation of the man who'd blown her brains out. "I'm not trying to hurt you," I said, working to lower my voice.

"Then what are you trying to do?" My mother worried her hands together, her raw knuckles scraping.

"I don't know," I admitted. And that was the awful truth of it. I'd thought when I'd come back to Ludlow that I'd known what I was looking for, that my purpose was laid out clear as an X on a map. But as the days went by, I felt more adrift than ever, running in circles, looking for clues that weren't there, finding answers that only led to more questions. Distrusting the people I loved, looking at familiar faces and seeing strangers instead. Putting my trust in someone I barely knew. I was lost and had no idea how to be found.

"This has to stop," my dad said. "We're your parents and we're telling you it has to stop."

I looked at him, this man who'd always played Abraham Lincoln during Ludlow's Fourth of July celebration. Not only because he was tall and gangly but because he radiated an honest-to-god goodness. Tom Dunning was a man you could trust, a man you could depend on. Except when it came to his own family. How long had it been since I'd been able to count on him for anything at all? Rage flared inside me, boiling over as it rose, my cheeks hot and burning. "Are you fucking kidding me?" I said. "Neither one of you has been my parent since the day Eliza died. And now you're going to sit here and lecture me? Tell me what I can and can't do?"

"Greer, we—" My mom had half risen in her seat, her hand outstretched toward me.

"I *needed* you!" I screamed, all my anger and resentment unmoored. Nothing left to hold it back or temper it. It was loose now, and we were all going to suffer for it. "Eliza was the one who died, but you were both gone, too. I was just a kid. Scared, confused, grieving. I needed someone to talk to, someone to trust, and all I had left was a missing-in-action dad and a mom who wouldn't look me in the eye!"

"That's not true," my mom protested, but her voice was weak.

She'd stopped reaching out for me, her arm back at her side. "That's not how it was."

"It is, though," I told her. "That's exactly how it was. The past isn't something you can change, Mom." I pointed at my dad, who was slumped back in his chair, eyes half closed. His pathetic attempt at momentary sobriety already fading. "You're going to look me in the face and tell me it's not true? Neither one of you gets to tell me how to live my life," I said, voice shaking. "You have no say. I've gone this long without parents. It's too late now. I don't need you anymore."

When I left the room, my father had covered his face with both hands, my mother silently weeping on the sofa. Both of them looking old and broken and alone. I'd said I wasn't trying to hurt them. But that turned out to be just one more lie.

. . . .

I'd wasted almost an entire day sprawled across my bed. A kind of numb inertia had settled over me, and I couldn't bring myself to move. I didn't want to leave my room and stumble across my parents, watch the pain and betrayal flash across their faces. I still hadn't heard from Cassie or Ryan and refused to be the first to reach out. That would feel like admitting something I wasn't ready to concede. Cassie was usually the one to break in these situations, making a peace offering neither Ryan nor I could resist. But thus far my phone had remained stubbornly silent.

I wasn't quite ready to give up and go back to Chicago, back to a job where most days I couldn't be sure I wasn't doing more harm than good. But I also didn't know what steps to take next. I had a feeling Dean either had already decided he was done looking for answers or was quickly heading in that direction. Without him, I felt unsure. It was easier to stumble around blindly in the dark, crashing into people's lives and making a mess of things, when you had someone just as lost right next to you.

So it was something of a relief when Dean called. I had almost expected never to hear from him again, the search for the truth about his brother slowly fading until its importance seemed distant, like a half-remembered dream. Maybe I'd be able to let it go, finally. But seeing Dean's name on my phone screen disabused me of that notion. I scrambled up to sitting, practically dropping my phone in my haste to answer the call.

Dean's voice sounded hollow and tinny in my ear, like he was calling from the bottom of a well. "Where are you?" I asked.

"Grandma's garage," he said. "I'm helping her clean out some old crap." He paused. "I think I may have found something."

"What?" I asked, sliding off the bed and already shoving my feet into sneakers.

"Can we meet?" he asked. "I'd rather talk about it in person."

He gave me directions to a spot on the outskirts of town, a place he said would be private and with low risk of being seen. I almost told him it didn't matter, my parents and probably the whole town of Ludlow already privy to our relationship. But despite what I'd said to my parents last night, there was a difference between them knowing about Dean and me and throwing it right in their faces. I guess I still had some kindness left in me after all.

The directions Dean gave me led to a barely paved country road surrounded on both sides by fields. The road itself didn't have an official name; most people called it "out there by Carl Murdock's place" because it was technically a dead end that dumped out onto Carl's land. But beyond where the road ended was a pond I knew people sometimes used for fishing. Carl never minded so long as they didn't make fresh ruts on his land and cleaned up after themselves. Dean had told me to meet him at the pond, and as I trudged across the open field toward the water, I felt a whisper of unease. Why here? And why now? But I told myself I was being paranoid, the past days of mistrust and anger burrowing into my head and kicking up dust.

Dean was standing at the edge of the pond, his back to me as I approached. He had his hands stuffed into the front pockets of his jeans, and even without being able to see his face, I could picture it clearly—pensive, serious, a little sad. I wondered if Dean had ever been carefree, if he'd ever been a kid who careened through the world with a permanent grin on his face. I couldn't picture it; he'd probably had to fight for every single smile.

"Hey," I said, not wanting to startle him, although he had to have heard my feet cutting across the autumn-stunted prairie grass. A cow lowed in the distance, a small huddle of them gathered around a weather-scarred water trough.

Dean turned his head and looked at me. "Hey," he said. He didn't smile at the sight of me, and that fact pained me more than it should have.

"This is an interesting spot," I said, joining him at the edge of the pond. A warning light flashed in my brain—*danger, danger, danger*—and I kept my gaze averted. A couple of fat bullfrogs, big as kittens, peered at us from the edge of the water, and I eyed them warily. As a kid, I'd always balked at swimming in ponds, had an irrational fear that a bullfrog would swim up from the depths and sink needle-sharp teeth into my flesh. No amount of reassurance from my parents would dissuade me from my conviction. I thought about telling Dean so he could make fun of me, but he didn't seem in the mood for childhood stories.

"Roy liked to come out here sometimes," he said. "It was a good spot to fish and not that many people knew about it. He didn't have to worry about anybody giving him shit or starting a fight. He told me once he liked how quiet it was." He shifted his body, and I felt his gaze burning into the side of my face. "But you prob-ably knew that already, didn't you?"

The whole world went still and silent, my head filled with static fuzz and cotton, my breathing short and labored like I was being suffocated. "What are you talking about?" I meant to sound fero-cious, a lion attacking, But I was only a rabbit, caught in a snare. Because from the second Dean had told me to meet him here, some part of me had known this was coming.

"My grandma never said the kittens were under the porch," he said, turning to face me fully. "The ones that Roy saved. During the trial she said he saved some kittens. But not where he found them."

"Yes, she did," I protested. "I remember."

"Stop fucking lying to me!" Dean yelled, and I flinched back-ward. "I knew you were holding something back that day in the cemetery when you mentioned the kittens. I could feel it, see it in the way you kept messing with your hair, fidgeting. I tried to tell myself I was being paranoid, tried to forget about it. But I couldn't. Because the last time I ignored a gut feeling, something terrible happened. So you know where I spent today? In my grandma's ga-rage, like I told you. Digging through boxes of crap for the trial transcripts. Roy's attorney had ordered a copy, but when Roy didn't want to file any appeals, he shipped them to us. I sat on that con-crete floor flipping through the pages. I read every goddamn word of my grandma's testimony, Greer. She never said anything about the porch. Don't you dare fucking stand here and tell me that she did."

I covered my face with both hands, told myself to breathe as silvery spots swam against my closed eyelids. This was the thing I'd been waiting for, the dark, hidden corners of my memory blown wide open, all my secrets spilling out into daylight. But now that the moment was here, I wasn't ready. Realizing too late that I was never going to be ready. I felt Dean's fingers rough in my hair, a stinging tug against my scalp.

"Roy was the one who told you the kittens were under the porch. You were the girl in his truck, weren't you? The one my grandma saw that summer. The one with the ponytail."

I nodded, trying to find my voice. "Yes," I managed, a hoarse rasp against my throat.

"Jesus Christ," Dean said. He sounded almost surprised, like there'd been a part of him, maybe a big part, that had hoped it was all a mistake.

I dropped my hands and looked at him. "I didn't know how to tell you. I didn't know how to tell anyone. Not before Eliza. And definitely not after."

"It's pretty goddamn simple, Greer. You open your mouth and say the words: 'I was fucking Roy Mathews.'"

"I wasn't," I said, shaking my head. "We just hung out for a while that summer, messed around a little, went on drives."

Dean stared at me. "You're gonna argue word choice with me now?" He shook his head. "How the hell did it even start?"

"At the refinery," I said. It had been a day in mid-July, hot and sticky, the minutes creeping by like hours. Eliza had been off with Travis. Cassie was babysitting, and Ryan had been busy helping his mom with something around the house. I'd felt restless for months already, itchy under my skin in that way only sixteen-year-olds can understand. I was bored of Ludlow, bored of the small circle of my life, bored of myself. And I hadn't felt like there was anyone I could talk to about it. Eliza and I had never been the kind of sisters who held late-night gab sessions, spilling our hopes and dreams and fears to each other. I could have confided in Ryan or Cassie, or even my parents, but a stubborn kernel in my gut refused to let me do it. I wanted to nurture this angst, had some stupid adolescent idea that it was changing me somehow into the person I was always meant to be. So sure I was the first and only girl who had ever felt this way.

It had been impulse that had led me to the refinery. Technically I wasn't allowed to drive outside of town; my parents would have grounded me for weeks if they'd found out. But I was feeling defiant, angry for no good reason, almost desperate to be caught doing something bad. It's no wonder parents are always terrified for their teenagers. The horrible split-second decisions we make, with no thought to the consequences, enough to keep even the most laid-back of parents up in the wee hours of the night.

The afternoon sun had been blisteringly hot, the kind of rays that made you wince when they fell on the back of your neck like a sticky hand. It had been a comfort to step through the doorway into the shadowy refinery, even with its trash-lined floor and history of bad deeds. At first I'd thought I was alone. I hadn't noticed another car parked in the weedy gravel lot, only found out later that Roy always pulled around back, the risk of a popped tire from all the old lumber and nails littering the ground worth it to have his truck hidden from any curious cops who happened by.

I'd heard him before I'd seen him. The sharp sound of shattering glass almost wrenching a scream from my throat. I'd managed to reel it back in at the very last second, nails pressing into the tender flesh of my palms. He hadn't noticed me yet, his back to where I stood frozen in the shadows. He had a paper grocery sack at his feet, and as I watched, he reached down and pulled out a green beer bottle, drew his arm back, and let the bottle fly with a harsh flick of his wrist. This time I was prepared for the sound, and instead of startling me, it made something close to relief flow through me. An unwinding, a loosening of too many things held tight.

"Hey," I said before I thought about whether I should. "Can I try?"

Roy turned so fast one of his tennis shoes skidded on the concrete floor, his leg sliding away from him. He righted himself quickly, eyes darting around the room. His hand fell to his back pocket, where I'd later learn he always carried an ancient switchblade. One of his eyes was swollen shut, and his upper lip was split, the knuckles of his throwing hand caked with dried blood. "Who are you?" he asked finally.

"Greer," I said, stepping closer. "What happened to your face?"

"Fight," he said, like it was a stupid question.

"Can I throw a bottle?"

He glanced down at the bag, shrugged broad shoulders. "I guess."

I reached in and took a heavy brown bottle, hefting the weight in my hand.

"Aim for the corner," Roy said. "Where the walls meet. Don't want any pieces flying back." His voice was deep and rusty, like he didn't have a lot of practice using it, and his words came slow. Not like he was dumb, exactly, but as if he had to think about what each word meant before it left his tongue.

I cocked my arm and threw the bottle as hard as I could, all my frustration and directionless anger sailing through the air along with the glass. When it shattered against the wall, I whooped, raising both hands in the air and doing a little shimmy. Next to me, Roy grunted in what might have been approval.

We'd taken turns with the rest of the bottles, slowly adding to the pile of glass shards on the floor. Once the bottles were gone, Roy finally introduced himself, pointed to a six-pack of beer against the wall. "Want one? We can throw the empties when we're done. If you want." He sounded almost shy, like he was asking me out on a date instead of offering me beer bottles for smashing.

I'd only ever had sips of my parents' wine, shared the dregs of a stolen bottle of whiskey that Ryan had brought to the gazebo one night. But I nodded like I was an old pro, sat on the dirty floor with this boy I didn't know, and opened a bottle. I knew I was being stupid, that probably thousands of girls the world over had ended up raped or murdered in exactly this way. But I was suddenly enamored with the idea of myself as a girl who took risks. A girl who befriended someone most people would have avoided. I was brave and I was wild, and nobody looking at me right then would think Greer Dunning was destined for a boring, safe life. Too young to understand that being able to take a boring, safe life for granted was a gift.

"Roy was different from my other friends," I said to Dean, cutting into my own memories. "And I was desperate for something different that summer. I was sixteen, and I was bored, and dumb, and so young." I swallowed a sob. "I don't have a better reason than that. I wish I did."

"Did you even like him?" Dean asked. "Or were you just fucking with him?"

"He was hard to like," I admitted. "He barely talked. He had a chip on his shoulder so huge I couldn't even begin to navigate around it. But he gave me something I needed that summer." I remembered riding around in Roy's crappy pickup, ducking down below the window line when we were in Ludlow, popping up again when we turned onto the wide-open roads. When we pulled into some random field, I let Roy kiss me, push his hands under my T-shirt, and pull down my bra. Never further than that. We shared cheeseburgers and Cokes from Sonic, chewing the ice pellets until my teeth screamed. He always paid, even when I offered. Now I knew he'd been stealing money from Merl to fund our dates, being able to pull out his wallet and buy me something more important to him than keeping his job. We threw bottles at the refinery and fished in this pond. Some days, we barely spoke a word. Other days, I talked and talked, eventually managing to pull a story or two from Roy like drawing water from a dank, hidden well. Roy was both my friend, in the loosest sense of the word, and my darkest, deepest shame. I wasn't fucking with him in the way Dean meant, but was I using him? Probably I was.

"Wow," Dean said, shaking his head. "I have to hand it to you. You managed to get both of us right where you wanted us, didn't you? All the sneaking around you and I've been doing, winding me around your finger, it must have seemed like old times."

"I didn't . . . that's not—"

"How did you convince Roy to kill Eliza?" he asked, talking over my feeble protest. "What did you promise him?"

I took a step backward, stumbling a little on the uneven ground. "No," I said. "I never even mentioned Eliza to him."

Dean raised his eyebrows. "You expect me to believe that? You were seeing my brother in secret. You've never told anyone about it. And he just happened to pick your sister and her boyfriend to murder? And then you randomly get a heart saying it was all for you? Come the fuck on, Greer. Nobody is dumb enough to believe that bullshit story."

"But it's the truth," I said, frantically trying to think of some way to get him to believe me. Knowing that my word was no longer even close to good enough. "Hanging out with Roy was the only thing I lied about."

Dean's laugh was harsh, scraping along my skin. "That's a pretty big omission."

"I know it is, but I never told Roy to kill anyone. I never hinted at it or even thought about it. I loved my sister. And Roy never said anything to me about wanting to hurt someone that way. I would have told Sheriff Baker if he had."

"Oh, yeah? Because you've managed to keep your mouth shut about Roy for years."

"Roy was my secret that summer. But we weren't hurting anyone. It didn't seem like anyone's business but ours. And it's not like we were ever a real couple. I knew from the first second I met him that we had a short shelf life. By the time Eliza died, we were already winding down. I wasn't showing up every time we were supposed to meet. I never even gave him my phone number. It was going to fizzle out. I didn't see the point in telling anyone. And after the murders . . ." I trailed off, not able, even after all this time, to give voice to the confusion and disbelief I'd felt the day I opened the newspaper and saw Roy's face staring back at me. It was like my whole world stopped, and it had never really started spinning again. "How could I tell anyone then? My parents were broken into a thousand pieces. The whole town was terrified and angry. Everyone would have thought exactly what you did, that I had something to do with it. I tried, though, in my own chickenshit way. I kept pushing and pressing, saying Roy wouldn't have acted alone, that there had to be something more to uncover. But nobody listened and then the heart showed up." I sucked in a breath. "I was sixteen, Dean, and too scared to do the right thing."

"You're not sixteen anymore," he pointed out, voice hard. "You're a grown woman."

"I know," I said, the words shaking on my exhale. "But so much time passed, and every year it got more impossible to open my mouth. I stayed away and tried to forget instead, buried it where I didn't have to think about it. And I've had to live with that every day since."

Dean cocked his head at me. "Are you seriously asking me to feel sorry for you right now?" Throwing my words from that first night at the Do back in my face. They were more painful than I'd thought they would be, made me sorry I'd ever aimed them at him. But isn't that always the way? We never fully understand the pain of something until we're on the receiving end; before that, it's all a game of pretend.

I shook my head, more tired than I'd ever been. I didn't want to stand there and make excuses or try to justify what I'd done. We were long past any of that.

"Then what?" he said. "You broke up with him, and your sister and Travis ended up dead?"

"We never actually broke up. Mainly because, at least in my mind, we weren't really together anyway. But he was angry when I pulled back. Hurt. He'd be aloof when we did meet up. Then press me to make future plans even if I told him I was busy. I think he thought we were more serious than we were."

"Of course he did. You were probably the best thing that ever happened to him."

"I couldn't have been that special," I protested, wanting to wrench away from the hot twist of guilt in my gut. "He was still seeing Libby the entire time."

"Because he was hedging his bets, Greer. Roy wasn't book smart, but he had decent instincts. He probably knew, on some level he didn't even want to acknowledge, that you weren't going to stick around."

"Maybe he was angry enough at me that he decided to kill Eliza?"

"No way," Dean said. "He wouldn't do that."

"How can you be sure?"

"I just am. Remember when I told you Roy was loyal? That loyalty didn't end when someone hurt him or abandoned him." He pushed his hair back and pointed to a scar along his hairline I'd never noticed before. "Roy gave me this when we were kids. After our mom walked out and never came back. I said something shitty about her. I can't even remember what. And Roy picked up a rock, a big, jagged thing, and clocked me right in the head with it. He couldn't stand, even after what she'd done, to hear a word against her. There's no way he would have hurt someone you loved to get back at you."

"Why then?" I practically screamed. "Why did he do it?"

"Because someone told him to," Dean said. "Someone told him it would help you."

I did it. For you.

"That's what I'm still trying to figure out," I said. "That's why I came back after all this time. I want to know the whole story. Including my part in it. I want the truth."

"Except you wouldn't know the truth if it bit you on the ass," he said. "All these weeks we've been trying to figure things out and you've been keeping a huge piece of the puzzle from me. Did you think we'd get to the end and your relationship with Roy would never come out?"

"No," I said softly. "I was tired of hiding it. I'm glad you know." Some part of me had wanted to tell him from the beginning, wanted him to be the person to hear it first. To know his brother had done his best to treat me well. Every moment Dean and I had spent together, the more I'd wanted to come clean. But, just like with Dylan's and Addy's murders, I'd waited too long. Fear and shame dragging my feet, turning me into a coward.

Dean laughed again. "Well, I'm not. I wish I'd never figured it out. I wish I'd never talked to you that day on the bench. It was better when you were just some girl whose life we'd ruined. At least then I didn't hate you."

"Please," I said, voice breaking, but I had no real idea what I was asking for.

"Please what?" he demanded. "Please forget you're a fucking liar? Please forgive you? Please don't tell anyone?" He threw up his hands. "We're done," he said, already walking away. "This is done."

I didn't try to run after him, cling to his arm, and attempt to change his mind. There was nothing I could possibly say to undo any of it. I wondered, sometimes, why it was a lesson I felt destined to learn over and over again.

Chapter Eighteen

didn't remember getting back to my car, felt drunk or high or suspended outside my body. I wasn't particularly surprised to find myself driving the back roads instead of heading toward town. The relief I'd always anticipated feeling in this moment—the solace of unburdening—hadn't arrived. Fear and guilt still wound a tight fist inside my stomach. As it turned out, Dean knowing didn't make the thought of everyone else knowing, too, any easier to bear.

I let my eyes drift closed for a second, breathed in the scent of autumn through my open window, both musty and crisp. Felt the breeze float over my face. I opened my eyes, saw the late-afternoon sun shining golden, landing with an amber twinkle against the grass. What was it about autumn light that made the passage of time so apparent? That made a hot lump of unshed tears form in my throat. No other season made me think of weeks passing, years gone, time wasted the way autumn did. The light itself a whispered reminder that there are a finite number of days left, for all of us.

I tried to conjure up the sound of Eliza's laugh and found I no longer could. Had trouble even with the tone of her voice. Had it been higher than mine? Deeper? My answer depended on the day. I felt guilty that I didn't miss her more. That the destruction of our family in the wake of her absence and the unintentional part I'd somehow played in her death were more painful than her actual loss. What kind of sister did that make me? What kind of person? I could no longer find the point where my guilt ended and my sorrow began. Tears rolled down the sides of my face and gathered in the hollows of my neck.

I drove until after darkness fell, trying to work up the courage to go home and confess everything to my parents. But when my almost empty gas tank forced me back to Ludlow, I found myself at the diner instead, pushing pieces of reheated meatloaf and mashed potato around my plate without eating any of it. I'd clearly been full of shit when I told Dean I was ready to stop hiding things because I didn't seem to be in much of a hurry to tell the truth.

It was long past regular Ludlow dinner hours and I was the only customer in the diner, all of Main Street empty and quiet. Across from me Mabel busied herself wiping down the counter, probably hoping I'd hurry up and finish so she could lock up and go home.

"What happened there?" I asked, pointing with my fork to a couple of broken chairs stacked to the right of the door. My voice sounded dull and lifeless, asking a question with no real interest in the answer.

Mabel clucked her tongue, coming around from behind the counter to top off my cup of decaf. "Garrett Bloom and his friends were in here earlier causing a ruckus. Drunk as skunks, all of them, and in foul moods, too."

My hand stilled on its way to reaching for the mug, eyes darting around the diner like Garrett might be hiding in the corner or underneath a table, waiting to jump out and teach me a lesson about squealing. "I'm guessing Sheriff Baker would have something to say about one of his deputies tearing up this place."

Mabel cocked her head. "He's not a deputy anymore. Haven't you heard? Got fired over some mess with Amber Stevens."

In the moment when I'd told Baker about Garrett, I hadn't cared what came afterward. And the fact was, Garrett deserved to be fired. But I couldn't help the way my stomach turned over, the little frisson of fear that lanced up my spine. Garrett wasn't the kind of guy to look at his own actions and take stock of what he'd done wrong. He would always find a way to place the full weight of blame on someone else. I wouldn't want to be Amber right now, and things probably weren't looking too good for me, either. "Do you know what happened?" I asked.

"From what I heard, Sheriff Baker'd suspected something wasn't kosher for a while. But it was only a suspicion until a few days ago. Somebody ratted Garrett out, and he was too caught off guard to even deny it. Losing his job over Amber Stevens." Mabel shook her head, started clearing away my still-full plate. "Sometimes that boy's dumber than dirt."

I left a twenty-dollar bill on the table while Mabel was in the kitchen and slipped out the back door into the alley. My car was parked in the tiny lot beside the grocery store, and my footsteps sounded loud in the stillness of the night, as if I was announcing my presence to the entire town, even though there was no one around to hear me. I had my keys in my hand, resisting the sudden urge to look over my shoulder, when I slowed, came to a stop. Someone had scratched the word "CUNT" across the driver's side of my car, the letters huge and jagged, paint scraped away in violent gouges.

I started forward again, moving faster, when a dark shape lunged around the back of my car, slamming my hip against the door and grabbing my wrist before I could get my keys up. "You fucking bitch," Garrett said, breath hot and rank with whiskey fumes. "I oughta kill you."

I pushed back hard, but he didn't move, his whole body pressed against mine. "Get off me," I said, chest heaving. I tried to use the car as leverage, shoved him again, but it was like trying to shift a brick wall. My back screamed where it was pinned against the sharp edge of my car window.

"I was always good to you," Garrett said from between clenched teeth. "And this is how you treat me?"

He was crying, I realized, the knowledge shocking me into momentary stillness. Tears and snot mingled on his face, his cheeks ruddy and eyes bloodshot.

"Garrett," I said, "I—"

Suddenly, his weight lifted off me, his body spinning away. Behind him, Eric had ahold of his shoulder, pulling him backward. "Come on, man," Eric said. "That's enough. She's not worth it."

We both watched as Garrett stumbled toward the street, still mumbling under his breath, and then Eric took a step in my direction. I shrank back, but he didn't touch me, his upper lip curled like he smelled something rotten. "You need to learn to mind your own fucking business, Greer. Go back to Chicago. You don't belong here anymore."

He held a beer bottle in his hand and he raised it as he walked away. For a second I thought he meant to throw it at my head and my arms came up automatically, but it smashed into the ground at my feet instead. A sharp explosion of glass, beer foaming around my shoes.

It was a long time before my hands were steady enough to drive. In that moment, there was no one I could call, I realized. Not a single person who wanted to hear from me. No one I hadn't disappointed. Not Cassie or Ryan. Not my parents. Not even Dean. The loneliness felt like death, heavy and suffocating. I could barely find enough air to breathe. I had finally burned every last one of my bridges, and I was choking on the flames.

. . . .

I went home and fell into bed, suffered bloated, sticky dreams. Roy morphing into Dean and back again. Eliza trying to speak around a mouth crammed full of rotting autumn leaves. Amber chasing me through a wheat field, the stalks sharp as razors when they flicked against my skin. Cassie and Ryan howling with laughter as they watched me run. Even after twelve hours of sleep, I woke fuzzy-headed and exhausted. I lay there for a while, listening to the silence of a half-dead house. My face felt swollen from crying, my vision blurred through puffy eyelids.

Eventually I dragged myself off the bed and shuffled into Eliza's room, a spot I'd avoided since the day of my return. I was hit all over again with its bland emptiness. Had my mother boxed up all Eliza's things, her dog-eared books, tangles of jewelry, and over-sized sweaters, and donated them to the Goodwill in Neosho? Or, worse, loaded them into garbage bags and put them out for the trash? I couldn't imagine it. My mother might not have wanted reminders every day, but I didn't think she had the stomach to rid herself of Eliza's possessions entirely.

The attic access in our house was in Eliza's closet through a panel in the ceiling that when pulled down released a rickety ladder. We usually only went up there twice a year, to drag down the boxes of Christmas ornaments stored under the eaves and then, after New Year's, to put them back again. But it was my mother's favored storage spot for things she couldn't bring herself to part with but didn't want cluttering up the house, either. The set of dishes she'd inherited from her own mother but deemed too ugly to use, an old dressmaker's mannequin that had been pressed into duty for a single summer when she'd had the idea she might start making some of our clothes, my dad's long-forgotten coffee mug collection. If

Eliza's things were still here, if she'd kept the photo Faith had seen, the attic was where they'd be.

The ladder was even more precarious than I remembered, missing a rung near the middle and squeaking ominously under my weight. Although it was autumn outside, the mornings sharp with oncoming winter, the attic was stuffy and close, as if all the summer heat had permeated the wood and couldn't find a way out again. Everything was as I remembered it except for a collection of boxes and plastic totes stacked against the far wall near the tiny gable window. I scrambled up the final step and stood on the narrow walkway of planks my dad had laid down the center of the attic to prevent anyone from falling through the insulation and breaking their neck.

As I'd suspected, the new boxes were neatly labeled with Eliza's name and a short description of their contents. I bypassed the ones labeled "Clothes" and "Bedding" and homed in on the two marked "Personal Belongings." I managed to make myself comfortable on the makeshift floor and opened the lid of the first box. The smell of dust and roses hit me in the face, the source of the smell apparent when I saw the desiccated remains of Eliza's junior prom corsage laid carefully on the top. I remembered the night Travis had slid it onto her wrist. White roses I'd deemed boring, but Eliza had been thrilled to receive. She'd kept it on the top of her dresser, slowly withering away, until the day she died.

I plucked the corsage gingerly from the pile and set it aside. Underneath were stacks of novels, her scrapbooks, a diary I'd already secretly read, although there wasn't much to glean from its pages. Eliza had been an indifferent chronicler of her own life. When I'd first picked the flimsy lock at fourteen, I'd been hoping for something juicy, or at least some venom aimed at me I could throw back in her face the next time we fought. But had instead been greeted with semiannual entries documenting what we'd eaten for Christmas dinner or her latest grade in English. It had hardly been worth the effort to snoop.

The rest of the box contained a shoebox filled with makeup and jewelry and a random assortment of congealed nail polishes. I lifted out the lipstick Eliza always wore, a pale pink almost the same color as her lips, and smoothed it over the back of my hand. Rubbed it in until only a faint shimmer remained. Eliza had done my makeup one night when we were in junior high. The two of us giggling as she tried to give me cat-eyes with black liquid eyeliner purloined from our mom's bathroom drawer. The results had been lopsided, at best. The memory made me ache. I put the lipstick back in the box.

I hoped the rest of her personal items would prove more fruitful, although I had no idea what I was really looking for. Something that illuminated my sister for me, maybe. Made her a living, breathing person again, at least for a few minutes. The second box held her yearbooks; the remains of her garbage wall, each quote carefully removed from the bulletin board and saved; the cards she'd gotten from Travis or our parents over the years; and a couple of truly cringe-worthy poems she'd written at some point. I pictured us sitting here together, laughing at her attempts to rhyme "adore" with "before" and turn it into something profound. Another thing her death had robbed us of, the chance to tease each other, to look back on our teenage years together with a kind of fond disbelief at what idiots we'd been.

At the bottom of the box was a romance novel, something with a bare-chested guy on the cover clutching a woman who could have been either in the throes of an orgasm or suffering a leg cramp, bosom heaving beneath a low-cut ball gown and mouth half open as she swooned. I huffed out an amused breath. I'd never known Eliza was a secret romance reader. I picked up the book and flipped through the pages, stopping when a flurry of paper spilled out.

242 · Amy Engel

They were photographs, I realized, grainy as if they'd been taken with a phone and printed out on regular printer paper. The edges cropped unevenly with a pair of scissors. There were half a dozen of them and they were all of me, taken the summer before Eliza died. What the hell? Me lounging on a towel beside the local pool, a shot from behind as I walked into the grocery store. And the rest, not just me anymore, but me and Roy. My hands went numb, the photos fluttering out of my fingers, the images barreling up at me from the attic floor. Kissing next to the fishing pond, standing over a pile of broken glass at the refinery. Roy and me in his truck, his arm hanging out of the window—the photo Faith had seen on Eliza's desk.

I sucked in a quick breath, tiny dust motes dancing in front of my eyes, the watery light from the window casting shadows I kept trying to blink away. My heart was galloping crazily in my chest, and I couldn't get enough air. How had Eliza taken these? Had she been the prickle on the back of my neck that entire summer? Had this been what she wanted to talk to me about on the night she died? The questions were coming too fast for me to find any answers, each one only bringing more confusion. Why had she been following me? Had she known about Roy the whole time? Why hadn't she said something earlier? I didn't understand, and the only person I could ask to explain was long gone.

Something was nipping at the edges of my brain, some detail I'd overlooked or ignored. I shuffled through the photos again, studying them closely, but the thought wouldn't materialize.

I stuffed the contents of the box back inside and gathered the photos in my hand. I almost toppled down the ladder in my haste to escape the attic, catching myself at the last second with one arm and wrenching my shoulder in the process. The pain barely registered as I slammed the ladder up, shut the attic panel with a bang.

I'd pay for the almost-fall later, but for now adrenaline was taking the edge off.

I grabbed my phone from the top of my dresser and sent Dean a quick text, telling him I'd found something, that it involved Roy, and asking him to text me back. If anyone would know how Roy might have reacted to those photos, it was Dean. I stared at my phone, willing the tiny dots to appear, but they didn't. I called him, and when it went straight to voice mail, I knew he wasn't going to respond. That he'd meant it when he said we were done. I left a message anyway, hating the tiny shake in my voice, the desperate plea behind my words.

I wished there were someone else I could ask, someone who might know what Eliza had been up to. But the only person she would have confided in was as long dead as she was. Was it possible Roy had killed her because he saw her following us? It didn't seem likely, even for someone as volatile as Roy. But what if Eliza had approached Roy, told him to stop seeing me? Would that have been enough for him to pick up a gun? Maybe the shadowy second person I'd always imagined being part of that night had been Eliza herself, unwittingly sealing her own fate when she pushed Roy too far. If that was the case, then her death was more my fault than I'd ever imagined, and I'd imagined a lot.

But if Dean was to be believed, Roy's way would have been to confront Eliza, push right back if she'd pushed him. He didn't plan, or lie in wait. The whole idea didn't feel right. Which I was well aware was a stupid way to decide if something was true or not. But at this point, it was all I had. That nagging feeling in my gut and Eliza's voice in my ear telling me that, finally, I was getting closer.

Chapter Nineteen

n the end, it wasn't Cassie who broke first but Ryan. I'd been sitting in my room most of the day, my phone in my hand, willing Dean to call me back. When my phone finally rang, I didn't even check to see who was calling before I answered. "Hello?" I said, voice just this side of frantic.

There was a pause on the other end, the muffled sound of voices. "Greer?"

"Ryan?" I was so surprised I pulled the phone away from my face, double-checked the screen to be sure.

"Yeah, hey," he said. Another pause. "Listen, I feel shitty about how the three of us left things. Cassie does, too."

"Yeah," I said, relief spooling outward from the tight center of my chest. I'd been more than halfway convinced I might never hear his voice again. "Same. I'm glad you called."

Ryan huffed out a laugh. "I wasn't sure you'd answer."

"Come on," I said. "Have I ever not answered for you or Cassie? No matter how mad I was?"

"Fair enough. I'm still over at Chet's, but I was hoping maybe the three of us could meet up tonight. Clear the air?"

"That sounds good," I said.

"I'll call Cassie. I was thinking we'd grab dinner. Chet had me working through lunch and I'm starving."

"Doesn't sound like Chet to miss a meal." It was still awkward between us, the conversation stiff with tension. But we were making an effort.

Ryan laughed again, a little easier this time. "He's very focused today. Let me get ahold of Cassie, but does six o'clock work for you?"

"Can we make it seven?" I didn't want to tell him this next part, but I also didn't want to keep lying. It only made everything worse when the truth inevitably came out, yesterday by the pond with Dean still cutting deep. "I need to go see Dean real quick."

Ryan sucked in a breath but, to his credit, kept his opinion to himself. "Okay," he said finally.

"I found something in Eliza's things. I'll tell you guys about it at dinner. But I want to show Dean. See what he thinks."

"Greer . . ."

"I know you don't approve of me hanging out with him," I said. "But you have to trust me on this one, Ryan. You and Cassie both. I'm not stupid and I'm not crazy. And this could be something important."

"Neither one of us ever thought you were stupid or crazy. Not for a single second." His voice was harsh and low. I'd hurt him simply by voicing the suspicion, the secret fear I'd carried since Eliza died that somehow I'd gone completely off the rails and everyone could see it but me. "We're worried, that's all. What kind of friends would we be if we weren't?" Ryan sighed. "Do what you need to do, okay?"

"Okay," I said, voice hoarse.

"Text us when you're free to meet up. We'll be waiting."

. . . .

The next time I called Dean, ten minutes after hanging up the phone with Ryan, he answered, his voice clipped and cautious. "You need to stop calling me."

"I know you said you were done," I told him, talking too fast, afraid he'd hang up if I didn't get the words out quickly enough. "But I found some photos in Eliza's stuff that my mom had packed away. I wanted you to see them."

"What kind of photos?"

I lowered my voice, even though I was alone in my room. "Ones of Roy and me that summer. Taken with a phone, I'm pretty sure."

Dean sucked in a breath, released it slowly. "You should show them to Baker," he said finally. "He'll know what to do with them."

I gripped the phone tighter, my stomach knotting. "Dean, please. Will you meet me? Take a look at them, see what you think? I'll go to Baker afterward, I promise." When he didn't respond, I forged ahead. "I'm sorry," I managed. "For everything. I'm sorry." My voice broke, and I jerked the phone upward, hiding my tears.

"Fine," he said. "Meet me at the refinery. I pass right by it on my way home from the farm."

"Okay. I'll leave now. Thank you." I hung up before he could change his mind and scrambled off the bed, shoving my feet into my shoes and the photos into my back pocket.

There were no other cars on the road, just a lone hawk soaring along beside me, then swooping down on what was probably an unsuspecting field mouse. I watched as he took off again, something clutched in his talons. By the time I turned down the road to the refinery, daylight was seeping away and the building looked bigger and uglier backlit by the setting sun. Broken windows and chipped concrete more prominent, barbed wire atop the chain link glinting slightly in the fading light.

Dean's SUV was parked out front, but he wasn't waiting inside it like I'd expected. I turned in my seat and wrestled my jacket out from under the box of Joanne Sawtell's junk I still needed to take to Goodwill. The evening air was already turning cold, autumn barreling fast toward winter when the sun wasn't shining. As I walked toward the fence, something niggled at me again, a tiny pinch at the base of my skull. I stood still for a second, closed my eyes, willing it to form into an actual thought. But it continued to elude me; the harder I reached for it, the faster it receded. Frustrated, I stomped across the gravel and shimmied underneath the chain-link fence, barely avoiding snagging my jacket on the metal in my haste.

I was still moving fast, distracted by what I couldn't put my mental fingers on, when I walked into the refinery. It was gloomy inside, almost dark, and Dean wasn't there. Or at least not anywhere I could see. My feet slowed, stopped. I listened in the growing dark, waiting for something I couldn't name. I should have known right then. Later, I would go over and over it, wondering how things might have been different if I hadn't been so slow.

"Dean?" I called, but not loud. Not a whisper, but most definitely not a shout. Like I was afraid of what might hear me. What answer might come out of the shadows. "Dean? Are you here?"

From above me the sound of something scuffling along the ground. And then Dean's voice, floating down. "Hey, I'm up here." His voice sounded pinched, worried, and the drumbeat of fear inside of me pulsed louder.

"Up where?" I called, still not moving.

"Up here," he answered. He beamed the flashlight from his phone down toward me and back up, where he was standing on the steps. High, up by the catwalk. "You need to see this."

"What?" I asked, but I was already moving, watching myself take the steps one at a time, climbing higher and higher. I passed the landing on the second level and kept going. Focusing on Dean's flashlight above me. When I reached the last step up to the highest landing, the catwalk to my left fading into the darkness, Dean was waiting. His hand was down by his side, the flashlight pointing at the floor so that I could barely see his face.

"What did you want to show me?" I asked, not moving any closer, one hand curled tight around the stair railing. I didn't know why I was afraid; I only knew that I was.

He raised his head and looked at me. "I'm sorry," he said, voice strained. "I tried to—"

The darkness behind him shifted, a shadow, a shape. Familiar and heartbreaking and impossible. It all hit me at once, the things I'd seen but hadn't put together, the things I'd known deep down but hadn't wanted to acknowledge. The photos hidden in a romance novel. The box of old books in the back of my car. A boy who lived to be needed. "No," I said. One foot slipped backward on the steps, and Dean reached out for me, caught my hand, and steadied me. He didn't let go, squeezed my fingers tight. "No," I said again. Like maybe if I kept saying it I could somehow make it untrue.

"It's okay, Greer. It's going to be okay." Ryan stepped out from behind Dean, his voice calm. A gun held lazily in his hand, as if he'd forgotten it was there.

"What . . ." My head was buzzing, my heart tripping, my voice floating away like helium from a spent balloon. The only thing keeping me grounded, tethered to this moment, was Dean's hand in mine. "I don't . . ."

"Come up here," Ryan said, holding out his hand. I took it automatically with my free one, without thinking, the way I had a thousand times before. Together he and Dean helped me onto the platform. But when I was steady, I dropped Ryan's hand, took a step closer to Dean.

"What are you doing here?" I asked. "What's going on? Why do you have a gun?" But I knew all the answers already, felt foolish somehow for having asked the questions.

"He followed me," Dean said, voice hard. "Right?"

Ryan nodded, not looking at Dean, only at me. "When you called, I knew you'd found those photos. Do you know how many times I looked for them over the years? Every time I was home, making excuses to help your mom clean, get stuff boxed up in Eliza's room." He shook his head, chagrined. "Where were they?"

It felt like he was speaking a foreign language, one I'd never heard before, every word taking an eternity to sort itself out inside my head. My own response came out delayed and hollow, the sound of my voice coming from very far away. "In a box in the attic. Inside one of your mom's old romance novels." The detail I'd been missing finally clicking into place.

Ryan laughed a little. "That must have been how Eliza got them out of my house right in front of me. You know my mom would loan a book to anybody." His face sobered. "I never meant for you to see them."

"I don't . . . I don't understand." Panic buzzed low and insistent at the base of my spine, and I wondered if I was in shock. Or if I was dreaming somehow, still tucked safely back in my bed. But Dean's hand in mine was warm and real, the dark of the refinery pressing in on all sides, the smell of damp and dirt heavy in the air.

"He was following you and Roy that summer," Dean said. "Stalking you."

"I wasn't *stalking* her," Ryan bit out. "For fuck's sake, Greer. I was worried about you. You'd been acting weird for weeks, so goddamn grouchy, arguing with us about everything. And then suddenly you seemed happier, but you were never around. You'd gone from irritable and unpredictable to secretive and quiet. None of it was like you. So, I followed you. I wanted to see where you were going, make sure you were safe."

"You had no right to do that," I said. "It wasn't any of your business. I never asked you to take care of me."

"You didn't have to ask," Ryan said, just this side of a shout. "That's what friends do, Greer. We look out for each other."

"You've got a seriously fucked-up idea of friendship," Dean said.

"You"—Ryan raised the gun and pointed it at Dean—"shut the hell up. You're not a part of this."

I squeezed Dean's hand, willing him to be quiet. I wanted Ryan's gaze off of Dean. I wanted that gun lowered. "But why the photos?" I asked, confusion still churning inside my brain, making it hard for me to focus on anything but the gun in Ryan's hand. "What was the point?" I resisted the urge to shake my head in hopes the movement would sort out all the scrambled pieces in my mind, slot everything back in a way that made sense.

Ryan shrugged. "I don't honestly know. At first I took them as proof of what was going on. I guess I thought if you didn't stop, come to your senses, I'd send them anonymously to your parents. Let them know what you were doing, the huge mistake you were making with that guy. They'd put a stop to it. He wasn't a good person, Greer. You have to understand that by now."

As he spoke, his gun hand fell, all of his attention centered on me. I felt Dean tense next to me and fear strangled my throat. I crushed his fingers in mine, trying to keep him still, but he pulled away from me. He lunged forward, quick and silent, hands already grappling for the gun. I heard a grunt of pain, the sounds of panting breaths, Ryan's shout. A blur of bodies and a single gunshot roaring through the darkness.

Dean buckled, went down so fast I couldn't even tell where he'd been shot, although the front of his shirt was already wet with blood. I screamed, tried to bend toward him, but Ryan kicked him hard. And then again. Dean slipped over the edge of the stairs, his body bouncing against the metal risers as he fell. I looked down at his body at the bottom of the steps, twisted and still, waiting for him to pop upright. Waiting for the joke, the laugh, the announcement that this was all the world's most fucked-up joke. "Dean!" I screamed when he failed to move, my voice echoing against the vast expanse of concrete. I took a step forward and Ryan's hand clamped down hard on my upper arm, dragging me back onto the platform. It was all suddenly, painfully, horribly real.

"Shit, shit, shit," Ryan chanted. "I didn't want to do that. I didn't mean to do that. He shouldn't have gone for the gun." He put himself between me and the stairs, pacing slightly in front of me.

"We need to call an ambulance," I said, my voice a high, fast babble. "He needs help."

"We're not calling anybody," Ryan said. "There's nothing they can do for him anyway. And we need to talk."

"*Talk?* There's nothing to talk about! You *shot* him, Ryan." I started forward, and he raised the gun again, not pointing it at me, exactly, but reminding me it was there.

I stopped moving, not really believing he would shoot me, but before this moment I would have put money on him not being able to shoot anyone. "Okay, you want to talk? Let's talk," I said, voice almost a shout. "You were responsible for Eliza and Travis, weren't you?" The answer was right in front of me, but I needed to hear him say the words. "And you killed Dylan and Addy, too?"

Ryan held my gaze. "Yes." He had the audacity to look sad, re-gret cutting across his features. "But, Greer, *I did it for you.*"

The noise that came out of me didn't sound human—the wail of a wild animal caught in a trap, the mourning sound of some creature being ripped apart and left for dead. I sank to my knees, then bent forward at the waist, covered my face with both hands and wept. I heard Ryan move, felt his body next to mine, one of his arms going around me, pulling me into his side. "Shhh," he said. "I'm right here. You're okay. It's okay."

And for a few minutes, I let myself believe that. Let my body sink into his, let myself forget Dean at the base of the stairs, forget what Ryan had done, what I had caused. I cried and howled and pretended it had nothing to do with the man who held me, the boy

I'd loved like a brother for virtually all of my life. But I could only lie to myself for so long. Eventually the tears slowed, and Ryan's arm turned into a vise around me, the smell of blood wafting upward on the cold night air. I pushed away from him, twisting out of his grip. I levered myself to standing and Ryan did the same, the two of us facing off in the near dark.

"How could you?" I said, the words a harsh rasp.

"I didn't want to. I never wanted to hurt anyone. But Eliza found those photos. She was helping my mom around the house one afternoon, sorting through her crap like usual, and I'd left the photos out on my desk. The one time I forgot to hide them." He shook his head. "She confronted me about them, but she wouldn't give them back. I tried to explain myself, tried to make her understand how worried I was. But she didn't care about anything I had to say. She only cared about me following you. She was going to tell you, make it seem like I'd been doing something wrong."

"You had been doing something wrong!" I screamed.

"You were my best friend!" Ryan yelled back. "If Eliza had told you, you'd never have looked at me the same way again."

"I would have understood," I told him. "If you'd explained it to me." But even as I said the words, I didn't know if they were true. Even if I'd forgiven him, he was right—he would have become someone different to me. There would have been no way to go back.

"I couldn't risk it," Ryan said, voice dropping. "Don't you remember what it felt like when we were that age? How much we needed each other? Nothing felt more important than that. I couldn't lose you. What would I have had left?"

Almost against my will, all of my teenage angst and bravado came rushing back. How my friends had been my entire world. More important to me than my own family. How every emotion, good or bad, felt like it had the power to change my world. I had been convinced no high the entire rest of my life would ever feel as good, no low would ever hurt as much. I had no frame of reference, no years of life against which to judge my experiences. Consequences were distant, cloudy threats, something to be worried about later, if at all. If someone or something had threatened my relationship with Ryan and Cassie, how far might I have gone to protect it? Not as far as Ryan had, but part of me could see how easily he'd gotten there. Could remember how painfully young sixteen was and how choices that now seemed ridiculous and dangerous had made a perfect kind of sense back then.

"You didn't do it for me," I said, needing, more than anything, for that to be true. "You did it to protect yourself."

Ryan shook his head. "It was for you. You weren't safe around Roy, Greer. I couldn't let you hang out with him and not make sure you were okay. He was dangerous and he wasn't going to let you go without a fight."

"Bullshit," I shot back. "I was already ending things before Eliza died."

"That may be what you thought, but he wasn't on the same page. He thought the two of you were real, if you can believe that shit."

"What did you say to him?" I asked, my heart cracking open. For almost half my life, all I'd felt for Roy was hatred, morphing him into some brain-dead, one-dimensional monster in my mind. But Dean had made me remember his human side, the guy who showed me how to funnel my anger, who stole money and risked his job to buy me an ice cream cone. The one who smiled, slow and tentative, every time I climbed into his truck. It hadn't absolved him, but it had turned him back into a person. And now Ryan was here, calmly giving voice to all the ways we'd manipulated Roy, used him for our own gain. It was still true that he'd pulled the trigger. But both of us, we'd put the gun in his hand.

"I wasn't planning on telling him anything. I barely knew the guy, befriended him a little to keep tabs on him, is all. It didn't take much. Man, I never met somebody so desperate for a friend. He was going to be a problem once you dumped him completely, but I figured we'd cross that bridge. But then Eliza found those fucking photos, told me she had to tell you, that it was up to you to decide what to do about it." He ran his free hand through his hair. "She didn't even care about you and Roy. That's what she should have been upset about. But all she cared about were the photos, me following you around. She had it completely backward." He took a deep breath. "I had to get Roy away from you and stop her. You get that, right?"

I didn't say anything. I'd slipped my hand into my jacket pocket while he talked, fingers grazing the edges of my phone.

"Take your hand out of your pocket," he told me, and my heart sank. He waited until I'd done as he'd instructed before he went on. "But I never meant for Roy to kill anyone. I swear to god, Greer. I told him that Eliza was the one keeping you two apart. That she'd found out and threatened to tell your parents. I thought he'd just scare her a little, maybe shove her around. Then she'd know that he was the real problem all along, not those photos. Not me."

"Did you know he bought a gun?" I asked quietly.

A choked sound burst out of Ryan. "Yeah, but I never thought he'd use it."

I shook my head. "You knew. You knew how much he needed to believe someone cared about him." Fresh tears rolled down my cheeks. "You knew what he would do."

"It wasn't my fault," Ryan said. "He wasn't a good guy."

"Who's a good guy?" I asked quietly. "You? You manipulated someone who didn't have the smarts or the will to resist you. You were responsible for the deaths of your friends. Then you killed two more people. Why Addy and Dylan?" I thought of Addy's mom baking pies, then slipping into her hot bath at night to grieve, and more tears fell.

Ryan winced, like the thought of Addy and Dylan hurt him in a way that Eliza and Travis, who had been his friends, did not. Or maybe it was more painful because with Addy and Dylan he'd been the one to actually pull the trigger. No way to make that someone else's fault. "That was hard," he said. "I hated doing it. Especially to Addy. I didn't know her, but she seemed like a good kid. I picked Dylan because he was an asshole, never could keep his mouth shut about how much he hated Ludlow and everyone in it." He shrugged. "If someone had to go, it might as well have been him."

I remembered what Dean had said about collateral damage and coldhearted bastards. Still, even now, I was having trouble reconciling that person with Ryan, who had always been one of the best, warmest people I knew. "Are you listening to yourself?" I asked. "Trying to justify what you did. What was any of it for?"

"It was for you!" His voice rose, his hands thrown up in the air, my eyes following the arc of the gun in his fingers. "Have you even been listening to me? I never would have done it, but you needed me to, Greer. I had to bring you back here. You were suffering in Chicago. Cassie told me the last time she went to visit that you were a shell of yourself. I couldn't let that go on. I thought maybe after the execution you'd snap out of it, but you didn't. And then, after Bethany and I split, it felt like a sign. I decided to move back here, and it seemed like everything was coming full circle. The three of us, we needed to be together again. That's the last time you were happy. The last time I was, too, really. I knew if you came back here, you'd be okay." He took a step toward me, his expression tender. "You needed to come home."

I coughed out a disbelieving laugh. "Did you ever think about just asking me?"

Ryan raised his eyebrows. "If I had, would you have come?" He didn't bother waiting for me to answer because we both knew the truth. "And deep down, you were waiting for it. Because the minute you heard about Dylan and Addy, you knew, didn't you? You knew it was a message. And you couldn't get here fast enough. When your mom said you were on your way back, I was sure I'd done the right thing."

Come back. The horrible part was that he was right. He knew me so well, knew exactly how to reel me in and pull me home. Knew exactly what message to send in order to get the result he wanted. He'd already done it once before.

"The hearts," I breathed out. "You drew a heart on Addy like the one you left for me."

He nodded. "I knew it was a risk, leaving that heart on Addy's arm, potentially tying the murders together. But no one knew about the paper heart but you and me. I drew the heart on Addy to remind me what it was all for. That sometimes we have to do hard things to help the people we love. It made it a little easier, in the end."

I could barely speak, picturing sixteen-year-old Ryan cutting the red paper, gluing on the doily, writing those words. And adult Ryan tracing a bloody heart on Addy's skin. I didn't understand how such goodness and such madness could coexist inside one person. "How could you be sure?" I asked slowly. "That no one knew about the paper heart but us?"

Ryan shrugged. "I just was."

"Because you knew what that heart would do to me," I said, voice rising. "You knew how guilty it would make me feel. You wanted me to feel responsible, to make sure I stopped asking questions and kept my mouth shut."

"No. I was trying to make you feel better. Let you know it had happened for a reason." But he couldn't meet my gaze, his eyes shifting away. "You should have left it alone, Greer. Now look at this mess. Look at us." He sounded sad and tired suddenly. A tear snaked down his cheek. "Why couldn't you have left it alone?"

"Because she was my sister," I said, stepping toward him. "Because I woke up every day choking on the knowledge that maybe I'd done something or said something that made Roy kill her. Because I knew he hadn't done it on his own, and it wasn't fair that he was the only one punished for it." Ryan was looking right at me, still and listening. It was the first time since I'd stepped into the refinery that I recognized him.

"Don't you think if I could rewind time, back to the very beginning, I'd pick a different path?" His voice was quiet, pained, all of his earlier bluster and excuses worn away. "If I'd known how much it would hurt you, hurt all of us . . ."

"But when you had another chance, you chose to do it again," I said. "To Addy and Dylan."

"I didn't, though," he said. "Have a choice. It's like I started walking this road when I was too young to realize what a shitty route it was. One with no off-ramps, no good places to turn around. So my only choice was to keep moving forward."

I shook my head. "You could have stopped, Ryan. You could have just stopped."

He blew out a shuddering breath. "If I'd stopped, then the whole thing would have been pointless. Because if I couldn't help you, then what would it have all been for, Greer? If you're not safe and happy, if our friendship isn't solid, then Eliza died for nothing. Then every step, every horrible thing I did, would have been for nothing. I had to keep going. I had to." His face twisted, and he looked so much like the Ryan I remembered. The boy who'd wept when his father left, the one who'd always been able to make me laugh, the one who loved me even at my most unlovable. My arms started to reach for him, and I forced them back to my sides. "And it worked," he said, his lips kicking up in a lopsided grin even as tears ran down his face. "For a little while."

He closed his eyes and bent down, set the gun gently on the ground between us. As soon as he straightened, I threw myself forward, scrabbling for the gun. I heard him move and my whole body tensed. But the sounds didn't come closer and I risked a look upward, even as my fingers closed around the gun and I grasped it tight in my hand.

Ryan was at the railing, his back to the rusted metal, hands raised in surrender. "I'm not going to hurt you," he said. "I could never hurt you, Greer. Don't you know that by now?"

"You did hurt me, though," I said on a sob, pushing myself to my feet. "You ruined my whole life."

"I didn't." He shook his head. "You have a life. You just haven't been living it. That was your choice, not mine. It's all in front of you. Your road is still wide open, Greer. But you have to want it."

"I should shoot you right now," I told him. Even as I said the words, I felt how easy it would be, how satisfying. Exacting revenge for all the people no longer here to do it for themselves. But my grip on the gun had already loosened, my finger not quite touching the trigger.

"You're not going to shoot me." Ryan kept his gaze on me, lifted one leg over the railing. The rusted metal groaned under his weight.

"What are you doing?" I asked.

"In my head, this was supposed to go a different way. Does that ever happen to you? You've got something all worked out and then life comes along and shits on it?"

"Yes," I said on a whisper. "Pretty much every day."

"I thought if you ever found out, you'd understand. Find a way to forgive me. That's the hope I've been living with these past few months. The only way I could even stand to look at myself in the mirror anymore. I kept holding onto the idea that together we'd get past it somehow." His voice broke. "But we can't, can we?"

I shook my head, unable to speak.

He drew his other leg over the railing. His hands gripping the metal all that kept him from plummeting backward into the darkness.

I took a step closer. "Please don't."

"Can you honestly see me in prison?" he asked. "Come on. I wouldn't last a week." His voice was light, almost amused, and for a split second it felt like one of our normal conversations. Banter as easy as breathing. My love for him rose hot and bitter inside me, and my vision telescoped crazily, trying to bring him into focus. I wanted so badly for this to not be happening.

"If you really are my friend, if you really love me, please don't do this." My words came out shaky and weak, and I lowered the gun. I finally fully understood Dean, how he could still love Roy, even after everything. How awful it must have been to watch him die. "I can't take any more."

"I'm sorry, Greer," Ryan said. "But I can't take any more, either."

He let go of the railing. I ran forward, throwing myself at him. Rusted metal tore along my inner arm, pain flaring. His face a pale oval rushing away from me into the shadows. His outstretched arm right there, so close, fingers brushing as he fell.

I'd wanted to kill him. I'd wanted to save him. In the end, I couldn't do either.

Chapter Twenty

Ryan had been wrong. Dean had a faint pulse under my fingers, a weak groan when I turned him over. My voice hoarse as I called for an ambulance. My hands pressing my jacket hard into his wound until the paramedics pulled me aside.

And then me being ushered into Sheriff Baker's cruiser, turning my face away when they wheeled Ryan out in a black body bag. It all felt very remote, like it was happening to a woman who looked like me, and sounded like me, but had nothing at all to do with me. I knew it would wear off, though, and I dreaded the reckoning.

I expected to be taken to the police station, so I was surprised when Baker pulled up at the hospital in Neosho. He must have registered my confusion when he opened the door and helped me out of the cruiser. "Your arm, sweetheart," he said. I looked down, saw blood dripping off the ends of my fingers. Vaguely remembered pain when I'd reached for Ryan.

A nurse helped me take off my ripped shirt, cleaned the jagged, deep gash on my upper inner arm. A glimpse of muscle, flecks of rust embedded in the wound, before I closed my eyes. They gave me a tetanus shot before a doctor arrived to sew me up. A long needle, thirty stitches, and I never flinched. Not because I was brave, but because I still wasn't feeling anything. A blissful numbness I wanted to float in forever.

After they were done with my arm and had gotten me back in

my clothes, they put me in a room by myself, a hot cup of coffee on the table that I couldn't lift to my lips without spilling. I sat on my hands in an attempt to still their shaking. When Baker joined me, he brought a blanket, draped it gently across my shoulders before he sat down across from me. "Your mother is here," he said, waited.

"She can come in," I told him. I was so tired of lying. And it was better to do this once. Flay myself open with a single swipe of the sword rather than die by a thousand smaller cuts.

When Baker opened the door, my mother rushed inside. Took the seat next to me and cradled my face in her battered hands. "Oh, my sweet girl," she said. "I'm right here. I'm here." I wondered if she still would be once I was done talking.

Baker took me through it slowly, making notes even though every word I said was being recorded. My mom made noises some-times, involuntary gasps or sighs, but never interrupted. When we got to Roy and me, Baker's pen paused and he raised his eyes to mine. I resisted the urge to look away. I told it all, and I spared no one. Especially not myself. There was relief in saying the words, in no longer keeping a dark and festering secret, one that was slowly eating me alive. Next to me, my mother had gone very still. I couldn't look at her.

"Greer," Baker said when I was finished. "It wasn't—"

"Don't," I said, harsh. "Don't tell me it wasn't my fault."

"Okay," he said. "I won't say that. But I'm gonna say something. And you're gonna listen."

I looked down at my hands. I had blood under my nails and embedded in the creases of my knuckles. Dean's blood. My blood. I could feel the numbness receding, and I tried to chase it, but it moved too fast for me. A sharp pain exploded in my chest.

"I already knew about you and Roy," Baker said. "I always knew."

My head shot up. I couldn't breathe, all the air backed up into my lungs. "What are you talking about?" I whispered.

"I saw you that summer. You think something like that goes on in my town and I'm not going to know about it, sweetheart? That I'm not going to keep tabs? Come on now," he said, voice gentle. "You know me better than that."

"Why didn't you . . . why didn't you ever say anything?" I asked.

Baker glanced at my mom with an apology in his eyes and then back to me. "I thought I was doing the right thing. I knew you didn't have anything to do with the murders. We had Roy, the gun, the confession. So I thought, why stir it all up, make everything worse? It would have just muddied the waters, and you were barely holding on as it was. But I see now that was a mistake. I should have helped you unburden yourself. Because you wanted me to know, didn't you? Way back then, when you wouldn't stop pressing? You wanted someone to figure it out, about you and Roy? Hold you to account?"

I nodded without speaking, tears dripping off my chin.

Baker sighed, a long, mournful breath. "I'm sorry I let you down. I wish I'd paid more attention, understood what you were trying to tell me. And maybe if I'd done that, instead of dismissing you, I could have figured out what Ryan was up to before he had a chance to do it again. That's on me, and it always will be. But whatever part of the fault for this is yours, and we can go back and forth on that all day, you've paid for it. A hundred times over." He tapped the back of my hand with his fingers, hard. "Are you hearing me?"

"Yes," I managed.

"You've paid, Greer. And now it really is time to let it go." He put pressure on my hand until I looked at him. "If you don't, if you can't, then you might as well have jumped with him. And that would be a goddamn shame."

I risked a glance at my mom, then wished I hadn't, tears coursing down her cheeks. I'd tried never to imagine this moment, mainly because when I did, I could picture clearly the horror on my mother's face. How bad the final rejection would sting, even after all the years of warm-up. I braced myself when she opened her mouth, steeling myself for what would come out. "Why didn't you tell us?" she asked. "All this time and you never said a word."

I struggled to speak, my throat tight. "I didn't know how."

"Is this the reason you haven't come home for so long? Pushed us away? Never wanted to talk about Eliza?"

Her words hit me like an electric shock, a sudden, sharp jab to my heart. All this time, I'd told myself the distance between us was what they'd wanted, the erasing of Eliza what they'd chosen. But really it had started with me, hadn't it? My resentment and denial a shield I held between us so they would never get close enough to find out the truth. "I didn't want you to hate me," I whispered.

"Oh, Greer. We could never hate you." She reached for my hands, folded them into her own. Her touch was gentle, her face soft. It broke something inside me, something brittle and hard that had needed smashing for years. "You shouldn't have carried it alone. It was too much for one person." She lifted our clasped hands and kissed my knuckles. She glanced at Baker. "Like he said, it's time to let it go."

I knew she was right, even though a part of me wanted to cling to my burden, its weight a kind of comfort. Who would I be without it? I had no idea anymore. But what I'd been carrying was too heavy. In order to keep moving forward, I had to set some of it down. The push of pain and the pull of love. Shame and forgiveness. Past and future. Maybe now it was up to me to decide which way I wanted to go. Maybe it always had been.

. . . .

When my mom and I got home, Cassie was waiting on my front steps, her face swollen from tears. She launched herself at me as soon as I was within grabbing distance, her arms so tight around me I could barely inhale. My mom laid a hand on my shoulder as she passed, shutting the door softly behind her as she went inside. "Is it true?" Cassie asked. And then, before I could answer, "I know it is. But I can't make myself believe it."

We lowered ourselves onto the front steps again, the sun barely beginning to rise over the treetops turning the air sugary pink. "Are you okay?" Cassie asked. "Did he hurt you?"

"No. He hurt Dean, though."

"Dean's in the hospital?"

I nodded. "I waited for a few hours, but they ended up moving him to Wichita. Last they told me, he's in surgery. Baker promised to call me as soon as they know anything more."

"Did Ryan say why he did it?" Cassie asked, after a minute of silence.

"He would say it was because I needed him to." It was the simplest answer, and the most painful one.

"That's such a load of crap," Cassie said, voice harsh. "You know that, right? Please tell me you know that."

"I'm trying to know it," I said. And I was, trying to tell myself that it was really all about Ryan. His need to protect, his need to guard a friendship he thought was in peril, his need to control.

"After I heard, I started thinking back, going over that summer. Remember how Samantha Leary accused me of slashing her tires and I thought she was crazy, so I broke up with her?" Cassie asked. "Do you think it could have been Ryan?"

"I don't know. Maybe. Probably. He didn't like the way she treated you. He could have been trying to protect you in his own spectacularly fucked-up way."

"I keep picking things apart. Like how he was always so obsessed with us being happy. Worrying every time I went through a breakup. Taking it harder than I did, half the time. And he'd call me after he visited you in Chicago, ranting about how sad you were, trying to figure out a way to fix it. Looking back, it was over the top. If it had been anyone else, it probably would have set off alarm bells. But it was *Ryan*. He'd always been overprotective. I never thought . . ."

"I know," I said, my voice breaking. "I never did, either." That's what we do for the people we love; we make allowances and excuses. We look past what's right in front of us in hopes we'll see something better.

"We spent so much time with him. How did we not know?"

"Because we didn't want to. Because we loved him." I paused. Took a deep, stinging breath. "The worst part is, I still do."

Cassie laid her head on my shoulder. "I do, too."

And I missed him already. Knew I'd live every day after this with a Ryan-shaped hole in my heart. Would ache to hear his easy laugh, see his lopsided grin, as long as I drew breath. Nothing he'd done was enough to erase the love for him that still lived inside me, as real as organ and bone.

"None of it makes sense," Cassie whispered, almost to herself. Across the street the wind picked up a swirl of leaves, sending them dancing along the sidewalk.

All these years, I'd expected that if I ever found out the real reason Eliza died, it would be something worthy of her passing. Something as big as her loss had been. Something that gave it meaning. But all I'd discovered was that the reason for a murder was almost never something earth-shattering. More often than not, it was something trivial, something so stupid and meaningless that you could hardly fathom how it would warrant the taking of a life. Six people gone because I picked a random Wednesday night to go to the refinery and ran into an angry boy throwing bottles. Lives ruined because my friend felt entitled to save me—to *kill* to save me—when I'd never asked for rescue. Dreams shattered because my sister discovered a secret she refused to keep buried. All of it so mundane, really, that the truth of it broke my heart all over again.

. . . .

I was baking cookies with my mom when they called to tell me Dean was able to have visitors. It had been two days since the shooting, two days of waiting for him to be stable enough for me to see him. "Go," my mom said as soon as I got off the phone. "I'll finish up here." We'd been spending more time together the last few days. Hours when she stopped cleaning, put down her bucket and mop and picked up a recipe, or we sat together reading on the front porch. She still cleaned more than she needed to, but at the end of the day she let me put lotion on her slightly less-battered skin. Sometimes we talked of Eliza. Our initial tentative reminiscing soon giving way to a torrent of memories. With every shared story I gave myself permission to grieve my sister in a way I never had before, without guilt and shame layered over the top of the hurt. It was simply sorrow now, and I let myself feel it—each memory an exquisite pain rippling outward into joy. I laughed, and cried, and allowed my mother to wipe away my tears. Slowly, carefully we were navigating our way into being mother and daughter again.

On my way out of the house, I peeked into the family room. My dad was asleep in his recliner, and I stopped to cover his legs with a blanket from the back of the sofa. I could smell bourbon on his breath, but there wasn't an open bottle beside him. I'd mentioned AA to him last night. Told him there was a meeting every Thursday evening in the basement of the Methodist church. He hadn't said he'd go. But he hadn't told me to fuck off, either. I guess that was our version of progress.

My parents and I weren't going to heal one another overnight. Or maybe ever. Forgiveness would come in baby steps, for me and for them. But I could stand the thought of seeing them now. And of letting myself be seen. Of being their daughter again. I had some hope for better in the future. It reminded me of one of the sayings on Eliza's garbage wall: "It's not the destination, it's the journey." God, I'd given her a special kind of hell about that one. "Of course it's the destination," I'd told her. "If you're going on vacation to New York City, you don't give a shit about the flight." She'd only rolled her eyes at me. That was one thing about Eliza; she never wasted her breath arguing when I was being an intentional pain in the ass. And the truth was, I still thought her wall was garbage. I still didn't really believe most of the crap she'd had up there. But I was trying. We all were.

. . . .

Dean was sleeping when I got to his room, his face pale and his hands crossed lightly on his chest. I grabbed the chair next to his bed, dragging it closer as quietly as I could, and took one of his hands in mine. His skin was warm, calloused, exactly how I remembered. Baker told me he'd been shot in the stomach, sheer luck that the bullet had missed any other major organs. The fall down the steps had dislocated his right shoulder, left him with a concussion, and caused any number of bruises and cuts. But he was going to survive, despite Ryan's best efforts.

I lowered my forehead to our clasped hands, searching for the scent of wheat or sweat. But all I got was hospital soap and a sterile whiff of antiseptic.

"Hey." His voice was scratchy, as if he hadn't spoken much in years instead of only a few days.

My head snapped up. "Hey," I said. I let go of his hand to brush an errant tear off my cheek, hoping he hadn't noticed. He turned his palm toward me, reaching for my fingers again.

"Guess I should have listened to those hand squeezes you were giving me in the refinery, huh?"

I choked out a little laugh. "Men. So stubborn. How are you feeling?"

"Like I got shot and thrown down a flight of stairs." He gave me a half smile. "What about you?"

"I'm fine," I said, but my voice wobbled and I glanced away.

"Are you?" He tightened his grip on my hand. "I heard about Ryan."

I shook my head, bit down on my bottom lip. "I know I should hate him. And part of me does. But the other part?" I paused. "He was my friend for a long time. A good friend. The best, really. No matter how much I try, I can't forget that."

"Don't be hard on yourself. Your history with him doesn't disappear just because of what he did."

I knew Dean understood, more than anyone, exactly how love and hate for someone could form a perfect knot inside you, forever entwined. I wished I'd been kinder to him when he'd tried to explain his feelings about Roy's death, wished I could have taken a step back from my own grief and anger and really seen what he was trying to show me. Been gentler with his pain. "I'm sorry for not telling you about Roy and me earlier. For not speaking up before his trial. If I had . . . maybe things would have been different for him." When I'd voiced these thoughts to Cassie, she'd assured me it wouldn't have changed the outcome. That at the end of the day, the fact remained that Roy had been the one to kill Eliza and Travis. I knew Cassie meant well. But the truth was, we'd never know for sure whether my silence helped cost a man his life.

"I doubt it would have made a difference," Dean said. "If Roy had wanted people to know about the two of you, if he'd felt like it mattered in the long run, he would have spoken up. For whatever reason, he didn't want to put you through that. He was protecting you, and it was his choice."

But how much choice does someone have in a situation like

Roy's? Especially someone not very bright and loyal to his core? Who's done something awful and already fallen on the sword? Does it matter to anyone what might have caused it, what portion of the blame might rightly belong to someone else? What the reasons might have been, faulty as they were? I know, back then, it hadn't mattered to me.

"You were right," I told Dean. "That day on the bench. They're all still gone. Nothing we discovered changes that." I squeezed his hand. "But I hope it helps a little, the knowing."

"It does," he said. "I'm a work in progress, but seeing the whole picture . . ." He gave a careful shrug. "I still wish I'd done more, paid more attention to Roy that summer. I doubt that will ever go away. But having answers, even painful ones, eases something for me."

"I'm glad." I swallowed hard, not trusting my voice. "I went to Roy's grave yesterday."

"You did? Why?"

"I owed it to him." I'd stood on that barren patch of dirt and let myself remember Roy in a way I hadn't allowed myself to do since the day he'd been arrested. He was a murderer. But he was more than that, too. He'd had a family and a life. He'd loved and been loved. And he'd meant something to me once, in a way I would never be able to fully articulate. Those things didn't cancel each other out. They didn't mean I forgave him or that I'd ever understand his choices, but I couldn't find it in myself to hate him anymore.

I let go of Dean's hand and reached up, ran my fingers along his cheek, felt the rasp of his stubble under my skin. "And I owed it to you," I whispered. Owed it to this man who could have so easily turned away from me, but held my hand instead. He shifted his head and kissed my palm, and I stood up, bent over him, and rested my forehead against his. We stayed that way for a moment, eyes closed, breathing in unison, and then he threaded a hand through my hair and brought his mouth to mine. This time when we kissed, there was only Dean behind my closed eyelids, no one else. Seeing him for the first time in the courtroom, stiff and tense in his ill-fitting suit. Sitting beside him on the memorial bench in the dying twilight. Riding next to him on Ludlow's back roads, searching for answers. Lying beneath his warm body on the cold floor of the refinery. His laugh, his furrowed brow, his strong hands. His un-dying resilience when it would have been easier to simply give up. A tear ran down my cheek, and I tasted it on his tongue.

He pulled back a little and looked at me, brushed his fingers under my eye, and caught my next tear before it fell. "In another life, we could have really been something," he whispered.

"Yes," I said, and nothing more. Because, after everything, what else was there to say? We were two parts of the same broken whole, but there was no way to piece us together. No way the shape we formed made any kind of sense. I wondered what might have been if Dean had been the boy I'd met in the refinery that long-ago sum-mer day. How different all our lives might have turned out to be.

When I sat back down, he took my hand again, ran his thumb across my knuckles.

"So what's next for you?" he asked, voice hoarse.

"I don't know exactly. I'm going back to Chicago in a few days. Cassie is coming with me for a week or two. It's her mission to help me turn my plain apartment into something 'Greer-worthy.' Whatever that means. It's been a long time since I've thought about it." I paused. "I'll be back for Christmas, though." When I'd asked my mom if that would be okay, she'd burst into tears and flapped her hands helplessly, laughing a little at her own reaction. Ludlow would never be the magical, uncomplicated home of my childhood.

272 • Amy Engel

But it could still be a place where I belonged. A place where the bad no longer eclipsed the good, but simply lived alongside it. *Come back.* It was a gentle murmur now, filled with the best kind of possibility.

"And your job?"

"I'm not sure about that, either. I think I'll finish this school year before I decide. I still don't know if I like it. Or even if I'm any good at it. But I've never put my heart into it, not really. I figure maybe I'll give that a try." I shrugged. "See how it goes." And now I had something more to offer the kids, didn't I? My honesty left me messy and raw, but maybe that's what they needed. My understanding of the foibles of youth and the shame of bad decisions. The healing power of forgiveness, especially for yourself. To see that even after the worst kind of mistakes, life can go on.

Dean smiled. "I think you've always been better at it than you give yourself credit for. But now those kids better buckle up. They won't know what hit them when they finally meet the real Greer Dunning. You're going to be amazing."

I smiled back, lips trembling. "What about you?" I managed. "Once you're healed?"

He sighed, tipped his gaze up to the ceiling. "I guess I'll keep on keeping on. Take care of my grandma as well as I can, for as long as I can. Work on the farm. Wait and see what life throws at me."

"I hope it's something good," I told him, voice fierce, like I was daring the universe to contradict me. I'd never meant anything more in my life.

He laughed slightly, the movement making him wince. "Yeah, you and me both."

When I left his room, I didn't linger. "See ya later," I said from the doorway, one hand raised in farewell. I was trying to memorize his face, the lines fanning out from his eyes when he smiled, the exact shades of brown in his hair.

"Goodbye, Greer," Dean said.

He was the first to look away, just so I wouldn't have to be.

. . . .

I paused on the sidewalk outside the hospital, scrubbed at my cheeks with both hands, then wiped my tears on my jeans. Out on the street, a car glided past. I caught my fingers reaching for my inner arm, and I barely resisted the urge to scratch under my bandage where my stitches were prickling, my skin slowly knitting back together. I tucked my hands into my pockets instead. Tilted my head back and felt the warm sun on my face. The light was pure gold, spilling down through magenta-hued leaves to puddle at my feet. I closed my eyes, the scent of apple pie flooding my memory, and took a deep breath. "The seasons are changing," I whispered. "My wound is healing. I am alive."

It was enough.

Acknowledgments

This book would not exist without the help, love, and encouragement of the following:

My editor, Maya Ziv. This book would not be the same without you. Thank you for pushing me to dig deeper. It's a joy to work on a book with someone who understands my vision and then encourages me until I get there.

My agent, Jodi Reamer. Thank you for always putting up with me and for knowing exactly how to respond to my emails.

My UK editor, Emily Kitchin. Thank you for your steadfast support and enthusiasm for all of my books. I'm so happy to be back with you for this one! And thank you to the entire HQ team!

Christine Ball, John Parsley, Sabila Kahn, Emily Canders, Caroline Payne, Lexy Cassola, Alice Dalrymple, and everyone at Dutton and Penguin Random House. Thank you for all your hard work on behalf of me and this book. Words can't adequately express my appreciation for all you do.

Cassandra Bushell. You had your work cut out for you taking my author photo. Thank you for your patience and humor and for making me look a hundred times better than in real life!

Brian, Graham, and Quinn. I know I'm not always fully present when I'm in the midst of writing a book, so thank you for bearing with me and being my biggest cheerleaders. Nothing would make sense without the three of you.

Holly. I don't know how many different ways I can say it, but thank you for being my best friend and the sister I never had. My life is so much better because you're part of it.

Meshelle. Sis, at this point you probably never want to see this book again. Thank you for all the times you read it, the advice you gave ("Vietnam!"), and for being my ride or die. We'll toast this book, and our friendship, in Paris!

Laura. If I don't text you twenty times a day, am I really writing a book? Thank you for your endless patience with my bitching and moaning. I feel very lucky to have a dear friend who also understands the sometimes painful writing life. We need to make a pact to always write books at the same time. I'm not sure I can survive the process otherwise.

Mom. Some of my very first memories are of you reading to me, even on nights when you were exhausted or I picked the longest book on my shelf. Thank you. I love you.

All my friends and family. Thank you for humoring my incessant talk about books and writing and for supporting me with every new novel.

Booksellers, reviewers, and librarians. Thank you for everything you do to get books into the hands of readers. Every author owes you a huge debt of gratitude. And a special thank-you to readers. You're the reason we write.

To the men and women I defended. Some of your cases were heartbreaking, some were infuriating, some were horrifying, but each one taught me that every person is more than the worst thing they've done. I'm forever grateful for the lesson.

And last, but never least, Larry the cat. Thank you for always keeping my legs warm while I'm writing.

About the Author

Amy Engel is the author of *The Familiar Dark*, *The Roanoke Girls*, and the Book of Ivy series. A former criminal defense attorney, she lives in Missouri with her family.